"As they say, " Some friendship are like ships that pass in the night" and in my rather mobile life I have enjoyed plenty. But others seem as bonded as night and the moon. John and Esther have been such for me for half a century.

One reason is that life for them is like the construction of a strong, complex and fascinating home that grows in usefulness and beauty. It has been so interesting to hear of some new exciting insight into the ways of human behaviour every time we met. Sometimes one insight would replace another but more often, add a new, more holistic way of understanding and helping.

So, I am excited on reading this book."

Rev Dr James Kime,
Retired Baptist minister, cross cultural worker and theological educator.

"In this book John and Esther bring a lifetime of both academic and practitioner experience to their writing. Through the deployment of narrative, they draw the reader into discovering insights into psychology and faith that impact the human condition."

George Savvides AM
FAICD, Chair SBS, past Managing Director Medibank Private.

"John and Esther Roodenburg have lived with a commitment to build strong relationships and to bring out the best in others. Combined with a depth of experience as practising and teaching psychologists, they have produced this book which is rich in insights. I expect that it will bring practical benefits for many readers and for some the experience of liberation from things that have held them back."

Rev Dr Peter Crawford OAM
Anglican Minister, Vice President CMS Australia,
former secretary EFAC Australia

"You know when you have a great teacher. You do whatever you can to somehow download their expertise, knowledge, and life experiences. Digs in Paradise is the gift that all students wish their great teachers could provide: a timeless snapshot of their learning, support, and worldview. Digs in Paradise offers the pearls of wisdom and thought-provoking story telling I was privileged to experience as a psychologist trained under Drs John and Esther Roodenburg. Readers will easily relate to the honest and captivating relationships, behaviours, and experiences of the characters in Digs of Paradise; gaining insight into the human condition whilst receiving subtle guidance for navigating their own world. I am excited for others to venture into the town of KP and learn from two of my great teachers."

Dr Simone Gindidis
Educational and Developmental Psychologist

"Cast your mind back to childhood and remember some of the games that you played. Perhaps you recall being on a road trip, and your parents asking you to name what you could see. While ostensibly something to pass the time or avoid the dread of boredom, something else was also happening. Buried in the experience of being entertained was an opportunity to learn! Had you been asked if you wanted to learn something, your younger self would likely have declined - but playing a game was always acceptable.

John and Esther Roodenburg bring their wealth of experience as educators and psychologists together in this teaching novel. Rarely will you have the opportunity to be so thoroughly entertained and yet genuinely learn so much about the inner experience of another person. The complexities of life experiences, behaviours, perceptions, beliefs and interactions are laid bare against a backdrop of tropical intrigue and self-discovery. Whether your goal is entertainment or education, this novel will undoubtedly deliver both!"

Dr Shane Costello
Educational and Developmental Psychologist
Senior Lecturer, Monash University

"John and Esther have devoted many years towards helping folk discover the vibrant life God intends for all of us. In this book is the heartbeat of this same calling, where distilled biblical wisdom, discernment, and authenticity, come to life through the characters and the challenges they face. A book which engages the reader on a number of levels."

Bruce Park,
Maths/Science and Design & Technology
Teacher, Past Anglican Parish Warden

PSYCHOLOGICAL DIGS
IN PARADISE

OVERCOMING THE TRAUMAS OF THE PAST
IN PURSUIT OF AN ELUSIVE IDEAL

DRS JOHN & ESTHER
ROODENBURG

Ark House Press
arkhousepress.com

Cataloguing in Publication Data:
Title: Psychological Digs in Paradise
ISBN: 978-0-6453714-8-2 (pbk)
Subjects: Trauma; Developmental Psychology; Relationships; Faith; Doubt

Cover art courtesy of Jean Bates
Design by initiateagency.com

AUTHORS' PREFACE

This novel is written as a teaching novel, at times known as social fiction. Initially we trained as teachers, then as two practitioner psychologists over many years. Later, again as teachers, we trained specialist psychologists in a graduate program at Monash University. We quickly learned that theory is best brought alive through storytelling, through real-life illustrations that support both the learning and the application of what is in question. Our appreciation of how and why psychology can contribute to a fuller understanding of what makes us as humans tick is the overriding rationale for why we've written this book, and as a novel.

Our living and our own learning has encompassed sometimes major adjusting to each other, in raising five children, and while also sharing the life stories of many who struggled to grasp what life was about. So our deep desire in writing this story is to make available some of what we've learned and understood, so that you the reader will be encouraged to enjoy discovering many things about yourself and others. We hope this book will encourage personal growth, and in turn will enable people keen to help others do so more effectively, through better insights into their understanding of personal skills required. The story highlights some of the psychological insights that we know are often importantly misunderstood, some that inevitably create unnecessary pain and dis-connection, both within and between individuals in our so-called edu-cated and liberated society.

Please note that although all these characters are fictional, they have grown out of personal experiences on the journey. Enjoy getting to know our characters in a little Paradise, and the brief meeting of some you'll hopefully wait to know more deeply within the next Psychological dig…

WITH APPRECIATION

Writing this book has seen many iterations. We are grateful to all those who helped shape it, generously giving of their time to reading, and providing invaluable feedback, recommendations and encouragement, from the first drafts through to the last. Our sincere appreciation includes those who wrote the commendations that appear on the rear cover and inside front cover, as well as from Ellie, Willem, Deirdre, Abbie, Ruth.

A very special thanks to Jean Bates for her original painting of the cover picture of Rustenberg Eilandt, with coffee plants, flowers and cherries in the corner. Jean's paintings can be seen at instagram@jeanbates2020

Finally, appreciation to Ark House for their professional support in seeing this book through to publication.

We would not have attempted this journey let alone finish it but for the prompting of the One who has called us to our vocation, and has blessed us in so many ways. Our prayer is that this book and any sequel will be an enjoyable journey for our readers.

Esther Roodenburg and John Roodenburg,
Melbourne, Victoria, Australia.

CONTENTS

PART 1

OUT OF TRAUMA...

1

Abandoned

Tara

How I love the coast of WA – I could spend hours just absorbing the salt air, the sense of the grandeur of the mighty ocean. Its might and power never cease to enthral me. Some days when it is too churned up to accede to its beckoning me in to ride an incoming and enticing wave, I find a more sheltered spot out of the wind, allowing myself just to reminisce. Life now is good, I conclude, in this beautiful city, with a good and satisfying group of uncomplicated friends who don't ask too much of me. And I have plenty of time to organize my life around my time at the beach, most days in fact. My mind free of busyness, I sometimes catch myself reflecting deeply; sudden memories come unbidden to my mind.

Much of my childhood is difficult to recall, or maybe I should honestly say, I haven't wanted to! What I do remember all too often is an evocative sense of absolute sadness, of feeling so alone. I do remember dreaming a lot, and so often the repetitive dreams had my mother coming back to visit me, with the excitement at feeling she had not abandoned me after all. Many of these dreams took place at the seaside, calling up echoes of our last visit there together. They always brought back memories of a time when I felt really loved. But then, the horrid shock on waking: the reality that my mother wasn't there. On realising it was only a wishful dream, I would lie there sobbing, sometimes for hours. How many times I remember I'd close my eyes, trying to get back into the dream, but all to no avail. On at least a couple of occasions I actually recalled realising that I must be in a dream, and I would fight to stay in the dream, clinging to my mother, for as long as I could.

After losing my mother at six, I was left in my grandparent's care. Yes, they provided well for my physical needs, but sadly it was a home where silence generally prevailed. My grandfather was a university lecturer, deeply absorbed in his world of economics. He would also typically bring reading material home. After my mother's death, my grandmother became really withdrawn. Nani would only speak in answer to questions, or to give me some brief and essential instruction. Mostly these focused on what I should not do, and that included instructions to never leave the house except for school. I felt so starved of affection and social interactions. I learned to live in my bedroom, losing myself in any books I could lay my hands on. No wonder I so love reading, even now into my twenties!

The drudgery of school holidays was broken only by the rare occasions when my grandmother allowed me to go to the beach with some school girlfriends who lived next door. How I absolutely loved those beach games and being with them – my only friends. I never forget the warmth of the sun on my body - it made me feel free for a time, and though ever so briefly, at least I could think it was good to be alive. But then, I have never forgotten the walks along the beautiful wide and ever-changing beach, the ever searching for unusual shells. So excited when finding some that were quite unique, I'd carefully carry them home to my bedroom, my safe haven.

I also still remember the thrill of walking along those sands, accentuated by then running to the water's edge, watching the white frothy line made by the highest most recent waves, breaking then disappearing along the shore. I felt as though I was challenging the waves themselves to catch me if they could! I even imagined the waves themselves had emotions, excitedly wanting to catch me, much like the infrequent but wonderful feelings I experienced when playing catchy with my friends at school. When I thought I'd teased the waves long enough, I would feel sorry for them and so, feeling elated at an opportunity to be kind, I'd want to let the waves catch me. Sometimes I would suddenly turn and run hard into the water, diving in, no matter what I was wearing, loving the sense of surrender to their complete wrapping of me in a warm embrace. I had enviously watched friends' fathers throw them playfully into the air. The surging water, the waves, powerfully throwing me this way and that, they were for me a father I never knew. Every time, that experience would make me feel exhilarated - happy, loved, and lovable. But then, just as I was fully enwrapped, frolicking with pleasure, my daydreaming among the turbulence would end when I had to answer a call from the shore. I would drag myself out reluctantly, imagining just for a lingering moment, that the noise of the waves was really their crying, calling out for me to come back. They seemed to share my feelings of abandonment, so I'd whispered: "I will come back".

Even now, years later as an adult, it pains me to recall that these visits to the sea had ended so suddenly. The night before my twelfth birthday, I had dreamed yet again of my mother, this time standing on a cliff overlooking my special beach. Then for my birthday, and knowing how much I loved that beach, my friends' parents had asked and had been allowed to take me with them. They clearly loved seeing how transformed into a happy child I became, having such fun on the beach, taunting the waves, temporarily escaping what otherwise seemed like interminable and sorrowful days.

On that particular day, I had sensed a very real likelihood that any joy that enabled me to escape life's heaviness here at the ocean was becoming more elusive. My imagination seemed to be stalling, giving into reality. I remember thinking: was this to be the last time? As I'd finally plunged into the welcoming water that day, I still remember the feeling of being overwhelmed by wanting to be with my mother. It was not the sea's arms I wanted, but my mother's warmth, holding me tight. That day, the sea's embrace became that of my mother, and I'd deliberately let myself go. My head under water, I had simply gulped in the water instead of air. A part of me wanted to swim to the top for air, but another part had then become far more determined; it had wanted all my sorrow to vanish, and gave the very promise of relief, to escape into my mother's arms. It claimed the water would drown my sorrow. I'd believed then that there would be no heeding the calls from the beach, no waking back into a world of loneliness where my now fading imagination was the only escape. Air was my enemy.

I still remember now what went through my head as I'd opened my eyes. All was white. Where was my mother? I had looked around for her, but only a machine was visible. A gross machine, with its tentacles of tubes and cables tied to my arm and taped to my face. I had realised then that I was in a hospital. Anger had swept over me as I aggressively reacted, pulling on all the tubes that now had me in their grasp. Alarms went off, and staff came rushing into the room, some quickly taking hold of me, pushing me back down onto the bed, demanding: "Tara, Tara, stop that, lie down!" Cruel world. How could they dare to pull me away from reaching my mother's impending embrace? Why! why had they not let me go? Oh, how well I still remember that ghastly, overwhelming disappointing day!

2

Sublimation

Tara

Of course, as soon as they realised the near drowning was no accident, I was sent to see a psychiatrist. Unfortunately, he came over as a little patronising, talking down to me, seeming to treat me as a mere child, without a brain. Though he couldn't know it, he had reminded me of my grandfather, though much later I conceded he perhaps had seemed a little more caring. Perhaps that's why those sessions felt like power struggles. I always felt the psychiatrist was contriving to manoeuvre discussions to getting me to be responsible.

Deep within, even as a child, somehow his listening had seemed forced to me, intrusive, clinical, coldly seeking after explanations, so unwelcome. Didn't he know? Didn't he understand? But clearly, I later concluded, he had been in purposeful pursuit of finding a way to prevent me from repeating my destructive behaviour; to release me from the apparent anger demonstrated by self-harming, and the lashing out at others reported to him by my mother's father. Without showing any sign that he really understood what I had been experiencing, the psychiatrist would simply express my grandfather's concern, saying that he wanted to facilitate my mental health, whatever that meant.

Those sessions had left me crying out inside: was he in any way concerned about me? I felt really resentful, on the brink of screaming at him, particularly when he asked how my grandparents and friends might have felt if I'd died. I didn't want to go to these sessions, but clearly, I was also expected to change my now frequent but uncharacteristic angry outbursts directed at those who were committed to 'caring' for me.

At one time, my grandfather had given me one of his many 'little lectures,' this time on the way to seeing the psychiatrist. Dada just talked, uninterrupted, not even turning to look at me when we stopped at traffic lights. He said I must let the doctor help me become the sort of person they could be proud of.

"You must not become like your mother, Tara, who caused your grandmother to sink into deep depression, bringing great shame on our family." His years in India had left him with a strong expressive accent.

The psychiatrist he'd organised for me, I later learned, was the same one who had tried to help my grandmother. Dada assured me this man was the best, a professor indeed, who only saw a limited number of patients. He tried to convince me I was so fortunate to be able to get direction from such a man, a man of great repute, high esteem, who had published extensively! As if I understood, or indeed if all this mattered to me. I was a twelve-year-old who had lost the only one who'd cared for me!

I remember a brief pause in his tirade, when my grandfather was clearly churning over some things he thought might be better not mentioned. Eventually he did share with me that the doctor had expressed some concern about my capacity with obsessive inclinations, my trying to escape into a world of fantasy. He said this was indicative of my 'potential for a disorder', but he couldn't remember which one. The other problem he had shared were indications of "an emerging oppositional-defiant personality that will ruin your life if your fantasising remains unchecked."

The psychiatrist, he told me, had even suggested that Dada should attend a session, so he could advise him on a suitable behavioural management program. I felt so angry, but no, I mustn't ever show it! What my grandfather did go on to divulge was that the doctor had impressed on him how very serious my problems were. And on he went, talking at me.

"You must listen to him, Tara, for there is no-one else better who can help you. Don't waste such an important man's time. And at home, you must listen to your grandmother more. Give more time to the jobs she gives you to help her. You must not waste so much time running away to your room to read silly books. Leave your childhood behind: it is time to grow up! Stop dreaming. The real world is tough."

When Dada had dropped me off that day, the angry part of me had become enraged, but I knew I must hide it, repress it, as I later came to understand what I had done in becoming simply stubbornly silent. Yes, listen I would, I decided, but that was all. No one ever wanted to listen to me, to hear my anger. When I let out my feelings, they all took it as an afront, a challenge if not a threat. I'd decided that no-one could understand, or even wanted to. Clearly, however, my grief, my sorrow and my loneliness should no longer find its expression in overt anger: the cost was too great.

So how else could I maintain control? How to keep people from invading my life? I suddenly became even more sullenly resolved, not just to keep to myself, but determined to control my emotions and imagination. This meant I had to deny emotions to others, and to do that, I had to even deny them to myself. That thought had made me feel safe. It eventually taught me that I could exercise such a steely resolve. Later on, I learned that throwing myself into any vigorous physical activity had me focus on the reality of the here and now, and effectively was more liberating than any wish-fulfilling imagination.

Thinking back to those early 'therapy' sessions, now with the eyes of an adult, sessions when I had been so easily provoked, I now understand how the repressed angry part of me had stumbled on a powerful covert release: sublimation. Turning the frustrated energy into what became a well-honed ingrained, reflexive, and protective defence mechanism made up of powerful passive aggressive skills.

Whenever reinforced, this means of roadblocking my anger then worked for me. I would sit unresponsive, looking at the floor. Obviously frustrated in finding it difficult to engage me in any discussion, the psychiatrist began using veiled promises, like suggesting I'd start to feel better if I let him help me. He asked me just to trust him, for my own sake. He wanted me to believe he was trustworthy because he was there for me: after all, he said, his professional obligation demanded a real duty of care! In addition, he further challenged this hurting, lonely and bewildered twelve-year-old by asking if I really wanted to feel better! Feel better? For me it had nothing to do with "feel better"! I just wanted my mother back, and obviously, no one could make that happen! I remember thinking it perhaps *was* time to stop any dreaming, accepting that life as it had been with my mother could never return. Dreaming, imagination, feelings: they were to be avoided.

I had managed to continue staring at the floor, closing my eyes to maintain control: that was imperative, I knew. The psychiatrist had at least allowed me that silence. While tentatively hanging on to some inner control, I also became aware of a deep struggle within. That had included being somewhat surprised by an innate sense of caring about others, a sensitivity almost completely lost during those weeks, months, and years of turmoil, finally culminating in the enforced ongoing therapy after the near-death experience. I even glimpsed a newly reawakened ability to read others, and I remember that awareness had caught me with surprise: I actually *felt* a little sorry for the man!

However, even then somehow I had known I could not allow that feeling to open up a likely vulnerability that would potentially create a chink in my protective armour, so newly formed. Yet somehow, I also knew I must break the impasse, but how, with neither him nor me giving in? Then it came to me: I must not return for more of these sessions! So finally, I had looked up at the professor. I had never before allowed eye contact. He'd looked surprised, and then somewhat relieved - I think at that moment he thought he had broken through.

Like a demure compliant child, I quietly said: "I want to go home now. I don't want to come again. I am good now." His response came quickly.

"You are good now?" he sounded somewhat surprised.

"Yes, I am OK. Dada has explained to me I must grow up and stop dreaming. The real world is tough. I must accept it. I will." I kept focussing directly on his eyes as I spoke.

"You are an amazing young girl. You have a wise dada."

He paused while I continued to look at him, and then reiterated that I was good now.

"Mmm. You say you are good. Does that mean you are prepared to promise me that if ever you feel suicidal again, you will tell your dada?"

I checked my immediate feeling of relief, sensing a potential escape, wondering, was this a trick? Was he really letting me off the hook that easily? Had I really won? I kept my guard up. But I did note that he had not asked me to promise an action, but only if I would be prepared to promise, and so I'd answered accordingly. I had used my clever bargaining ability, which had often been necessary to thwart the demands of my over-controlling grandparents.

"If I am prepared to promise, will you tell Dada that I don't need to see you anymore?" I had nervously waited an expected and more clever response from the great man.

The professor took some time to think.

"Well, of course, if that is what you want" he had said, "but I do think you need to work through some things to become a happy person."

"Then I am prepared to promise." The meaning of my clearly given response was not double checked, as if he really needed to believe me, and I wanted to give him reason for confidence in my intentions. So, I had added quietly, without in any way making myself vulnerable: "I never planned to drown myself. It just came to me. . . . when I was under water." The silence seemed interminable.

"OK, Tara, then it would be wrong for me to insist on seeing you more just now." He had briefly gone on speaking, trying to encourage me to find someone who could help me deal with "some issues that otherwise will become a problem, and we don't want that, do we."

For me, even at twelve years of age, this implied I was the problem that had to be solved. I walked out to the waiting car feeling like I had a trump card in hand, telling my grandfather the professor did not think I needed to see him again. But my grandfather was not so easily convinced.

"If you show us that you can be a good girl, with no more nonsense, then I will concur with the professor. I will talk with him tomorrow. This is very quick after he told me just not so long ago that you have serious problems. But maybe it is so quick because he is such a knowledgeable man. But Tara, remember, the slightest indication of any trouble, and we will send you straight back."

I remember I'd wondered what 'concur' meant. But I know now, looking back, that I had felt incredibly relieved. In hindsight, those early sessions had successfully convinced me that life was about coping; coping with the expectations that others put on you, and learning to hide your own emotions, so important if you were to maintain control. Further protective shells grew around my persona. But I struggled with forming an identity: accepting and knowing who I really was, the never feeling OK about myself dominating my self-perceptions. I was sure that no-one really cared that there was no-one who could provide me with a healthy sense of being, and no-one I could really trust to form a wholesome attachment to.

Though only so young, I recall that I decided to keep relationships superficial. That way I would also avoid any risk of any more suffering through the pain created by loss. Little wonder that my teenage years were marked by high risk, thrill seeking, and quite self-destructive activities at every opportunity. Looking for fun involved only the most superficial of relationships. Nor did this pattern really end when my grandparents insisted on an arranged marriage that took place on my seventeenth birthday.

Only six months after *that* event, at eighteen I had finally decided to escape what had quickly become an abusive controlling marital relationship. It meant escaping from my grandparents as well. The huge step to independence took me to a refuge in Perth, far out of reach on the other side of the country. I began to feel a little safer. Habits though are not so easily changed. I slipped into a somewhat tortured personal lifestyle, trying all the while to find myself. One point I was resolute on though: I did not want family to find me.

3

Help!

Tara

Another free day, with some happy reflections! I am so thankful for the friends who happily have allowed me into their group activities. They had simply accepted my explanation of my move to Perth for study purposes, with no questions asked nor any answers given by me that might have given them any reason to doubt my straightforward and uncomplicated lifestyle. On the surface I guess I came over as a confident young woman, with a strongly developed sense of independence, so that's how they simply and unquestionably accepted me.

But another disturbing thought, when I am compelled to rethink about what I have done about the life I'd lived which my new friends had no inkling of – nor did I ever want them to know! But my sense of shame and embarrassment seems to have surfaced again, and I have no idea why. I had been very needy when I first left the women's refuge, and it was easy to just do what many of the women had been doing to fill in their time: making out with some guy they introduced me to, only to find he wasn't at all likeable, then accepting another blind date, forever living in hope. Some offered financial benefits, others simply wanted free sex, but with no strings attached. There were one or two opportunities to take up good work options, but these also came with hidden expectations which I had hated them for – and ultimately hated myself as well!

After several years alternating between experimenting with new guys, followed by periods of total abstinence, I became quite disillusioned with relationships in general. It was only after meeting socially with a small group of serious students in my final year at Uni did I dare to think that maybe life had some good things to offer after all. I'd enjoyed some tutorials with two women in particular who were my own age, and they eventually persuaded me to join them socially. My life's focus then had suddenly made a complete turnaround, which included an acceptance of these friends who were unselfishly committed to honest caring for each other, but which clearly was largely based in their authentic desire to be in a right relationship with their God. Accepting this truth for myself eventually brought a huge relief, removing so much fear that had previously been associated with relationships. My spiritual eyes slowly opened, and my faith journey began, bringing hope and some inner joy, with a growing genuine interest in learning what it means to be concerned with more than the physical surrounds. For the first time in my life, I had a growing sense of purpose beyond myself.

Little did my friends know during that time, however, of the inner turmoil that sometimes caused my own well-constructed sense of equilibrium to vanish. At those times, I would withdraw even from my friends, under the excuse of being too caught up by the demands of work and study. And although I had so recently come to appreciate what it meant to somewhat trust in a God who cares, I often felt under some condemnation – as if I would never really be good enough to count on the forgiveness and love promised for any who put their faith in such a promise. Only this last month, after battling with a tremendous sense of life being too difficult had I looked up and found an address of a psychologist, hoping that this time the move towards wellness would release me from my cleverly hidden but negative mental attitude to my own life story. Nothing seemed to satisfy. Even my surfing, which had offered such relief in the last year or two whenever I felt such aloneness, had now lost its attraction.

I made an appointment, and my first visit had been reassuring. Rather than having me feel a failure because I was expressing negative thoughts about life, the psychologist had simply assured me that many people have such thoughts and feelings but because they refused to admit to them, such people had to develop ways of masking them, or pretending that by shoving things under a carpet, the dust would disappear! That way the huge lump under the carpet eventually causes the stumble that could really hurt!

She listened to my brief account of my life in Perth, basically covering my life at Uni, my friends, my work, and love of all things physically demanding, all so apparently innocuous and indeed now quite healthy. I didn't go into great details of my profligate life during those early years after moving to Perth, but enough to paint a picture that showed I had experienced some depressive thoughts about life in general. In sharing these elements, I tentatively shared that sort of becoming a Christian had given me hope. I was really surprised but relieved when she admitted that she also understood what that meant, sharing the fact that she also was personally convinced of who Jesus is. So why was I so unhappy, so unsatisfied, I asked?

It was then that Em, obviously an experienced middle-aged wise lady, clearly discerned there was more to be known, and her questions became more specific, without seeming to be invasive of my privacy. For example, she asked about my life before Uni, and gently asked what life had been like before I started my tertiary studies. And what had life as a single person been like before faith became more real? Were there things I still felt guilty about? Gradually more of my story was revealed:

I felt Em was genuinely interested in what life had been like for me, and though initially I focused on good things, it became important to share some of the things that had deeply impacted my sense of well-being.

That first 50-minute session had been time enough to share details of my marriage and the awfulness of believing in love that had so quickly and destructively been dispelled. Clearly Em recognised and so appropriately responded to my distress about that loss, with sympathy that made me feel neither uncomfortable nor sceptical, as she in no way falsely claimed she understood how I might have felt. But she did assert, however, with a quiet reassurance, that such a let-down, such a terrible disappointment was enough to unsettle the most secure person, especially at such a young age! And that she also accepted that my rationally expressed ideas about feeling unsatisfied, feeling life to be out of control were quite understandable, even if they were the only distressing things I experienced.

Of course, I had to admit that the failed marriage, and its physical abuse, was in fact not the only thing that I had experienced, so another appointment was made. Before leaving that first session, Em encouraged me to spend some time before the next session to write down a list of things that had, potentially at least, destroyed my healthy view of how life should be, and with each item, to list what feelings I think any *other* person might have felt, should they have experienced what I had. This took a huge weight off my instinctive self-criticisms, because it was always easier to excuse others' feelings, but not my own.

My task suddenly seemed to become much less onerous, so that week each night I spent some time reflecting on my life. Once I started, there was no stopping me. And because I was committed to truthful, honest reflections, regardless of how upset I might be, I was amazed at just how sorry I felt for someone else who might have suffered what I had been subjected to. I still maintained a rational, objective attitude to the facts, as if these details were about some Jane Doe, not Tara! I somehow knew, however, that this would not remain possible after my next session, sharing with someone who was as insightful yet personally respectful as Em.

After a brief but relaxed intro, interacting about small but pleasant things of the week, for both the counsellor and me, Em began her session with a smile:

"So Tara, have you been your conscientious self with your reflections this week?"

"Oh yes, and here is my list, Em – unbelievably long, I'm afraid. I must admit I surprised even myself what things needed to be included". I wait a few moments while Em peruses my neatly typed up list, expecting her surprise but this didn't happen. She simply said:

"Well, Tara, I think it must have been a revelation to you that you were so able to report someone else's feelings, should they have shared this lived experience".

"Well, yes, in some way it was! I have always, well, since I was a young teenager, always prided myself on being rational, not inclined to let my feelings rule me. But I can see they have in fact become my nemesis, my Achilles heel as it were. Because, unbeknown to me, I have often been involved in stuff that was leading me up proverbial garden paths, or perhaps rather, down terrible ravines, simply because my feelings were not *obviously* leading the way! How stupid, Em, but I now can't understand why I behave so differently towards myself than I would towards others!"

"Sometimes, Tara, the principle of doing to others what you would do for yourself gets tripped up by other, hmm, less conscious beliefs".

"Like what?" I ask, concerned that I am really screwed up in my logical attempt to be caring.

"Oh, there's nothing wrong about your obvious care for others, Tara – but something is not quite right about being so down on yourself. Can you tell me about a time when you were really happy, when you felt loved and more than acceptable?"

I now force myself to remain controlled, because immediately a memory of a loving mother jumps into my mind – the day when we had spent time on the beach together, and all was wonderful.

I share this memory with Em, then of course she asks, "so what went wrong, Tara?" My tears could no longer be held back, and as I weep quietly, Em hands me the box of tissues, assuring me it is a good thing to know that when you share feelings, you honour the one who listens to your grief.

After several minutes, Em reaches over to lightly touch my hand, saying:

"Tara, are you prepared to let go of any belief that is unhelpful, that threatens to spoil your life as a mature adult?"

"I think so – but I'm afraid that if this one about treating myself nicely means I become a dithering, blubbering child, I'm not sure I want to go there!"

"I can understand that, Tara, but balance is more likely when this is done with complete respect between the parts of your mind that look after you. I believe we have been fearfully yet wonderfully made, and that when our minds desire to work in cooperation with our Creator, each part of our mind will seek to look after us, not try to be harmful, nor even be disruptive".

"So am I right in saying that the part of me that has blocked my positive feelings about myself has really not been helpful?"

"I would prefer you ask yourself that, Tara – because it may be that the *intent* was quite good, but the chosen behaviour in the end became detrimental to you".

Em then asked me to envisage looking into a 3D picture, one where I could see a little Tara at the beach. She encouraged me to use all my senses – to note the sounds, the movements, the sights and even the smells. As I settled into a trusting relaxed mode, I gradually could hear waves, though the picture was just a still picture. Then I imagined I was sitting on the sand, holding a book with blank pages. As suggested by Em, when I asked the part of me that had shut me down to feelings to draw a symbol of itself, immediately a small frightened emoji face appeared. I asked that part what she was frightened about, and she wrote the word DROWN, in big purple letters. As I silently asked whether she would ever feel like doing something like that again, she shook her head vigorously, so I asked whether there was another part of her that would. She simply nodded.

As I reported what I saw, Em would then suggest the next question: to ask that other part to come along side this frightened face, with its own emoji. Almost before the question was finished, a self-confident face appeared, and after an invitation to be connected, they each tentatively reached out a hand to each other. Em then began to explain how caring for each other means we work together, while always seeking to honour the words of Proverbs 3, verses 3 – 6…accepting that our good Creator will always direct us in positive healthy ways, never offer solutions that would be destructive. I listen carefully to Em, as I watch the two parts facing each other, each admitting various problems they had each suffered, when over the years, one part then another would try their best to rule, yet each finding they couldn't help each other. It was like they were meeting for the first time – as if separately they couldn't trust the other to be achieving worthwhile results. I simply sat and watched, almost as if I was a relaxed but intrigued third person.

After what seemed like a long discussion between them, with me not always knowing what was spoken, it seems clear to me that they are now agreed there were better ways of supporting me towards becoming a caring, confident adult, while also now wanting to assist me to take care of my own needs more appropriately. I finally allow them to dive off into a playful embrace as they disappear from my visual awareness, leaving me to disengage from the picture and to gratefully look back towards Em.

"That was amazing, Em! Did you see the two embrace?"

"No, Tara, I don't read your mind, though some think psychs do!" She laughs, as she assures me: "but I do see facial expressions and body language, and these tell me your mind is quite relieved about the agreements made, is that right?"

"Absolutely! I have not felt such internal peace, ever – its like the fight within has stopped, though I'm not even sure what alternatives may yet emerge!"

"That's a great start, Tara – and I look forward to a catchup session in a few weeks, so you can report on how its all going! Of course, we have just looked at the first thing on your list...you may want to decide to rearrange the priorities on your list, because these sessions are always about your needs, your agendas, and in your own time frame. Sometimes we want changes to be much less about depth, and more about speed. Some of that must depend on your choices, Tara. I will always respect that." I glance down to my copy of the list, and make a mental note that I want to work on feeling in control, and need to put that at the top of my priorities.

I leave that session with a sense of hope for the future, but one that also leaves me feeling surprisingly emotionally drained – this time, however, not so much negatively exhausted but in due respect for myself as a human being, one who has experienced a life far less perfect than it should have been. I am also importantly aware of how my own choices have contributed to that fact. But I am more committed to growing up, not to flagellating myself for my behaviours that had been resorted to, in a childish attempt to cope with insufferable pain and loss. I know I will cry myself to sleep, but more from relief and the release of pent-up emotions, not with self-pity.

4

A Dour Scot

Iain

"Coffee time, Iain." The clinic's receptionist Jenny burst in through my open door. The only decent coffee is around the corner from work, at the Il Lido Italian Canteen just off Cottesloe beach. It is always good to get a leg stretch. Coffee in hand, we wander over to the beach.

"Why is it, do you think, that the far away horizon brings such relaxation, re-energising for the remaining afternoon?" Jenny asked.

"Mindfulness" I suggest, as I go on to explain that it is about focusing far into the distance, almost out of focus, drawing attention away from all the demanding immediate busyness. I start staring off into horizon myself, relaxing at the sight of small insignificant sails dotted along the seascape. But just as it is beginning to captivate me, Jenny's question starts a train of thought. I am distracted. A question pops up. Is this the only way people experience mindfulness? Insatiably curious, I allow my eyes a quick flick back to the busy beach right front of us. A few people are lying down, soaking up the last of the summer warmth, and a couple reading. They all look enviably relaxed. Another form of mindfulness no doubt, at least for those with closed eyes?

Then the ever-present surfers. What is their enjoyment? Excitement? Is there some sort of mindfulness happening, despite their frenetic activity? Is it activity that distracts them from everyday stressors? I recall one of them had told me how surfing made him feel invigorated, and at one with nature. That is inconceivable to me. How can vigorous activity be restful, even enjoyable? What is it they enjoy? What sort of people enjoy surfing? I look around. Towards the end of summer, great time of the year in Perth - wonderful! The surfers here are mostly young board-shorted and bikini clad sun-blonded surfers. Well, no surprise. That's typical for this beach in Perth at this time of day, even during the week. Fit, active, young, grasping the moment, enjoying an unfettered lifestyle. Yes, inextricably, majorly preoccupied with the next wave, such focus, such obsession just not allowing time for any of the encumbrances of modern-day capitalism to stress them. Maybe they had no need for formal mindfulness – they are always so mindful of grasping then staying on top of the next wave. I feel a little envious of what I assume their state of mind to be, but not of their physical exertion!

Ah, I notice a few older surfers among them as well. There is an older wiry looking guy, long grey hair, loose and tangled, skin leathery and quite wrinkled, even from a distance. Then I notice a female surfer. She looks Mediterranean, or I ponder, perhaps Middle-eastern background? A dark complexion and thick black hair that's not tied back. It's hard to tell from here how old she is. She is wearing an all-black wet suit, no hijab though I muse. Somehow, I don't know why, but she looks an unlikely surfer, and that fascinates me. I want to see how she surfs, but time is running on.

She is back in the water. The speed with which she manages to swim and paddle out again on her board surprises me. Then, a large wave is coming in and within seconds she has climbed to her feet on the board and is riding it. I wonder about how tall she might be. Around five feet, maybe even less. Is it a low centre of gravity that allows her to get up with such seeming ease? I've been told that women have a lower centre of gravity anyhow. Interesting. I continue to watch as she comes back in. Even to my untrained eye every movement looks so effortless, fast, effective, and elegant in a way that reminds me of a gymnast or classical dancer. Maybe she is a dancer? It is not what I had expected when I first saw her.

I am intrigued. I have questions. How can I manage to get a good look at the surfer's face? I find myself wanting to see her face up close. How old is she? Does her face tell a story? Is it lined from the sun, and how does the sun affect such a dark complexion, so different from my fair Celtic skin and ruddy red-head complexion?

Jenny reminds me that it is about time we head back. I am about to move off when I notice the dark surfer going for her towel, unclipping her board leash from her ankle. Is she going to sit down? No. She looks energised. She is starting up the embankment towards the carpark, due east. We are north of her, and our walk back to the office is north. No sense in trying to cross paths by walking south.

But when the surfer gets up to the path running north-south along the beach dune, to my delight she turns north! She must be going to the northern car park, and that means walking right past us, unless she gets off the path and cuts along the grass. Jenny gives me a strange look, half impatience, half wondering what I am staring at. I feel a little funnily embarrassed. She looks where I am looking. She looks back at me with a wry smile and then starts to move off. I imagine her thinking, 'men, can't help themselves when there are pretty women in scant attire'. Oh well, I tell myself, think what you will, that's not it. I notice I haven't finished my coffee. What a convenient excuse: I ask her to just hang on so I can finish. That will be just long enough for the surfer to walk past.

As she comes closer, darn it! I can't see her face for the dark mop of hair blown across by the Fremantle Doctor! The Freo Doctor is a regular afternoon cooling breeze that's now seeing most people getting up from the beach. Makes me conscious of my own hair, and I brush it aside, only to notice she is doing the same. As she sees me, she hesitates, then to my surprise, indeed my delight, she stops, and I see her gaze has gone from my face to my arm.

"Um, would you mind, can you tell me the time please?" She smiles as she continues to look at the sleeve around my wrist.

Answers come flooding in to satisfy my questions. Clear voice, Australian accent. Dark skin does not look all that weathered. Doesn't look like she spends all day everyday surfing. Yet she was so skilful. Almost one with the water. I wonder how else she may have developed such superb motor skills, such a love for water. Bright clear blue eyes, not the brown ones I expected. No drug indicators. Not really a dropout surfie. Athletic yes. My intrigue has distracted me.

"You have a watch?" she asks, looking down at my arm. I'm a little embarrassed at my delay.

"Oh, yes, sure, its, its three thirty, afternoon of course." I am feeling more than a little awkward, as I try to jest.

"Thanks" she says, looking back to my face. She turns to walk on. But then pauses like one would do when a further question comes to mind.

"That's some Scottish accent!" It's not a question waiting for affirmation as is usually the case in such situations. Without pausing she goes on.

"I often wonder how such a cold country can produce such a warm accent. Do you like watching surfing in Scotland? Do you perhaps surf? You looked to be watching us so keenly while your partner was off enjoying the distance."

Sprung. What do I say? Was my interest so obvious as to be intrusive, and was she checking me out? I wanted to joke.

"Warm accent bespeaks warm people."

"And as for surfing?"

"Oh I'm no surfer. Surfing is a mystery to me. Watching you is just fascinating." Oops, I'd better make sure it is not just about her. "I find myself trying to work out what makes all of you surfers tick. But, then, you are all so different."

"Watching doesn't tell you anything really though, does it?" She smiles with a tilt of her head.

"I guess not. So, what draws you to surfing?"

"It's free. It's freedom. Ah, it's a great leveller". She pauses, then says "You look like you are built for it. Ever thought of trying it? No knowing without doing."

She spoke in a way that suggested to me that she might enjoy challenging and teasing people. And, yes, I *am* a little surprised that she seems to have taken so much in about me, not just that I had been looking. For a stranger, its rather straightforward, direct. I put it down to cultural background perhaps despite no accent. As I find it kind of attractive, I pick up on it and joke - that appearances can be deceiving and take it as permission for me to ask a few more specific questions about her obvious love of surfing.

Jenny has been watching. She takes an opportunity to break in to remind me that we need to get going, suggesting it's getting late. The surfer looks over to her for the first time as if only now aware of her, and sounds apologetic:

"Oh, sorry, didn't mean to hold you up." Then, as if playfully choosing her words with intentional double meaning, she thanks us for the time.

As we head back to work, I want to look back but don't. I have some phone calls to make. Ha, I still have my coffee in hand, and still half drunk! As we walk back Jenny ribs me:

"I've never seen you flirt before!"

I protest that I am just interested in people, being polite and social. Jenny just grins.

Back at the office I make some calls, while drinking the cold remaining coffee. I sit back in my chair when the surfer's cheeky face comes to mind, rather more vividly than I am used to. I must have been quite intrigued. I am enjoying the recalled image, those eyes, the smile, the tousled hair, quite appealing. Maybe Jenny was right. Before I realise what I am doing, I google surfing. The memory of her face brings a sense of warmth. Silly, I tell myself. Primacy effect, yes, remember the danger of first impressions.

Its 4am. I have had a week of the unknown surfer intruding, uninvited. Nothing serious. I have just woken but feel wide awake. I'd been dreaming. What was all that about? All I could remember was the surfer, yet again, but this time holding up her arm and saying, 'look, no rings!' What was I dreaming that led up to that? It has faded, but her face has not. What is the continuing curiosity really about? Is it some sort of an attraction? Maybe she reminds me of someone?

That's it! She is the exact opposite of my ex-wife. I turn over restlessly. I finally go to sleep.

5

Sheila

Iain

I had left Sheila, and I had left Scotland too, mainly because of her. She was blond, tall, and dark eyed. Every boy in class had been after her. She was the minister's daughter, and I was an earnest young man her father approved of. I was besotted when she responded to my advances and even more so when we started going out. But I now know, it was not her I was infatuated with, but rather, the ego stroking prize she represented. Well may I have been an earnest young man on the surface but hidden away were hormones driving unfettered desires. Nothing is so untameable as an addiction you deny. We couldn't wait to get married, and at 20 years of age her father licenced our illicit activities, leaving me thinking any guilt I considered bothersome would be no more.

In the ensuing two years there were two pivotal points. The first was when I came to the realisation that lust combined with ego in fact is no basis for intimacy but devastatingly destructive for any relationship. Our fights increased. Nothing I could do seemed to be able to satisfy Sheila in any way. We found ourselves looking and turning to others to satisfy seemingly insatiable desires. One night, Sheila lay sobbing on our bed after hitting me with the breadboard. She was sick of me taking stuff too seriously. Life was to be lived. Thinking was for nerds. Serious talks were what her father did, all the time. I vividly recall her going on at me, screaming that there was no way she felt I loved her enough, could *ever* love her enough, and if I was such a thinker, had I never thought about why she just couldn't ever love me. She'd married me, she said, because her father had told her I was God's man for her, and he had been so relieved when we married. Ignorantly, I had not realized Sheila had simply wanted to escape his demanding, authoritarian ways. She'd learnt to be compliant.

It was not as I'd hoped: nothing seemed right. I felt despair, tinged with bitterness. Then came my feeling devastated, hopeless. No matter what I did to try to fix things, it just seemed one mile too far when Sheila went on to tell me about a clandestine swingers' group she had been going along to. There, she said, they were real men: they really made her feel excited and loved.

Following many a sleepless night on the couch, when one night I had finally made it clear that I had decided that there was nothing left but separation, Sheila had later emerged from our bedroom trying to cuddle up and meekly saying that she didn't want our marriage to end. I suspect with the benefit of hindsight that it was because she feared her father's reaction, knowing the shame on him. Couldn't I just love her more, she pleaded?

The cuddling worked. We agreed on counselling. It was the counsellor who finally asked Sheila to consider whether her need to be indulged was insatiable? He ingenuously even suggested she might have a borderline personality disorder. Unless she came to terms with and sought help for that, he'd said, she would never be satisfied with anyone loving her enough. At first, she surprisingly seemed to accept that this might be the case, and indeed, she said she recognised that to be true. She'd never felt loved at home. Then just as the session was about to end, she asked what might also be wrong with me: did I have any responsibility when it came to a satisfying marriage? Sure, the counsellor had answered, but that was for the next time. She left and in the ensuing days became quite angry, saying she wouldn't go back to a counsellor who heaped it all on her, and moreover, nor did she ever want to see any counsellor in the future!

I hoped that time might bring sense. I soon concluded that nothing would change as I saw her continue to disappear in the night knowing it was to meet up with her swingers' group. Not that I didn't have my own struggles, one of which was alcohol. We lived in a small Scottish community where everyone knew everyone, and my ego was such that I was uncomfortable even walking around town. Friends seemed to know more about Sheila's clandestine proclivities than I did. My marriage was clearly over.

I wanted to better understand people, and what makes for good relationships. So it was that I grasped the opportunity to take up a scholarship to further study psychology. After finishing graduate degrees in Edinburgh, I emigrated, getting away as far as possible from my failed life, in the end becoming a practitioner in Perth, Western Australia.

I now knew I was in search of myself, needing to find myself before I could ever be ready for another relationship. For a while I put aside any potential considerations for intimacy with a female. I even considered whether I might be gay, but soon realised that wasn't me. Slowly, ever so slowly as I journeyed. I learned much from my studies in psychology, notably benefiting from Frankl's Logo Therapy, in my search for peace, realising the wisdom of answering the questions about life in the right order: Who am I, where am I going, and then who goes with me? Gradually I also slowly became aware of a healing spiritually, encouraged as I read C S Lewis, with some important personal growth, born out of never having quite abandoned my struggle to find a trustworthy understanding of God. But I was never sure I would ever find *myself* sufficiently to entertain unadulterated intimacy, though I admit I had not even a remote idea as to what that might actually look like.

In the ensuing years, I have enjoyed some mildly romantic relationships, but none have ever come to anything worth persevering with. Sometimes I ponder why they never go anywhere. Maybe it's because a lot goes around in my head most of the time. It's easy to slip into my bubble. I enjoy the internal dialogue, teasing out ideas. You can probably tell that from my writing. I enjoy watching people: all so different. They fascinate me, they intrigue me, though still I battle to understand anyone in any intuitive way. Don't get me wrong, I like people, and do like talking with people, one to one. I care quite deeply in fact about others' wellbeing. That's one of my drivers in my work. As for groups, well, they are OK, if there's room for some good discussion. I can't stand parties though, or dancing, or trying to engage in small talk.

So, what stops me getting in any deeper with anyone? Somehow the relationships just peter out. One woman had even called me a dour Scotsman! Another asked why every discussion always had to be so serious. I didn't think I was that serious. Don't think I can't enjoy some fun nor can play a prank or two. In fact, playing a prank was such a shock to one girlfriend, that's what ended the relationship. On reflection, she was a rather serious person herself, possibly one I connected with more than any other. But the two of us? We just didn't fit!

I have tried to work myself out through attachment theory, and my valued older friend and colleague Em has talked with me about that as well. But, despite all my study, I don't think I have any real understanding of what such a connection would *feel* like. Sure, I *know* about it, I just don't seem to be able to *experience* it. Maybe I don't allow myself. But how can I be blocking something others consider so fundamental? Is there some reason why I need to keep everything cognitive, above nose level? Sure, I am a little cautious about experientialism, even in my spiritual journey. Even there, any sense of what I think is attachment doesn't come from any spiritual experiences, but rather my knowing Him seems to come from my knowing *about* Him. I accept He loves me not because I feel it, but because I have carefully come to the conclusion that the Bible is reliably inspired, and it tells me so. For me, knowing is a point of trust in revealed truth as well as discovered truth: Bible and science respectively. Sometimes I ponder how much this is me and how much it is my Presbyterial-Scottish cultural heritage.

In the end, a spiritual experience is all very well to think about, but I don't pine for what I do not know, nor for what, if I am honest, I am a little diffident about. Occasionally if I do have some pangs for what might be nice, I find it easier to simply bury myself in my work. But now at almost 37 I have come to the conclusion, simply, that, well, I am just one of those people, as an introvert, best off in my own world.

So, this is background that I hope helps any reader understand why I find myself again asking about an uninvited dream: How can it be that, so counter to any intention and even any desire or sense of need, I find myself *attracted* to a complete stranger? If that is not superficial, what is? It involves an emotionality that totally confuses me. When people speak of love at first sight, I think of that sort of talk as romantic self-deluding nonsense. My rational mind tries to understand. Is there some sort of latent wish fulfilment? Is it time to get back to read some Freud? After all, that's where the attachment style stuff has its roots. Psychodynamic stuff seems so more appealing than cold logical cognitive behaviourism. Somehow, when it comes to the deeply personal and relational, it seems to make more sense to me to dig down to mental activity and memories so deeply hidden from consciousness. That's it, explanations by recourse to the subconscious recesses of an unconscious mind. Hey, Iain, keep it simple! Complexity just gets you running around in circles. Besides, what's the evidence at the base of that stuff?

With a repeating dream of the surfer, I am fascinated as to why it seems to be almost, if not exactly, the same dream. I have never had that before. If that's not the mark of some sort of an irrational obsession, what is? Maybe it's time to accept that I may be using work as an escape? Or perhaps it's time to get serious about a real girlfriend, not some imaginary fanciful idea?

'Whatever,' I think, but for now I need to stop the silly dreams. I come back to using the familiar behavioural techniques I use with clients to dismiss the intrusions, to extinguish any crazy thoughts. They work. I didn't get back to Freud. I simply bury myself in my work again and feel content, or so I think.

6

Caught by Surprise

Tara

My relatively brief stay at the refuge after escaping Melbourne had certainly taught me much about life. It was my first real taste of an unrestrained opportunity to do what I liked. There were plenty there who encouraged me to believe in that freedom. Fortunately, it had also provided some positive benefits. Finally enough confidence to move into my own unit, and this provided time: for myself and for some serious study. Some good conversations also gave me insight into a personal need to start taking responsibility for a future that I had never thought possible. I then enrolled at the University of WA, and from there learned that my early love of the outdoors could be rewarded if I studied hard, like early on I had also played hard. I made some difficult decisions, and I think I have stuck to them!

During my undergrad years, I soon learned that my natural abilities lay in the observational sciences, and I discovered I definitely did not want to be a social scientist: people were too unpredictable, unreliable, and often even uncaring. So when I finally met some students who were both fun to be with, but also serious about life, involved with social concern for others less fortunate, I began tagging along with them. As I mentioned earlier, as I'd watched and listened, I became convinced that their religious beliefs were not really heavy, though they were indeed unselfishly very focused. In time I understood I could also do what they did, because I asked for and received an amazing gift: the wonder of feeling loved and empowered by the spirit of an amazing Creator, a graciously loving and forgiving God. I thankfully responded to knowing it was not about keeping laws, but about relationship. I had much to learn, but I then felt I was on a constructive wholesome track. There was a sense of innate goodness, of the way things should and could be: hope restored!

During this time, I had accepted a traineeship called a scholarship, studying while also working with a successful company in Western Australia, initially developing menus mainly for the air travel industry. This led finally to my gaining a master's degree in food technology and sensory science. I had taken up a position within their research and development department. I had thrown myself into my work, and I still really love it. It allows me many opportunities to spend time outdoors, researching plants and the best environments in which these should be grown. Always so good to be away from many of the interpersonal challenges some of my colleagues complain of. Ever the observer, it gives me plenty of time to enjoy observing and recording details of our diverse and quite fascinating creation. I loved seeing and learning about plants as edible foods, but also as examples of incredible global variations in nature that we have come to understand and appreciate within our multi-cultural society.

I had also happily deflected several well-meaning attempts at match making at a Church I had started to attend, but thankfully now, people have learned to leave me alone. I appreciate that my church family is there when or if I need it, but currently it almost seems somewhat like my childhood family: while people cared, the church family has never really provided any depth of friendship. As the years have passed, I realised people have naturally become more involved with their own life demands.

I look back on the student years with gratitude: a time when fun, discussions, even doing things for others was mostly unpressured, relaxed even, a privileged time! Gradually over time it has dawned on me that the After-church Coffee which offers a time to talk, is always so rushed. Even though I try to engage more deeply, mostly people keep it pretty superficial, as if in a hurry to get away. A small study group I joined for a while sadly offered nothing more personally engaging either. I am left wondering if it is because I don't share the common ground of being a couple, or not having to cope with raising children. Some seem to assume I might well be gay, but that clearly was not a subject they have ever dared to raise.

I reflect on how I so appreciate a couple of close friends at work, though, who are also single. But sadly, while we share a lot through work, and even occasionally socially, they don't share my greatest and newly found treasure: my faith. However, along with being by nature quite introverted, my faith serves me well, for I love solo activities like reading, and on the other hand, I also really enjoy any physically demanding activity. Time in the garden is always so enjoyable, too, particularly producing some veggies I can share with neighbours and others at church. Always invigorated by physical activity, I look for any opportunity to escape any boredom I might feel, like surfing and rowing or simply walking the beaches.

There's something wonderful about the sea, isn't there! It never ceases to capture our full attention: photos just can't cut it somehow, no matter how we try. Beautiful, powerful, yet also, relaxing, draws you in! And for me, it's at the sea where any memories of failed relationships are kept well out of mind, helping to keep any small desire for intimacy well sublimated, indeed effectively displaced by the sheer enjoyment of the physical exhilarations I so enjoy!

I've almost turned 33 and today here I am back surfing again, straight after work. But as I note the warmth disappearing, I shake off the sand, and pause to take in the beauty of the massive, surging ocean, before slowly heading back towards the car. Suddenly a couple on the shore catch my attention. In a way that's not unusual: I quite enjoy observing people, though I do it matter-of-factly, quite dispassionately. The man is tall, while his partner is short, similar in fact to my own height. For a split second I find myself uncharacteristically wondering what it would be like if I was that woman. I notice how the wind blows the man's red hair across his face. Strange, unfamiliar thoughts! Then I realise the couple seem to be watching me, well, the man seems to be focussed on me, if not the woman. I feel somewhat embarrassed. Did they think I had been rude, standing staring at them? Why on earth have they so caught my attention? Maybe it's the amusing intrigue of seeing a couple who are so obviously different, not least in size! For whatever reason, I decide to deliberately trek past them on the way to my car. I casually stop, ask him the time, though feel a bit stupid really, because I always know pretty much what the time is!

The man tells me the time, and then I am quite surprised that he goes on to ask me a question: "what is it about surfing that you enjoy so much?" Somehow, inexplicably, I feel his question is not just a pleasant curiosity but is genuine, warm, interested, and yes, personal. I'm right - they had been watching me. I can't resist challenging him about his interest in surfing: life is about doing, not just watching. The passing comment turns into a short discussion, though I can see the woman is a little irritated, almost trying to upset the interaction with some of her quite trivial comments. I really want it to keep going; I am enjoying his warm Scottish accent.

Reluctantly I say, "I must be off too" and turn to walk towards my car, not comfortable with whatever I am currently experiencing. I can call it some sort of a conflict within, almost like a warning not to be silly. I have no explanation for what had just happened. After all, this was just a stranger on the beach. Why any need for a deep-down part of me to be *feeling* so defensive? What am I thinking? I pride myself on being a rational, pretty self-controlled human being. I am often impatient with anyone who suggests they can't help themselves, and I can be quite dismissive of anyone seemingly run by their feelings. My failed arranged marriage and a series of disastrous relationships after all taught me so much. It's years now since I had decided I wasn't able to understand or even want any sort of committed relationship. My Christianised conscience had tapped me on the shoulder, and I well remember gladly giving up on accepting one-night stands - never again! I remember how that hadn't really been too difficult: they were always so serially shallow and unsatisfying. In fact, I am now glad to say they had all but desensitised me to any desire for a relationship with a man. Life on my own is far simpler, much less painful.

But here, completely by surprise, my heart seems to be suggesting some sort of attraction. What's going on? My head starts spinning with wrong, wrong, wrong. As I close the car door, and before starting the engine, I yell out loud: 'Tara, get a hold of yourself. Don't judge a book by its cover! And after a decade of reasonably successful celibacy, why this stupid emotional reaction?'

Over the next few weeks, I find whenever I am not busy, his face or his voice keeps popping into my head. It's so irritating, but I can't stop thinking about him. What am I doing, allowing myself to indulge in thinking about a married man! "Wrong, wrong, wrong" I even yell at myself, hoping that would stop it! How come my thoughts, my decisive plans are so out of control? I clearly need to stay away from the beach, in case we meet up again. I'll go rowing instead, on the beautiful Swan River. That's obviously the best thing to fix these mindless imaginings!

Unfortunately, however, any time I relax, the beach scene and the discussion with the Scotsman comes unbidden into my conflicted mind. Then again, 'wrong, wrong, wrong 'echoes around in my head. It even occurs when I am sleeping; suddenly I'll be awake, hearing myself calling out in that sleep limited speech: 'wrong, wrong, wrong!'

I am now feeling desperate: this battle has raged on for two months! I try prayer, but that brings no relief! I can't share concerns with any of my church friends, either - in fact, they have no idea that I had ever been married! How can I smash their perception of me, an ardent stoic? I'll have to go get help with this obsession, find a way to put *him* out of my mind. It is ridiculous!! How can I be so simple minded as to let a Scottish brogue get to me? That's it: Scottish brogue. Maybe a visit to Scotland would cure me. But no amount of talking to myself, no matter how intense or vigorously I exercise, nothing seems to stop the intrusions. In fact, they only seem to become the more intrusive the more I deliberately try to abort such thoughts. Maybe it's time to revisit Em, the lovely older psychologist who helped me a few years ago, when dealing with past negative destructive inter-personal behavioural patterns. At least she knows me well and won't make me feel even more stupid!

Only a week elapses before I find myself sitting once again in the waiting room at her clinic.

7

—

Digging the Unconscious

Tara

Em herself comes to the waiting room door and warmly beckons me to follow. Together we walk down the hallway towards her consulting room, chatting comfortably like old acquaintances catching up.

"You're looking well, Tara. It's been, what, almost ten years?"

"Yes, must be all of that." I am quite relaxed, knowing any serious conversation will only begin in the privacy of her room. But nearing Em's room, suddenly a man pops out from an adjacent room, and I go into shock: He looks like the man from the beach! Is it? Or just my ridiculous obsession? He is heading off to the waiting room I just left. I hear his Scottish accent. It *is* him! I want to run, but what to say to Em? I almost stagger into her room, and slump into a chair.

"Tara, you look like, well, as if you just saw a ghost!"

"That Scotsman, he's the trouble!" I blurt out but can't say more. Poor Em looks taken aback. Who knows what she is thinking, but she looks worried. But she, always so sensitive, just quietly waits for me to explain. It takes me several seemingly long minutes before I collect myself sufficiently to find how to continue.

"He, that guy, is the reason I came here today."

Now it is clear to me that the psychologist in Em is completely baffled. She knows me to be a direct, matter of fact sort of person, but I've not given her much to go on. She simply nods encouragingly, so I try as fast as possible to continue.

"I am committed to a single life, you know that, Em, and that's been going pretty well since I saw you last. I was really happy with how things were. And now, well, I can't get him out of my mind. I don't even know who he is, and … Em, you helped me last time, but this, well this is undoing all of that. I feel as though my feelings are getting the better of me again. You must help!"

I fall silent for a minute or so. Em clearly wants to ask specific questions but knows that I would react as if in an inquisition if she does. She was always good at summarising, mirroring what she thought she had heard, so thankfully she does that now, giving me time to catch my breath:

"So Tara, you are saying you simply can't get this guy out of your mind, and yet you don't even know him? Yet somehow, you know he is a Scotsman?"

I feel stupid, but I know I must tell her all about what happened back on the beach. As clearly as possible, I honestly share my innermost thoughts and feelings about the intrigue and conflict I had and still feel over this man. I admit my total confusion, my conflicted internal dialogue that plays havoc with me, both when I'm awake and even when sleeping.

"I have even stopped surfing or going anywhere other than work, for fear of seeing him again. So now, Em, I desperately want your help, because I must know how to stop these crazy intrusions!"

Em just nods again, so I launch into more revelations about my uncontrolled thoughts.

"It is so infuriating. He just keeps intruding. He is even stopping me properly getting on with my work. He is making me feel things I have never thought before, or is it thought things I have never felt before, or whatever – see how I am confused? I am a rational woman. I consider self-control a matter of good character, but he, well, he just comes in completely uninvited. I have tried to distract myself, and just as I think I have succeeded, he pops in and takes over my thinking again. I can't understand how he does that. And now, I have just seen him, here! Oh dear! How much more is he going to distract me after, after today? I even wake up at times, with him coming into my dreams. Really, its a nightmare! Am I going mad?"

Em responds quietly and non-confrontationally: "So it seems to you that *you* have no control in this matter?"As always, she cleverly refrains from asking specifically about my feelings, for she had already assessed me, way back, that I am a realist for whom feelings are never the way into my concerns. She so nicely reflects to me what I was most alarmed by: my lack of a sense of agency, visibly without my necessary sense of being in control. She gives me time to clearly put my rational case before inviting me to explore whatever eventually emerges in our discussion.

"Yes….. yes, I think that's it, I need to get control."

"So do you mean control of yourself?" she asked me carefully, almost tentatively.

"Well yes, of course! I need to get control!"

"So it's not really someone else doing this, is it? This is part of your own mind, seemingly working against you, yes?" She begins to push the point that she knew I had learned from her years before.

I remember how she had taught me that 'talking therapy' by itself is very limited. Good therapy usually involves exploring unrealistic and often quite unconscious expectations that eventually must emerge, as these try to meet repressed, unacknowledged, or even denied needs and desires. Any straightforward approach to identifying the motivating repressions inevitably finds them subconsciously well defended. Indeed, a front-on challenge can serve to defend and deny them even more robustly. I vaguely remember that the path to uncover those hidden, unconscious thoughts and feelings needs to be indirect and client led.

"Yes, I know it's my stupid and frustrating mind. But how do I get that control back?"

Em then asks what seems like a question a bit off track:

"Do you get anxious very much at all now, Tara?"

"No, not really. I don't think I am an anxious type of person. Oh, except maybe when I don't feel I have control. Is that why you are asking?"

"Well, when we worked through things last time you were coming to see me, you said quite openly that getting close to anyone made you break into a sweat, and I suggested that sounded like being anxious."

"Ok, yes, I remember. Well… I like my friends, but I don't ever want to let myself get too close to anyone."

"Is that because when you think about getting close to anyone, you are afraid that you may actually lose control?"

"No, it's not control of what I or even what the other might do - I have learned that one, the hard way! I am older now, and I'm happy to say I think we sorted that out! No, it's not that, but as you know, relationships in the past have brought me nothing but pain and unhappiness…. and well, I am content to accept that I am just not cut out for romantic relationships. I am just not the romantic type. Nor the maternal type either. Once you helped me understand that there are different types of relationships, well, I am enjoying many good platonic friendships. I am really happy now with my job and friends."

"Except, now, for this intrusion?" Em smiles at me, almost as if she wants me to relax in the idea as perhaps being OK.

"Yes, and I don't want it; it's no good for me and he is probably married or has a partner or something." That is something deep down I now really want to ask Em: to know if the Scotsman is in a committed relationship with anyone. She probably senses that, but I daren't ask! I'm thinking fast, like there are two likely results of knowing: if he is committed to someone, then surely, I could regain control, because he is out of bounds. But what if he isn't? That hits me again as a terrifying thought. Briefly I'm confronted with the old approach-avoidance conflict. I decide it is better not to know. So I say:

"How do I get this nonsense to stop, Em"?

Em doesn't yet give me an answer. Instead, she continues to try to capture what is going on inside my head.

"What makes you think there's a part of you wants to bring this episode so close to the surface all the time, when the rest of you is so up in arms struggling to keep control?"

"You tell me! I just want control!"

"But you can't get control of these thoughts….. Repression never brings peace: you have to settle this within."

"There is nothing to settle. I don't need romance. I am quite happy with my lot as it is. I have made a conscious decision. My mind needs to obey. I need to shut this part of me down."

Em looks at me knowingly. There is a deep sense of caring in her eyes. I trust this woman. She speaks firmly, decisively, and I know her well enough for her to have that right.

"You are such a determined person, Tara. Self-disciplined. Self-controlled. But that can make you your own worst enemy. You can give yourself, deep down, a really hard time, to the point of bullying! Yes, self-bullying! That is what we otherwise call repression. Conflicts are never resolved by bullying, and none more so than when they are conflicts raging deeply in our own soul, breaking out in our subconscious mind. It's tearing you apart. We need to do some work!"

"Are you going to help me gain control?" I ask plaintively, hoping she will.

"I think you are missing the gist what I am saying. It's not about control. It's about listening."

"Listening?"

"Yes, listening. How about I get you a drink: hot or cold?"

8

Don't Bully

Tara

Em comes back with a cup of tea. She's forgotten that I am not a tea person, but that doesn't really matter. I am almost oblivious to what I am drinking anyhow. The brief pause: purposeful on Em's part I have no doubt, skilful. It has given me time I needed to digest what has been said before we move on. She gives me a further minute or so as we sit there, each with cup in hand, sitting forward in our chairs like a couple of old friends.

"Tara, remember how we did some work negotiating with your subconscious mind last time?"

"Yes, I remember. You got me to relax and clear my mind and then to talk to myself? I think you called it some Gestalt-based work with the unconscious."

"Yes, so you remember it pretty well. And do you remember what happened?"

"How can I forget? I knew consciously all the raging conflicts, like a disorderly class of kids. You pointed out that we spend most of our day doing things automatically, having trained ourselves; most of what we do I accept is done by our subconscious mind, with us acting out of habit. I remember being a little amused when you suggested that talking to yourself is not the first sign of madness but is a really healthy thing to do - to be fully in touch with yourself. I do it all the time, more consciously now, and usually that's great! But it's not *working* now. I keep telling myself, even yelling at myself to stop, but I can't convince some recalcitrant subconscious part of me to behave itself." I am feeling quite angry, frustrated at this point.

"Do you remember when and how I got you to not only listen to the thoughts coming into consciousness, but to talk directly to yourself, as if to various parts within your subconscious? Even asking such diverse thoughts expressed by them to be resolved quite subconsciously, almost as if asking your conscious mind to just respectfully listen to other parts of your mind?"

"Yes, I do. And it made sense when you pointed out we all quite commonly say 'a part of me wants to do this and another part wants me to do the opposite.' Just like St Paul said about his own mind and conflicting behaviours. That way of describing the subconscious was a convincing moment."

"So, while we reflected together that while it happens naturally in everyday life, when we concentrate in a relaxed mode, in a more specifically focussed deeper way, we can more effectively deal with a behaviour or feeling that we consciously don't understand at all, yet need to resolve."

"Yes, I remember."

"Are you happy to do that now?"

"Anything! That is, anything that will allow me to control this bubbling up from my unconscious that is mucking up my life!" I sound and need Em to know that I am quite determined.

"Well, no, that would be bullying, Tara. Remember, we want the conflicts to be worked out by negotiation and consultation. We want to achieve peace, not victory! A bully never *really* wins. That's why we have the word pyrrhic – only won by too great a cost. Any wins from bullying are always pyrrhic at best and never without problems."

"Mmm; well, I am certainly conscious of a major battle going on deep down there. Peace would be a victory" I say, finding myself now smiling with a tinge of hope.

In agreement and with a clear memory of the process to resolve such conflict, I immediately close my eyes, at the same time settling myself more comfortably, thinking "this is the same relaxing chair I remember from previous consultations." In fact, even before Em starts to give her normal relaxation spiel, I find myself saying: "I can already sense some floating inside my brain." Em picked up on the process. She well knew that highly visual people tend to talk to themselves through pictures and writing, while more verbally oriented people hear things, almost like shouts normally coming into consciousness, but when there's a relaxed focus, it is possible to obtain clarity of one's thoughts in a more ordered way. She leaves it open now for me to find my preferred way of listening to my subconscious parts; slowly and quietly she asks an open question, joining the conversation but only as a facilitator.

"So what's happening down there?"

"There is a lot of yelling and arguing - just as I was getting consciously aware."

"Ask for quiet."

"So… yes, now there is quiet! Wow. Hey, there's a part that seems to be hiding" I am finding it easy to maintain a relaxed concentration on the internal dialogue, fascinated in fact! It's like I am observing from outside myself.

"Ask that part of you what it is trying to do for you, while needing to be in hiding?"

"Says it wants to look after me - but all the other parts are getting loud and saying 'no, don't listen.' I told them to be quiet and now they are. It seems this must be a part of me that wants me to be romantic."

"Check it out" Em then suggests.

"It doesn't make sense, Em. It's gone completely quiet in my subconscious; just this one small voice saying that I need to allow the gentle spirit of God to lead me, to free up my mind to listen to some external truth. But that's what I have been praying. I thought I was doing that. Whoa, this makes even less sense."

I am forced to pause, reflecting on all my thoughts as I consciously process all that is going on. "The thoughts coming are that, well, those thoughts I am experiencing about the Scotsman, though unbidden, may be God inspired. What does that mean? That can't be right! There's this other part of me intruding, yelling now, 'stop, stop, stop' and says it is protecting me - it doesn't want me to get hurt and its objecting." I'm given some moments before Em quietly seeks to facilitate deeper understanding.

"I believe your creative part is committed to your best interests, under the Lordship of Jesus, so Tara, ask that part to get together with the two differing parts, to respectfully sort out their differences."

"Not very strong, that creative part in me I am afraid, but I will suggest that." There are some moments of silence, giving my mind time for a peaceful solution to the internal conflict. Time seems to pass without any limiting awareness. When that internal conflict is finally resolved, I now feel I want to open my eyes: I want to share my more lucid and reassuring thoughts with my wise counsellor. I silently enjoy the peace. Then I speak slowly and quietly.

"I couldn't follow all the discussion down there or is it up there! But it was so quick and soft, and yet, surprisingly respectful. What came through is that love is God given, and romance is one expression of love, though I had never thought of that before! The now agreeable parts suggest I need to keep an open mind and to listen, patiently trusting God to lead my thinking, believing He always wants what is good for me. It sort of makes sense, but then it doesn't. All I can say is that I have a sense of peace. I don't feel in such turmoil anymore."

After a quiet pause, I continue, now more confidently: "I guess my thinking about this Scotsman will go away now, which is fantastic."

"Maybe Tara, maybe not. But some good lessons from deep within your own mind, eh? Enough for today! So now I presume you are going surfing, hey!" Funny how I never feel Em is laughing at me, but more joining me where I am at, with a sense that life is for living!

After such a satisfying session, alone that night over dinner, I deliberately make a decision. My stupid reaction to the Scotsman is not going to stop me doing what I really love doing. I WILL go back to surfing! It won't be any problem either. Such relief! Perhaps I should plan to see Em in a month, just to let her know all is OK. I reflect on how it is always so good to share with someone you know understands and cares! Can't do that with many people.

9

A Soldier

Iain

I am about to see a difficult client. He is a Vietnam veteran living on a secluded bush block. He is exceedingly angry after having his guns confiscated, after he'd had an altercation with a neighbour though unarmed in any way.

I replay the previous session in my mind before getting him from the waiting room. That initial session had been one of trying to establish trust, and every time we made progress, he'd doubled back and accused me of trying to get into his head. Slowly, the story unfurled as he, always on alert, insisted on standing, *and* near the door.

Both he and his neighbour are returned servicemen. Mates cover each other's backs, even if the mate now happens to be a policeman. Tom's fists were clenched, and he'd punched hard into his left arm. The policeman's wife however was declared to be no mate. She made it quite clear she didn't like him. After the altercation, he had heard her screaming at her husband, threatening to leave. Who did they think they were, armed police and an armoured vehicle? He, a decorated soldier! Were they going to take away his medals as well? The language was colourful, every second word a profanity, the volume at points maxed out.

"You bastards, you are all the same. Youse just want me to spill my guts! I've seen people with their real guts hanging out. Now *you* couldn't take that, I'll bet! Just get me my guns and licence back! You owe me. Didn't fight for my country just to get kicked in the guts. F***ing bastards."

Over fifty minutes of a yo-yoing-doubling-back rollercoaster, I was able none the less to sufficiently assess him to be as confident as I need to be that this man is, for all his expressed anger, not a threat. Sure, he is angry, an anger associated with all the symptoms of full-blown PTSD in fact. But he has provided me with cogent evidence that he is incredibly respectful of life, and seriously conscientious in his disciplined handling of any firearms. It is self-evident. I figure that if he was ever going to harm anyone, he would have done so long ago. Rough diamond, but integrity is an intrinsic part of him. Honesty. Duty. Hmm. I am comfortable with my reasoning.

There was no sense telling him of my assessment. In fact, he would probably feel insulted that I had ever had any questions about him. It was so clear that guns and hunting remain an intrinsic part of his identity. He has been wronged. I had told him I want to see him get his guns back.

"You are just fooling, it's a trick to get me back here," Tom challenged me.

I knew no argument would convince him. No bargaining. No way would he give up any sense of control in his world, least of all to a stranger, a psychologist. The only thing that I had was that he saw me as associated with the department of Veterans Affairs, so that made me sort of army, even a kind of mate. Even so, he was fighting every step of the way to my helping him. Little to play with, rationally, I figured he was the sort of person who was likely to respond to a challenge. Acknowledge some understanding of where he is at and then challenge.

"If I was you, I wouldn't be trusting anyone. You have made it very clear that you are here just because you want your guns back. Nothing more. I respect that. I cannot make you do anything that you'd not want or choose to do. I can only assist you to get what you want. I am convinced enough to commit to doing all I can."

There was guarded suspicion on Tom's face.

"F*** all, f***ing why. What's f***ing in it for you?"

"Justice. You are a soldier who has risked his life for his country, and you have been misjudged, wronged, discriminated against because you suffer from PTSD. Disgraceful. Humiliating."

Silence as he takes it in. I continued on, as finally, he …yes! Tom takes his seat! Yes! Progress!

"You could so easily borrow another gun from one of your mates, couldn't you. It's not having a licence that makes anyone like you dangerous. But I reckon that demonstrates a strong incentive for keeping to the regulations."

In my replay I see again his quizzical expression, almost disbelief. Tom sitting still, no longer the agitation evident in moving from leg to leg. That tells me heaps. After a brief pause, it's time to press on.

"And, as I see it, you have three weeks to get yourself together before you must face the appeals panel. I hear you. In your present state I reckon you are about to go down there and give them a piece of your mind. But doing what we *feel* like doing doesn't get us to our goal. It only releases feelings. And will guarantee, Tom, that you *don't* get your guns back!"

Tom lets out some expletives, peppered with colourful descriptions about the sorts of people he sees as typically making up such a panel. His voice was still so loud I was sure people can even hear him down the passage in the waiting room. I wanted to push hope, real hope. I wanted him to experience someone trusting him, believing him. He desperately needs someone to believe him, and to believe *in* him.

"You want your licence back. I believe you deserve it back. I want you to get it back. I think I can help you do that. Try me." I have chosen my language carefully so as to clearly leave ownership and control with him. It is not something I can fix for him. He looks intensely at me, clearly a little incredulous. I needed to be more concrete: a direct suggestion of what to do.

"The last two psychos threw me out" he mutters. Tom had expected me to do the same. I know that. I have seen their reports, DVA files. I ignore this: I need to get down to action. We need to get down to action. He learns by being shown. I need to show him. I am probably the last stop and am aware he will continue to test me. That's why I asked him to 'try me.' A soldier has learned to accept orders, so that's what I realize I must do. I give him a challenge, but almost spoken as an order. Training. I hoped he'd understand that.

"We have a job to do. Come back the next two Mondays and we will role play you being in front of the panel, and work on a strategy for convincing them to give you back your shooting licence. In the meantime, Tom, think carefully about what you would say when asked why you really want your guns back, and clearly give these to me next visit."

He'd sat there for a few moments, then without a word, stood up and walks out the door. My heart sinks as I watched Tom go. Never sure about how that would pan out.

10

A Woman Intrudes

Iain

So now, it's a week later. I had seen Tom's name on this morning's list, not knowing until then that a few days after seeing me, the veteran *had* come in and made another appointment. He is down as my last appointment. It's already been a full-on day.

I need a break as I brace myself. I am making myself a cup of coffee in the staffroom when Em comes in. She goes over to make herself a coffee but then starts to engage me in a case discussion. That's not unusual. We as colleagues support each other. But right now, I have come here to prepare for a potential struggle: I will need to think on my feet. Caffeine should help.

"Did you notice my last client as you passed in the corridor just before?" Em asks.

"Not really."

I was trying not to sound too available.

"Well, this is a tricky one."

I want to turn away. I don't want to start a case discussion about someone else's difficult problematic client. No distractions: It's been a long day. 'Please Em I think….' I think that, but that's not what I say. Instead, I respond by trying to sound as disinterested as I can without being impolite.

"Ah ha."

Normally Em is quite sensitive to such signals, but ugh, not now: she is continuing - oh bother.

"I have seen her before, years ago, and she learned really quickly to effectively deal with some pretty terrible childhood traumas. She is a very driven and disciplined woman."

"Hmm." I respond now by turning away a little, trying to sound somewhat more disinterested. That's difficult though. Em is always there for me. Ugh, still she is not getting the message. Time just to be honest and say that I am about to work with my own very tricky client. But I don't.

"Seems that she has found herself unwillingly a little obsessed with the memory of a man she saw on a beach a couple of months ago after she came out from surfing."

By now I am halfway to the door. A warm tremor runs down my back. It stops me for a moment, and without turning, I find myself looking up to the ceiling. I see the beach scene as if it was only half an hour ago. Flashbacks of her face in the dream then intrude.

No, it cannot be, I tell myself. It's just one of Em's clients. For a moment I feel some sort of inexplicable and undeniable excitement. Then I wonder: why such a hapless intrusion? Irritation, and it flows into annoyance. I thought it was under control. I feel the tension of needing to get cognitive control. It all happens in microseconds. What can I say? I don't want to hear any more, not now.

"Sorry, just got to fly. Difficult client waiting. Talk later."

And with that I rush off to my consulting room. I become completely absorbed in the session with the returned soldier. It's intense. There are moments of seemingly breaking through to some sort of trust. It is quite moving. Hope shimmers on the horizon. Tom is mostly retaining control of his temper. He pushes back savagely with expletives any time I am not listening enough. That feels encouraging in itself. It speaks of an inner strength. I like that. It means there is substance to build on. But still the two attempts at role plays wind up as merely giving him opportunities to vent aggressively. I am not sure that they might not be doing more damage. He is clearly emotionally exhausted and just sits back in his chair, despondent.

I search for another angle. We cannot keep going this way. 'Oh God, where are you? If only you would help at a time like this! I have to be able to humanise the review panel members somehow'. But how?

I am aware that we have not addressed the ignominy of the armed police at his house. I am aware it could have turned into a shootout if he had really been a violent man. Power provokes war. Should I explore this? Is this the block?

Again, my silent cry for help goes up. Surely, God also cares for this man!

I suddenly wonder if I could find out who is on the panel. Tom continues to sit there looking dejected, and I wonder whether he is sitting there long enough to get himself together enough to get up and leave. I search the web as fast as I can, googling images on my laptop, looking for a picture of the panel. That should help make them concrete for him. But I cannot find any photo. I click "All" and there! I find the police minister's press release announcing the appointment of the panel members. I click the document hoping to find a picture. There is none. But their names are there. I look at their names. It tells me where they are from. Two are ex-police officers, and I notice one is ex-army.

"Here we are" I turn around, feeling a little triumphant: "we have the panel. Look, their names. One is ex-army, Tom. Maybe you know of him?" I am hoping.

He says nothing, shrugs his shoulders, but he doesn't leave. Tom is now willing to run through a role play again; the change is palpable. The session goes well overtime. But there is more to be done. Next week then. He agrees. I have hope. This makes my job worthwhile.

The office is already empty. As I make my way home, I find myself pondering a little about how the next session will go. Doubts intrude. Will the progress carry through? And… was He really there?

The earlier sessions of the day seem like a distant memory, as if weeks ago. That's not unusual on such a full day. I need to switch off. Rebound from the caffeine is setting in. Fatigue. Watch where you are walking. Mentally I'm spent. I need sugar, mindless distraction. Turn on the television. Sit down. Microwave for dinner. Game shows offer nice trivia. Then a recording of last night's MasterChef. I know I am not up to looking at any news.

It's one of those rare times when one becomes slowly aware that one is dreaming. It grows even more vivid. It is the surfer! No face, just holding up her hand. 'Look no rings, show me your hand' she had just said, yet again in her Australian accent. In my dream I find myself not wanting to wake. I don't want her to go away. I am trying to recall the earlier parts of the dream, but as I do, she fades, fast, and I wake. I am on the couch. The TV has turned itself off.

I recall Em's discussion in the kitchenette. Was she talking about the same person? I find myself so wanting it to be her. Absurd! I hear from deep down. Why was she telling me? I feel a little confused. I am now fully awake. What am I thinking? I look at my watch. It needs to be recharged. I look over to the oven clock. 3:30 am the digits scream. I stagger off to my bedroom, realising that I am quite cold. Madness: I want to ring Em, but it's the middle of the night. There is sleep to be had. Tomorrow is another full day. I tell myself to get a hold of myself. Sort it out in the morning. A part of me doesn't want me to go to sleep, just savour the dream, imagine if it had been true. When I wake at seven thirty, I realise the battle must have lasted a couple of hours. I last remember five thirty as I lean over to touch my apple watch on its stand. Lord, how tired I am!

11

Accountability

Iain

I wake. It's 9am. The power has been off. My watch has not recharged, so is flat as a tack, and my alarm hasn't gone off! By now my first client will be waiting. Ugh. I rush to my laptop to check before I ring. Ah, fortunate, my first is at 10 am. I breathe more easily and check the rest of the day's schedule as I start to recall the restless night, then the dream and the wakeful hours all coming back to me.

Just as I look away to reflect, I note the last appointment for the day: '5pm - Peer Supervision.' I look back, and, Ha, I think, timely. Should be able to talk about this darn intrusion. I don't understand that those pesky intrusions are back again, waking me each night. With the thought of tackling that tonight, I rush through a shower and get dressed, leaving just enough time to down a coffee and some muesli. I am well on my way as the caffeine kicks in.

Work absorbs me. As always, each session has me in a bubble of its own. Then there is the hour set aside for phone calls and report writing. It stretches into most of lunch time. Before I have had time to think of anything else, I am with the next client, and suddenly it seems, it is five past five.

Coffee. I need a coffee. I wander towards the kitchenette wishing I had time to get a decent coffee around the corner, but I don't. Must ask Jenny to let Em know I am on my way, but she is not at her desk as I go past. Maybe I should nick up to Em's room, but then the trouble is we might start talking, and I need that caffeine! Darn it, I vacillate - a sure indication of how tired I am, and it reminds me of the sleepless night. Oh dear, I hope Em has not forgotten and gone home.

As I walk into the kitchenette, frazzled, there's Em and Jenny with their backs to me, talking. They hear me and turn around.

"Talking about me?" I joke.

"Absolutely! So much to talk about!" responds Jenny the receptionist as always, cheekily smiling, and there is Em, holding a takeaway coffee and a Mars Bar I eye off covetously. She waits a few seconds, and then stretches out her arm.

"Jenny got you this: we thought you might need it for our session." Thoughtfulness. Always there for others, these two. How come I never seem to think of such things for them? At least one relief, Em has not forgotten our supervision session. But why should she? She, unlike some others, consults her diary! I wonder why I am so reliant on Jenny reminding me. Maybe it's the bubble I get into, and my utter lack of any sense of time. How would it be to always be so aware of what's going on around you, I ponder, so much interruptive information to cope with. Hang on, has Em just given me her coffee because of how I looked at her cup? I am about to check when she turns around and grabs her coffee, along with a Cherry Ripe.

We settle into the easy chairs in Em's office. She seems to know to let me collect myself, and I just sit there sipping the coffee. Thoughtful again!

"Been a full day, eh?" she asks at last. I am still collecting myself, and simply nod.

"Your turn to set the topic tonight, remember? Or are you a bit too exhausted and should we postpone tonight?"

She is perceptive, but this jolts my mind into action even before the caffeine has had time to do its work. 'Set the agenda?' Our peer supervision is mostly focussed on talking through our respective cases. Should we talk about the soldier?

Then, the waking hours from last night intrude. I yearn to know more about the surfer and there is a pang of secret hope she may be the person Em mentioned as having passed me in the corridor yesterday. Maybe talking through her case would bring the idealisation that has somehow formed in my mind to come crashing down to earth. Had I not learned the folly of creating idylls from the lesson of my shattering experience with Sheila? How is it that despite resolving never again to allow myself such an indulgence, I find myself slipping into this again? Yes, that's it, a dose of reality will solve the problem. Better speak.

"Yes, full on day, but that's nothing new. Just need to catch myself for a few moments. Nearly there. Are you OK with a few case discussions?"

"Yes, sure, if you go first."

Blown the chance. Oh well, the soldier then. After that maybe we can get back to the surfer. I want to get through it quickly, but we do have a detailed and constructive discussion. I slowly explore my feelings of compassion for this man, and a sense of owing him on behalf of society, the society that is now afraid of a man who knew what honour meant: that you were prepared to risk death for your country. I am encouraged that Em agreed with my assessment that he appears to be a conscientious and responsible individual. My empathy is appropriate and has not clouded my judgement. The notes of our discussion go into his file. Accountability. Responsibility. All part of the benefits of the required professional peer supervision. A flash goes through my mind about the surfer. Why can I be so balanced with a most difficult case such as the soldier, yet do not seem to be able to be objective, analytical, self-protective about a complete stranger? Good for next discussion.

I am ready to move on, but Em raises a few more points and so the discussion continues for a further ten minutes, but all the while I am growing more impatient to move on. Perhaps the delay is providential? While anticipation of talking about the surfer had been building, so did a certain level of discomfort. What are the ethics here? Conflict of interests? Am I the dispassionate colleague that I need to be in any case discussion? Is my interest in the client's interests, or simply serving mine? Privacy issues, but surely not! Then a thought takes me completely by surprise. If I enquire and Em shares anything about this person, then ethically, and by the well-established professional standards for psychologists, I am working as an associated professional, privy to professionally shared information. And that means that I can entertain no intimate relationship whatsoever with this person for at least two years.

I hear myself thinking, that's good, out of reach, putting paid to any further thoughts, and no doubt the pesky dreams will stop. And just as soon as I have thought that, another thought: what if I really like what I hear? Hang on, am I not a confirmed single? The confusion now distracts me from Em's final summing up of the case of the soldier, and she seems to have noticed my absence.

"So, what's on your mind now?" she asks.

The only thing I am sure of is that I am too confused to want to talk about the surfer. So I blurt out the next thing that comes to mind.

"Unwanted intrusions" is all I can manage to say. I am aware that I am not Em's client, nor she mine. But at times of peer supervision, we discuss those things that may impact our work, our functioning. Em had eighteen months ago shared in her being devastated by actions of the pastor at her church. She had so appreciated his clear capacity for teaching and apparent care and had regarded him a good friend. But he had a dark secret. He finally had been called out, having had inappropriate relations with some of the younger women in the church, and for some years. An enquiry had received more than thirty complaints, and yet there were those who would not hear any ill of him. He had simply moved on to another church, claiming to have been maligned because of his "right" theological positions. We had shared what for her was a really tough time. In a sense, this has given me the green light to share my current though more minor personal frustration.

"Unwanted intrusions?" she asks.

"Yes, I am having these dreams that wake me up…. about a person I once saw, and she is holding up her arm, saying, 'look, no rings.' I lie awake for hours after that and that is crazy. I don't even know who she is. It happened a while back, but now it has started all over again. I am concerned that a part of me just doesn't want to stop the repeated intrusion. Irrational, eh?"

The last phrase is an attempt to steer Em away from any potential to ask more about content. I simply want to talk about how to be rational in blocking the intrusions, probably with us running through some sort of gestalt technique. Em does neither. Her question takes me by surprise.

"Iain, what are you afraid of?"

"Nothing… Nothing! What on *earth* makes you think I am afraid?" I ask, clearly somewhat perplexed.

"But you *are* afraid of something, Iain!" She looks directly at me, a look that she was not going to avert. It feels an intrusion, and from anyone else would be unwelcome, and possibly with any other colleague, inappropriate. But with Em: we'd worked on her trauma. She has earned the right here. I sit silent as the sense of intrusion subsides and defensiveness arises.

"What do you mean, afraid? I am pretty well not an anxious sort of person!"

"I am not suggesting you are either prone to anxiety or generally fearful. Listen again to my question. What are you afraid of?"

"I don't think I am afraid of anything, and my faith means not even really being anxious about the ultimate fear: death." There is an awkward pause as Em is clearly assessing the moment, intently observing my every expression and posture, as psychologists are trained to do. After a brief moment, she moves on:

"What of your addictions?"

"My addictions?"

"Yes, first your addiction to Sheila, then to drinking, then as you have shared with me, a stint of gambling, and now to work. We both know that addictions are a means of escape."

"But" I protest, "Sheila was no addiction! And drinking, yes well, my father was an alcoholic, so that was a biological propensity, and anyhow, that's under control now."

Somehow, I hope if I can but rebut the first two, her hypothesis will fall, but I know the ploy too well in clients, so it is half-hearted. In fact, I should know that for a clinician of Em's experience, recognising addiction is no hypothesis but a clear insight. I have trailed off as the realisation runs home. Em smiles as she recognises my realisation. She says nothing, waiting for me to go on. I try a new tack.

"What am I trying to run away from then?"

"People."

"But I work with people every day. I care deeply about people," I protest.

"I know you do, Iain, no question about it. You are incredibly caring. Look at your work with the soldier, even today. Patience, compassion, and a passion for justice for him."

Relief, we can agree, I am not afraid of people. I now want to go on to confirm that:

"Em, how often haven't we spoken about the very centre of our work being to bring about the very heart of the Gospel: grace and relationships? So how can you say that I run away from people?"

"Sure, I agree. People sense how much you really do care. It shows in the way they trust you too. You are there for them. They let you into their lives, no question about that. You see lots of soldiers, along with a great variety of hurting people."

Em pauses before then going on more poignantly:

"But Iain, other than me, who do you really let into your life? Who do you trust? You are so controlled. Seeing people, professionally, well, they are all at arm's length."

"Boundaries" I reply.

"Ah, boundaries yes, and guarding your heart is all good and well, but boundaries can go too far. They can become over self-protective, denying relationships where we need them. They are appropriate professionally, but in your personal life?"

I feel like I did at six, having been pulled out from under the bed as I was repeatedly when caught hiding from my drunk father. I want to deny her inference, so I try to turn it into a joke.

"I am just a dour Scottish Presbyterian!"

"A dour Scotsman without passion? Ha!" Em is in earnest. She is not about to let me off the hook. It is a moment she has no doubt been waiting for - maybe a long time.

"And you really think you have no need for anyone, letting anyone in? So, what have your addictions really been about then, Iain?"

I know she is right. I sit there wondering about my next move. I feel very vulnerable. This is a professional supervision session, and we are touching on the personal. I know that I have a choice. Do I continue to ingress my personal life? It's my choice. Em, ever respectful, is not pushing any more. After a few minutes of silence, she finally goes on, very quietly, in sync with the gravity of the moment:

"And now, this woman intrudes into your dreams! What's that telling you? What are you afraid of, eh? What does your training tell you?"

Em has continued speaking to me softly, gently, but I sense firmly, and I know deep down, in love, the kind of tough love that forces an issue with a respected colleague in peer supervision that needs to be addressed. She has left me no room to run away. I ask myself - who else would dare to breach my defences? Finally, I reply in quiet resignation.

"I know." Em sees the resignation on my face.

"Yes, you do, and I think we have gone far enough tonight! The rest is up to you, and I need say no more. Now, I think we need to go and have a game of squash, eh?"

Em seems to know what I need. All my pent-up emotions seem to explode into what is one of the most energetic games I have ever played. I rarely beat Em, but now, I am unbeatable. I go home and fall into bed too exhausted to bother with dinner.

I wake up after dreaming yet again: the surfer. I no longer feel ambivalent. I sense a strange calm. Getting back to sleep no longer seems important. But I have work tomorrow. And then I realise a new sense, that work no longer feels like it should be all consuming. There is more to life than running away. I need to find the surfer. What is that release I feel as I decide I must find her? A struggle has ended. I *will* find her. But not through Em. In moments, I roll over and am back asleep, deep contented sleep.

PART 2

SETTLING INTO PARADISE...

12

On the Way

Iain

Five years have gone by. I am in a plane. I slip into a short shallow sleep, several hours after taking off from Perth. It has been an exhausting month, planning, packing up, saying final goodbyes to our friends, while still dealing with clients right up to the last.

I wake. I enjoy looking over to my wife Tara on my left, obliviously devouring a scientific paper. She is excited to be fulfilling a long-held dream, of further research involving field work that is outdoors! Turning to look through the plane's window, I see the setting sun's red streaks on wispy clouds, and then a darkening blue sky where it meets the deep blue green of the Indian Ocean. We are flying to Kleine Paradijs, Dutch for Little Paradise, on the island of Rustenberg, a large atoll just north-west of the Cocos Islands.

I ponder our decision to move here, made less than four years after we married. Tara has won an industry post graduate award from the Western Australian government, to undertake a doctoral research project into the sensory characteristics of a long-lost heritage coffee grown in the mountains of Rustenberg. The island had initially been settled by the Dutch East India Company in the late 17th century, as a hidden location for the experimentation and development of high-class fine coffee varieties, in the seclusion of its seemingly inaccessible mountains. There were rumours that a particularly remarkable and unique Arabica had been developed, only for the plantation and nursery to be completely decimated in a tropical cyclone that followed, in what is regarded as possibly the world's worst modern climate catastrophe. That event was caused by the Mount Tambora eruption on the nearby Indonesian island of Sumbawa, in 1815.

On researching the rumours around the coffee, Tara had found some records indicating there had actually been a secret initiative to reopen the search quite recently by the very company she now worked for, but the previous researcher had died in a road accident on her field trip to the island. For Tara, a self-confessed coffee fanatic, the opportunity to explore and research coffee species that might bring new flavours as well as provide a variety more adaptable to climate change is quite exciting. But ever the addict of detective stories, the possibility of her own detective work into the myth holding real potential, that was beyond excitement, even for a measured person like her! In fact, it has been great to see that excitement more evident, as the plans to come here finally eventuated.

I reflect. While I am feeling quite excited for Tara, I'm guardedly becoming excited for myself. I had never contemplated taking deliberate time out to reflect, but somehow with Tara, life is no longer all about work. A wonderful relief.

I reminisce. We have revelled in the incredible times of togetherness, with shared love and excitement pervading even things that used to seem so ordinary. But having been seen to be a confirmed 'bachelor' for so long, when time was mine to use as I wished, togetherness had naturally created conflicts, some of which my psychological training had not prepared me to deal with at a more personal level. It also became apparent that, although prior to meeting me Tara had resolved many of the hurts experienced in her childhood, there were times when obviously some memories of past issues were triggered, and still remained a mystery. She would become distraught. I knew only too well how to handle someone in such a state in the consulting room. My role and objectivity there, the appropriate professional boundaries were clear. The first negative episodes that intruded on our married life together had thrown me back, and there had been times of wondering how it was ever going to pan out.

Slowly though, as trust had grown in working through such issues, I realised I was *experiencing* a new type of relationship: an intimate connexion. Here I experienced a sense of personal attachment that registers vulnerability. And this, to someone who usually had seemed so strong and in control. I ponder attachment styles, and how my original attachment to Sheila was so not really any sort of attachment at all. Just romantic lust.

But here is my really first soul mate. So it is that Tara and I have noted on numerous occasions that we've grown enormously through our sometimes none the less quite volatile exchanges. These have definitely become less frequent. And now we have a new pattern. When we talk *after* such interchanges, with raised feelings slowly diminished, there is laughter as we share the realisation of how silly it had been!

Talking with Em was now on an altogether other footing. She no longer takes on a professional role with Tara since we were now all friends. While Tara was never my client, she had been one at the practice. So, to ensure any relationship was ethically progressed we had been carefully supported through consultation with another senior psychologist. And as this advanced further, this had quite naturally been more possible by including Em's husband Jack in our social interactions. And, sharing our journeying as friends had opened the door for Em to share some of her own experiences in an oft lonely journey, reminding us that in this broken world, those who *seem* to have it all together have simply learned how best to cope with life's curved balls.

The future awaits. I also find myself wanting some time to make ordinary everyday friends, with a freedom not to be 'the psychologist.' I have promised myself time to think and to meditate. Maybe even get some of my own bad habits under control. The island adventure seems so inviting, idyllic in so many ways. Especially now, with early reports of a global pandemic being so terrible – thankfully as yet mostly overseas. Certainly not on the island we are going to! I know, I know, deep down there is a little slightly repressed thought that a picture gained mostly from tourist information may make the grass look so much greener. Sure, today we are all so susceptible to the spin we want to believe. Don't we all like to fantasize a little about paradise on earth? For the moment, just for once, I want to indulge in the possibility of the spin. I know that reality will set in ultimately, but it's fun to dream!

I pull up my satchel. There's some mail I'd collected as we finally went past the office on the way to the plane. One of them is a card with familiar writing I regularly see, about once a year. I know the writing well. It brings back memories of how moved I'd been the first time I saw the author's writing. It's from the soldier who got his licence *and* his guns back.

REPORTING IN TO HQ AS REQUESTED
OUT BUSH
CONTRACT SHOOTING PEST CONTROL
GOING OK
YOU KEEP WELL
I KNOW WHERE TO FIND YOU
THERE IS NO NAME, NO ADDRESS.

I am highly visual. I replay our last meetings, already several years ago. It had been a cold day when Tom had come in demanding to see me on the spot. Jenny, ever the watchful receptionist, had tried to put him off, asking him to make an appointment, but I was just then walking down to get my next client from the waiting room, so he saw me. He simply charged forward, holding out a shoe box as he said:

"Got me guns back. Thanks. Receptionist says you are too busy to see me. I need you to read this. Found 'em when mum died. She's kept 'em, every one. I didn't know. I'll fetch 'em from you next week."

With that Tom had turned and was out the door before I could even ask him anything. I had peeked into the box, seeing a bottle of wine and what looked like a cache of envelopes. I had put them on my desk as I engaged with the next client.

I forgot the box that night, so it was over lunch next day that I opened it. There were letters, the letters of a nineteen-year-old conscript in Vietnam, writing back to his mum. His writing was neat. His language was entirely comprehendible despite no punctuation, just capital letters where sentences mostly started. No paragraphs. The descriptions were vivid. Some lines here or there of important information that had been obliterated by a thick black texta. Corners had been torn from nearly all the envelopes, no doubt to collect the stamps. Here and there was an army stamp indicating they had been screened by the censor.

As I read, what caught me most were the cries from the heart: a frightened young man describing the most horrific scenes, and how he felt, yes how he felt like a murderer. I had to stop after one where he described an engagement with Viet Cong: the Australians had thrown grenades down unearthed tunnels after receiving fire from the area. They were ordered to do a body count only to realise that the dead were mostly female. Tom had watched a mate roll one over. He had felt sickened on seeing the partial face that remained: she reminded him of his own younger sister.

As I'd carried the box home that night, I felt it was something sacred, incredibly precious. As I had read numbers of the remaining letters over the ensuing days, I was deeply moved, not only by their content, but by a sense of privilege that this man should trust me enough to share these precious valuable letters. Such vulnerability from a man with such a well defended persona. Tom had tried so hard to challenge my trust at every turn. By the grace of God, I had experienced a strength and wisdom I can only explain as from outside myself. For Tom, however, finally someone had accepted him, unconditionally, and trusted him at the right time, even with his ever-present anger!

I continue to reflect on why so many like Tom are misunderstood, even shunned. Why had he not been listened to, especially by those others with training, supposedly concerned for his well-being, such as when discharged from his compulsory time in the military? Like so many others, he had simply been de-mobbed on his return and sent home. Is it because we in our western individualism have accepted a lie, that it is all about me, my comfort, needing to look after myself first? How often don't I too find myself blind to discerning character, but responsive to how comfortable or otherwise someone has me feeling about myself.

This soldier, superficially a tough rough diamond alright, but inside a scarred and traumatized boy remained, and he had let me see a glimpse of that. His story needed to be heard, but he would have none of my suggestion that he get it published, even under a pseudonym, nor sent to the national war archives, even anonymously.

During one session, Tom told me of a chaplain in Vietnam who had helped, so that was my opportunity to ask if he had any sense of a god. His answer had been 'not of a god but yeah, God! He was there alright, somewhere, I knew 'cos I talked to Him, all the time, otherwise I wouldn't be here now, would I?' Sometimes without realising it, we have been sent as ministering angels to people *He* loves but few others find they can. What a privilege!

13

Landing

Tara

The seat belt sign comes on and the steward announces our impending arrival. I put my computer away, unplugging a USB Flash Drive. Iain is watching and asks me why I have not copied the contents to my laptop. I explain that it is from my predecessor, Gena, and is encrypted in a way that doesn't allow for files to be copied across.

"Ah Gena, the Gena who died in that accident on the island, some years ago?" he asks.

"Yes"

I notice it is not only Iain who is curious. A man across the aisle suddenly appears interested in us, though he is looking from behind a hand half hiding his face. Before I can talk further, I am distracted by a young man behind him now groaning, eyes closed. Anxiety? He looked fine when we boarded the plane. Introduced himself as Kyle and we had a nice friendly chat as we waited in line to board. He was with his father, a big man who showed no interest in talking to anyone. Even now he seems oblivious to his son's groaning, intently looking out the window.

The cabin crew are scurrying with final checks in readiness for landing. We are sitting opposite the dickie seats reserved for a couple of flight attendants. The two attendants flop down chatting to each other as they fasten their seat belts.

"Looks like we come in from over the sea" Iain says addressing the attendants as much as me.

"Yes" one of the attendants replies, "It is often a bit tricky this one, with up-draughts just at the shoreline where the runway starts, and at the other end, which is also at the beach. They call this the 'shudder-in-shudder-out runway." Smilingly she adds: "Either way, if we under or overshoot, we land in the drink." We all laugh.

Prophetic words. Moments later the plane lurches upwards as it crosses the beach and then bounces heavily onto the runway. Then sudden hard braking and the engines screaming in reverse. Our laughing flight attendant isn't smiling any more but is ashen grey.

"Geez," she exclaimed, "never been that bad before. I think we only just made it. I thought I was exaggerating before!"

"Well, might be wiser to keep that sort of Aussie humour to ourselves," I hear the other attendant quietly whisper to her colleague, just as another loud groan comes from the young man across the aisle. He is now leaning forward onto the seat in front of him, spewing into a paper bag he'd managed to sequester just in time. I notice the inquisitive man I'd observed who'd been sitting directly in front of the anxious youth has now jumped up and moved away, standing aside to allow the steward past to open the above head lockers. They seem to know each other and there is a brief exchange. Maybe a frequent passenger to the island?

It doesn't take long to disembark and joining the end of the short line of travellers, we walk across the tarmac to the airport building. Large letters across the top announce

Kleine Paradijs International & Domestic Airport
Welcome to Rustenberg Eilandt.

As we get closer, we can read the sign above two adjoining entry doors. The one on the left door indicates 'Domestic Terminal,' the other 'International Terminal.'

We enter via the domestic door leading into a single space where the separation between the international and domestic areas is simply created by a row of chairs, back-to-back. Even more surprising is an unrestricted gap in the row, allowing for free movement from one side to the other. A couple of people in the international area are busy on their computers. At the end of the row of chairs, one on each side, we see the requisite metal detection arches and baggage belts. Next to each, an open exit gate through which we now walk together. No staff in sight, except for a young man busy playing on his phone in the kiosk-come-coffee shop. Bags can take some time to come through, so we interrupt the young man for a coffee.

Coffee drunk, we soon find our luggage on a trolley at the front door, the last remaining bags of the small number of incoming passengers who travelled with us from Australia. A brief stop in Broome had seen only two people board the plane, but a number of crates loaded suggested this was an important aspect of regular service to the Island, as a carrier of supplies. Just in time, we manage to catch the departing small shuttle bus heading to the town centre. There are two other passengers already there. We are only all too happy to allow the driver to find our booked hotel. We are also glad the next few days will be without the stress that packing up and leaving our home of almost three years in Perth had been for both of us. We have arrived - an exciting new beginning!

The Hotel Ibis is, well, a hotel. I just take time to set my computer up on the hotel desk, plug it into its recharge unit, before kicking off my shoes, stripping off to flop onto the bed. Meanwhile Iain puts the last of the luggage into the small wardrobe. We had not spoken much as we individually took in the scenery on the way. The mountains behind the town rose sharply. But now, suddenly the impact of the journey, the farewells, the packing, the excitement of a new adventure, all the uncertainties, the long plane hours, and especially the mildly humid heat suddenly hit us. Everything has caught up, leaving us both feeling exhausted. Despite my curiosity about the town, for me the bed looks clean and inviting.

But for Iain, perked up by his nap on the plane and shot of caffeine at the airport, the thought of looking around is stimulating. Knowing my need for sleep, he quietly says:

"I'd like to go out onto the street, just walk around the block, get a sense of the lay of the land".

I have no wish to argue, but simply nod my head. My eyes are already closed, as I doze off into a welcome and dream-free land of deep sleeee......

14

Walkabout

Iain

I am experiencing a strong urge to find my bearings, to orient myself in space and time. I know that whenever I am in a new place or situation I need to look around before I can settle. Then I need a plan. Once done, I am free to become absorbed, get into stuff. For me that usually means working in a bubble, oblivious to the world around, even to any sense of time or temperature.

I look at Tara lying there. She is happy just to flop. It amazes me how she always seems so acutely aware of her immediate surrounds, and what is happening. I also envy her ability to orient herself adaptively to wherever she is. Here she is, quite happy just to respond to her body's need for a nap. Her breathing tells me she is asleep. How lucky is she!

If I slip out now, when I come back, Tara will be ready to go out to eat. I close the door as quietly as I can, and wander into the narrow shopping street below. I need another coffee if I am to do without a nap.

It is a bustling early evening, with a market just opening up further down the street. First, a coffee. I stand back at the first coffee stall. Two

Mazza grinders, an ageing Nova Simonelli espresso machine, and a tattooed barista. Mmm, it looks promising. Tara had taught me well. Extracting good coffee requires someone with the right equipment (tick), properly roasted coffee (the two lines advertised looked promising (tick), technical prowess of the barista (hopefully!), the obsession of an artisan (tattoos and frazzled hair looked the part, another potential tick), and with the perfectionism that dogs many artists (maybe): all in the pursuit of an elusive elixir. The barista works quickly, experience evident from his staring upward into space and then down the line of stalls as he waits for milk to texture. I step forward.

"Short black, please."

As the barista turns, the angle of his face suggests someone of mixed cultural heritage: a short well-built Eurasian, most probably of Dutch-Ceylonese extraction I'm thinking. His hands are more like the northern European coal shovels in contrast to the elegantly fingered ones typical of Asians. I reflect momentarily of the amusing dry humour of some Dutch friends as they describe the needs their forefathers had lived with: living on a swamp of a country, natural selection favoured those with big robust hands the tell me. Like the marsh-wiggles in Lewis's science fiction trilogy, their laughing taunts suggested that had modern industrialisation not come along, they would surely have developed webbing!

The beautiful skin now catches my attention. It was light enough to show off his tattoos: exquisitely detailed trees and birds. I reflect on Tara and her Anglo-Indian background. With my own light ginger hair and associated freckled complexion, I can never tan but simply burn to a lobster-look-alike. I like the way familiar European features blend so aesthetically with somewhat lightened Asian and Indian skin toning. No irritating burned lobsters here.

Sipping the coffee is so good as I pull my phone from my pocket and turn on google maps. I head to the home of the reformed church minister. I had contacted him and asked if he knew of anywhere quiet:

perhaps someone in his congregation might have a place for us to rent for a year, maybe even just a holiday rental?

The Reverend van der Leer had called me in response to my email a couple of weeks ago. After announcing 'van der Leer here,' I noted that he hadn't shared his first name. I'd informed him that we'd like to finalise somewhere quickly, and that it needs to be comfortable for me, but particularly for Tara who needs to have a decent place to write up her research. He said he thought he had a place we could use, at least until we found somewhere more permanent. I had indicated when I would be arriving and that I would drop by as soon as I could. I have also planned a visit to the real estate agent. However, it's now Friday evening, and seemingly the Island has shut down for anything other than partying. I suspect that van der Leer is not the partying type. He should be home.

Twenty meters to go according to the map, and now some distance from the market, I round a corner into a narrow-cobbled street lined with single fronted, well-kept, white-washed attached stone cottages. Number 7 has a clear sign in two languages.

Hervormde Pastorie - St Martins Kerk
Reformed Church Manse - St Martins Church
Dominee/Minister in Charge - Ds J. J. van der Leer.
Afspraken/Appointments - Telephone 9966 2241

I knock at the door. I hear loud deliberate footsteps coming toward the door.

"Hello, yes, what can I do for you - oh, vait a minute, you must be Jan?" The tall bespectacled man sounded to have an even stronger Dutch accent in person than on the phone. He had a napkin in his left hand which he now raises to wipe his mouth. It was clear he was just having dinner, so no time to talk now.

"Yes, um, I'm Iain, letting you know we have just arrived. Wonder about a suitable time to catch up about a possible rental." I was conscious that my accent was suddenly much more broadly Scottish than usual, as if somehow someone with a strong Dutch accent would understand it better!!

"Very goot, wel, let us say eight in de morning, ya? after de prayer meeting. You are most velcom to come to de prayer meeting. It is at six-tirty tomorrow morning, every Saturday morning."

"Thank you very much ...." I feel a little awkward not knowing how to address him. I wonder now whether reverting to a strong accent was a subconscious way for me to signal I was a cultural foreigner. Van der Leer broke the brief awkward pause:

"Ya, tot siens den," and he closes the door, only to open it again a few seconds later to call after me as I am just turning around: "Oh, ya, de prayer meeting, it is here, at de pastorie, most velcom." The door closed again.

I head back to the hotel. The map has taken me to the side of the hotel. I orient myself to find the front door. Suddenly the side door flings open, and I am bowled over by a solidly built hooded man charging out. He doesn't stop, just runs off. I pick myself and dust myself down. He sure is in a hurry. I see him disappear in the distance.

It is then that I notice that he has dropped something: a computer mouse! I pick it up and call after him, but he is already out of sight around the corner.

As I walk around to hand it in at the reception desk, I look at the mouse to see if there is any identification when I notice it is the same brand Tara uses. But nothing strange about that... until I notice a couple of marks that identifies it as potentially, really Tara's. I wonder: could it be hers?

A surge of adrenaline, I am suddenly fully awake. I race past reception, past the lift and up the stairs.

15

Unwelcome Intrusion

Tara

Unlike my usual pattern of awakening quickly and alert if I have had a daytime nap, it's been a deep sleep. Stirred now by the cool air from the air conditioner, I open my eyes sleepily and there at the desk with his back to me is Iain. Strange, he too must be feeling the aircon cold: he's put on his jacket, and even has the hoodie over his head! I love making him jump in surprise. I know he'll be in one of his thought bubbles, so ever so quietly, I creep up on him and fling my arms around him! No noise from him, but the startled Iain jumps up, and without turning, he savagely elbows me in the stomach! I'm the one now so startled, flung to the floor, but without any hesitation he bolts for the open door, slamming it shut as he goes.

It takes me only a few seconds to realise that the man was not Iain at all. I'm so shocked! And so frightened. I hardly have any time to do anything other than race to lock and chain the door, throw on my top, then begin looking for my phone to call Iain, when I hear scraping at the door. I call out "Who is it?", using a voice that I hope sounds confident enough to scare anyone away. Relief. It is Iain's voice:

"Its me, Tara!"

I open the door, and fall into his arms, feeling fear as well as relief. I ask Iain where he's been, but he says "tell you later, Tara, but…are you Ok? Did anyone hurt you? What's happened?"

I try to steady my nerves and my trembling body, telling Iain what I remembered about the hooded guy. Immediately Iain then says:

"Oh, that must have been the guy who virtually knocked me over in his hurry to get away."

"Did you see his face?" I ask.

"No, but he dropped this – I'm pretty sure it's your computer mouse! That's why I rushed to get back in here, but you'd chained the door. I was really afraid for what might have happened to you, babe!"

"You are here now, and so glad you weren't far away, Iain…I was petrified he'd come back!"

With no further delay, we call reception with what has happened. The manager comes within minutes, and quite quickly after that, the police also arrive. The manager seems to know the two police officers quite well, introducing them. Dirk, the Detective Inspector has a remarkable resemblance in face, demeanour, and dress, to the actor Peter Falk. Carrying a cigar butt, he could have been cut straight from the old Columbo TV series, or maybe better recognised today as a male version of the more recent Vera, of British police fame. Dirk's assistant is introduced as his sergeant Sabina, in contrast simply casually dressed in shorts, sandals and a tropical tank top. Apologising for having not been quicker, the inspector mutters something about being called away from his Friday night happy hour by the beach - "good for collegiality" he says, looking at the floor.

They take our story seriously and announce that this is a crime scene, so we are not to touch anything. We tell them that in looking around we think he seems to have only taken my mouse. The intruder seemed to be trying to get into my computer and maybe he was clutching the mouse when I disturbed him. It seems bizarre.

The sergeant takes out her phone and starts to photograph the scene, while the DI pulls a couple of large plastic zip-lock bags from his pocket.

"Always be prepared" he mutters, as he hands a pair of plastic gloves to his sergeant and asks her to close and pick up the laptop. Then he asks for the mouse Iain had picked up, and also puts this into the plastic bag, along with a couple of other items on the desktop that look to have been pulled from my computer bag.

"Fingerprints and DNA" he is muttering yet again as he turns to us both and asks: "you don't mind if we take these for a while - probably can do without them while you are on holiday eh? …anything else you think may have been touched by the intruder?"

Then there follows a series of further predictable questions, with the left-handed DI taking notes on a small pad held in his right hand in which he is also holding the extinguished half cigar. After the item bagging and looking around, the sergeant had been looking through our papers, while also quietly observing us.

"At least all your papers seem to still be intact. Looks like the intruder may have been looking for drugs. Do you have any, perhaps extra ones, doctor? Perhaps the intruder knew you were a doctor?" the sergeant asks.

"I'm not a medical doctor" Iain replies. "It looks to me more like the intruder was after information, but goodness, we have nothing worth stealing."

The DI looks somewhat perplexed, if not confused. But his sergeant continues to suggest answers:

"Except that identity theft is on the increase and it is surprising how many people carry that encrypted information on their computers and leave things like their passports, wallets, and computer code out on the desk when they first arrive. At least you disturbed him before he managed to get into your computer, and he missed your passports! No wallet missing?"

"I had my wallet with me; remember, I was out," Iain replies, and I tell them mine is still in my bag.

"Best to keep all such in the room safe. Whether after drugs or identity, young lady, you look like you could do with a drink." The DI's voice was raspy, and he was again looking down at the floor in front of me. Funnily enough, it seems he must have a caring side.

"My sergeant here can organise a victims of crime referral to the local counsellor if you think that would help. Not that you should need it, if you think it through, though. This is an island. The local law breakers, even when drunk, are mostly mischievous rather than bad or dangerous. Yes, just think about it, you are pretty safe here in KP."

Somehow, by the way he was almost talking to himself, it seemed the detective was trying to convince himself more than us that KP is a safe place. The DI goes on, muttering even more quietly to himself now:

"Unless a nasty visitor comes in. And we tend to pick up quickly on any of those at the airport or harbour. No need for Neighbourhood Watch here. Everyone seems to know everyone else's business."

Later Iain tells me he was fighting the impulse to take the next plane back. Primacy effect and mild trauma, he was telling himself: don't let first impressions be the lasting ones; the world is full of the unexpected. In his current state of shock, I can tell that he is bravely trying to tear himself away from thinking what might have been! He can be quite pessimistic.

The sergeant now speaks with concern to the hotel manager.

"The entry security system: do you have any video? We need to talk to you next downstairs and have a look at your system. But first, how are you going to ensure these two people can feel safe from further intrusions?"

Surprising concern for us from the officer.

The manager then turns to us.

"This is a crime free hotel. But be pleased, at all times I advise you most strongly to make use of the safety chain and the safe in your room. It is of the utmost importance to us that you feel safe at all times. You feel safe, yes?"

Soon after the brief reassurance, Sabina and the two men retreat.

16

The Debriefing

Iain knew they needed to debrief. He was trying to work out why Tara was so unresponsive to his reaching out. Was she angry with him, for not having been there? Or was it that she needed time to process what had happened? Why did he so quickly assume that when Tara was not happy, he was at fault in some way?

This was when his training kicked in. A picture of an inflated bladder came to his mind, like when feelings build up until the bladder is so full it becomes a complete distraction from anything rational. To deal with the trauma they had just experienced, they needed to make sense of it. He, being who he was, needed to get it into perspective. Tara also needed to feel she could do something: perhaps it would simply be to ensure they were no longer vulnerable, the room secure. Each in their own way needed to feel safe. They needed to validate each other's understanding.

But first, before reason could have its way, Iain knew they each needed to vent, discharge their respective balloons, deflate their raised emotional states that normally demand fight or flight. It might well feel like riding an out-of-control hot air balloon. Iain knew that he would have to lead this process. He knew that he could not wait for Tara to ask after his feelings; not because she would not care, but because she didn't like acknowledging emotions, not even her own. She was inevitably solution focused. Empowerment came through doing for her. He looked over at her. She looked troubled. He felt the silence had been long enough.

"You look like I feel: troubled and shaken. Not exactly the best of experiences, of first impressions of the island, eh?"

"Things happen. I guess we will get over it in a few days. Rather annoying though," replied Tara. Clearly in the pause, she had been gathering herself together, regaining control.

"Just annoying? Any other feelings?" Immediately Iain thought he may have moved to feelings too quickly, and her answer confirmed that.

"I can feel you" she said, her troubled look turning into a mischievous smile as she leant over to tickle him. Iain felt relief. Her withdrawal had not been because she was angry with him in any way, but because she needed the silence to think. He was glad he had paused. He took her hand, and this time she squeezed it back.

"Yeah, yeah, but really, are you feeling OK?"

Tara's face went into a neutral kind of stare as she tried to reflect inward.

"Yeah - I just wish it hadn't happened!"

"So do I, and that's just telling me what you think, what you wished hadn't happened. What are you feeling though, right now?"

She reflected again for nearly a minute.

"A bit shaken up …. …. I suppose."

"A bit shaken up?"

"Yea, just a bit shaken up. Well, actually, if I'm honest, I think I've had, like, a massive shot of adrenalin! A bit like after a close call, like in surfing."

"Aha, your physical feelings – so maybe you are feeling frightened, or anxious, feeling like this place is unsafe?"

"I can't tell if the trembling which I think is caused by adrenalin is anxiety or not. I know I just want to get the heck out of here. Reason is telling me I am safe, but I don't feel safe. It reminds me of when I was young, around the time my mother died. I decided when I was twelve that I would not let myself feel that again, but I guess here we are, and I am feeling that, if it is a feeling."

Iain allowed some more time for reflective silence, and then asked her specifics about how the events had unfolded for her. She told him about thinking it was he who was sitting at the desk and the shock of getting knocked down. In fact, she said, if she had realised he was an intruder, she may well have tackled him, but that would have been foolish. Finally, she admitted she could identify a sense of violation.

"But Iain, where were you?"

Reconstruction was important; however, Iain didn't think it was quite time yet to share his experience and his own feelings. He could feel her hand, cold and clammy and still holding his hand quite strongly as he had been speaking, which told him there was more Tara needed to talk about.

"Tell you in a minute," he continued: "but now, you said you feel violated; do you think you are feeling anything else, perhaps now more aware you have identified feeling violated?"

Tara was quiet for a minute or so, before answering, slowly, more reflective than usual, as if struggling to identify correct words to explain how she was feeling:

"I think, well, now that I have identified being violated, well, it's like there is a rising anger, yes, I am starting to feel really angry!"

For Iain, this was progress. Such anger indicates motivation to take charge, moving away from any sense of being a victim. He knew that such events can turn into long term traumatization, where there is an unresolved sense of dis-empowerment, victimization. Tara being who

Iain understood her to be could now progress to what she might do. Action would give her a sense of empowerment.

Dysfunctional reactions can result in seeking and even more so, in taking revenge. Options are needed, to allow anger to motivate constructive outworkings, but Iain realised that before that could happen, it would be good to allow her to release some more of the anger.

"So, you are really feeling a lot of anger now, eh, very angry?"

"Really angry, yes."

"Do you get a sense of what or who you are feeling angry about?" Iain was wanting her to consider the object of her anger as a prelude to contemplating positive action.

"Mmm, it's not just that I feel violated, but, mmm, if it turns out that the person was a druggie looking for stuff to support his addiction, then I am angry at a lack of help, at the things that drove that person to it. After all, I was there once. But if he is a criminal of some sort, well, I feel angry with him. He should be responsible."

"And angry at the Hotel, or maybe me for not locking the door properly?"

"Well, I thought of that, but I am not sure how that person got in as the door cannot be closed without locking, and you need a card to get in, and it has to be held open to not lock. So I don't think you or the Hotel are responsible. Maybe you didn't quite close it, Iain. Anyhow, where were you? Where had you gone?"

While the anger reduced somewhat by her sharing, other more hidden feelings needed to also be uncovered – feelings not normally admitted to. How quickly the psychologist in him had come to the fore, recognising a pattern to need to take charge in a traumatic situation. But this was not a client but his wife, and the experience was a shared one: time for him to now share his own thoughts and reactions, starting by responding honestly to her questioning.

"You heard me tell the police how I had slipped out and was coming back when the intruder ran into me at the side door, with me picking up what I realised was your computer mouse! I was terrified you may have been harmed in some way! That thought was absolutely overwhelming, and you have no idea the relief in finding you alive and unharmed."

They both suddenly hugged each other, needing the reassurance of closeness, togetherness.

"I guess we are both in shock - look at us" suggested Tara, with a small laugh. "But we are unharmed. Can we talk over some dinner? I am suddenly *really* hungry!"

So it was that over a late dinner they reconstructed yet again what had happened, questioning what the intruder might have been looking for. The small intimate restaurant had a comfortably tropical and quiet ambience, allowing Tara to recall for Iain what the DI and sergeant had said about safety on the island. They were also able to reason that since Tara had not been touched, the intruder had hardly been a potential murderer or rapist but simply a thief. And then, as Iain recalled the incident at the hotel side door, a whiff of a sweet perfume came into his mind. That caused Tara also to recall a known perfume. Was this imagination? She remembered something like an Opium Eau de Parfum, one of her friends' favourites. On asking Iain who the perfume might have reminded him of, he thought for a few seconds and then suggested her friend Judy. They laughed at the thought of the slim Judy in drag, cushioned up, having followed them to the island, playing a prank on them. Then, when realising the details suggested a female intruder, their conversation continued.

"But if it was a girl, she was a big woman. Come to think of it, though, it better explains the long straight hair with a purple streak coming out from the side and covering the face under the hoodie. I noticed when I was down the street before, that dreadlocks, not plain long hair, are popular here among younger guys." They both agreed they didn't expect that the strength of the perfume to have meant that it was likely to have simply rubbed off from a girlfriend.

"Better let the police know," and that conclusion had ended their speculation.

Nor did they get into one of their frequent discussions, enjoyed so much by Iain, and more likely endured by Tara. But even without such a discussion about whether providence was for real and what might this event have any purpose, their forensic deductions brought a sense of empowerment. The thought of a female thief seemed much less threatening; at least Tara felt less vulnerable, though there was still the question as to how 'she' might have opened a locked door. And now, having finished a bottle of red wine between them, they enjoyed their shared sticky date pudding while chatting congenially with the owner.

Everyone seemed to know everyone, and they were clearly identified as new arrivals. On hearing that Tara was a plant biologist researching coffee, the owner had sat down and chatted about her own passion, interrupting the discussion only to make and bring them each one of her special decaffeinated liqueur affogatos. Iain and Tara had felt the welcoming open atmosphere, which served to expel any lingering concerns that had made them feel this might not be the safe piece of paradise they had originally expected.

Relaxed now, with the humidity reduced in the evening, and in a socially warm atmosphere combined with the effects of the relief of debriefing, the pudding, red wine, the affogatos, and a congenial discussion, with arms around each other they walked back to their hotel, passing by other alfresco diners along the way. Back in their room they took no time to fall into bed.

17

Local Contact

Iain

The sun starts peeping in through the hotel window. From her breathing, I assume Tara is still heavily asleep. I snap to fully awake as I remember: the prayer meeting! Tension: to go or not to go? But then, as I look with delight at my sleeping wife, my mind is made up. I can't leave her alone again just now. It's not that I should be here when she wakes, it is simply that I want to be! That's a realisation for me – this event has woken me up to being more naturally, more spontaneously aware of someone other than myself! I must finally be growing up, maturing! Well, I reflect, I *am* over halfway to three score years and ten!

After breakfast I decide to ring the Reverend van der Leer. The phone rings out. No answering machine or message bank. By the time I finally manage to get through, it is late afternoon. I ask if there is a convenient time to come and see him.

"Not tonight. I am preparing for the morning. After the morning service?" comes the straight unapologetic reply. I had already thought about going to his church sometime in the future, but now I'm feeling a little irritated: I am expected to go to the reformed church service in the morning, or the possibility of finding suitable accommodation through van der Leer may evaporate.

But next morning, we reluctantly attend The Reformed church. Fortunately, I had filled Tara in about my brief interchanges with him, so she also knew something of what to expect at his church. The service runs much along the lines I remembered days long gone, back in my hometown strict Presbyterian church in Glasgow, except no hymns, only psalms. I've rarely thought of that since! There is also no data projector here, like back in WA.

When the sermon starts, we are offered some sweets by the man in the seat in front of us. We look around to see many of the parishioners digging out lollies. Mostly older folk, though a couple of children on one side who I knew would appreciate the sweets! Later that day, Tara reflected on this practice as perhaps intended to help maintain attention with a sugar fix! She had braced herself for a dry exegetical exposition, and she is not disappointed. The sermon is a straightforward three-point talk, logical, deductive, analytical and cerebral.

At one level I am in my comfort zone, having been brought up on such sermons. Just when wondering what practical applications the minister might draw out, however, he abruptly finishes with a simple admonishment: "Paul honours Gott in every vay, to de deps of his being by putting his trust in de truth. To inherit eternal life, we too must put our trust in Gott and His Word. And dat means obeying him in every-ting. May He give us all de strength to do so. Amen."

Tara looks across at me and I smile. I'm sure she wonders what my smile might mean, what I am thinking - about the sermon or other things? I feel somewhat awkward, but there's no time to explain now, as we walk across to where the obligatory morning tea is being served. Before anyone else can engage us, the minister, still in what seems to us as his anachronistic black gown, comes across to us.

As van der Leer is shaking my hand, I introduce Tara. He looks back and forth from me to Tara several times without speaking.

"Ah, so dis is your wife, ya?" he asks. Continuing to shake my hand, and without waiting for an answer, still looking at me, he asks rhetorically:

"So, is she originally from Rustenberg Eilandt den I see?"

Tara steps in:

"What makes you think I might be from here?"

The hand shaking stops and he turns to Tara:

"It's just, well, you look somewhat like a local burgher, and so I thought at the very least you might have family here."

"A local burgher?"

"Oh, ya…, local burghers….., they are people of mixed race, mostly Celonese, or I should say Sri Lanken now, mixed with other European, Dutch or…or I tink, mostly Portuguese."

"No, no, I am not a burgher. I was born in Australia, my grand-mother from India."

His next statement is another unguarded, blunt, somewhat rhetorical question:

"So with that background, you are a Christian believer, no?"

For Tara, it is not such a simple straight forward matter of right belief. Understanding faith to her rests on understanding her story, her journey, and culture. Accordingly, she can't resist the temptation to tease out his question.

"I was brought up in Australia in an Anglo-Indian Hindu family" she says with a smile. Though she didn't share with him that there'd been little of Hindu beliefs modelled to her, and only small aspects of her cultural heritage were ever really explored. Meanwhile, van der Leer is obviously perplexed. Tara allows a poignant pause, watching the expression of the minister's face. This gives the minister an opportunity to reflect before asking his next question:

"So, you are not religious at all?"

"No. I am not very religious, or spiritual if it comes to that." She has identified somewhat with her cultural roots, but religious ritual had left her cold; she finds mysticism elusive.

"Then do you believe anything?" His tone is just a little despairing.

"I believe, with the certainty of an informed agnostic." Her response is quick and confident.

"So, that is, you do believe the Bible, maybe a little?" asks the minister, now with a more hopeful tone entering his voice.

Clearly Tara now decides it is time to end this discussion before getting too serious.

"If you mean, do I believe Jesus is the Son of God? Yes, that I do believe, sincerely and so deeply that I want to grow in knowing him more. But loving someone isn't really religious, spiritual or mystical, is it?"

With those last words van der Leer looks relieved, making me break into a wry knowing smile toward Tara. Love for her, she often says, in the here and now, in the being and doing, not some esoteric or romantic mysticism. Well done, girl, I think!

"Dat is good den" he said to Tara before turning to me again: "Your wife, how do I say it, she is quite philosophical."

There is just a discernible surprise in his heavily accented voice, suggesting he might not expect this from a woman! Or perhaps it reflects his thoughts about someone of colour, I wonder. But I am glad to reflect that neither of us would be worried about this presumption. Tara knows that in fact she is not particularly philosophical at all, though I am! For Tara in the end, it is the tangible evidence that makes sense. It is tangible evidence of the historic reliability of the New Testament documents and the tangible evidence of the life transforming effects of the message for her and her friends that has convinced Tara. Meanwhile, Tara will also I have no doubt muse to herself that van der Leer hadn't actually asked if she had in fact committed herself beyond *desiring* to trust Christ.

This made way for the opportunity I had been waiting for: to ask about the cottage that in our interchanges van der Leer had suggested might be available for us to rent. Pondering whether I needed to push him, I am surprised that van der Leer has done his homework. He gives me a note with contact details of an available rental property, owned by one of his elderly parishioners. He tells us it will be available for at least twelve months! It is available to take up tomorrow. God is good, he tells us with a sudden almost mischievous smile that seems to imply that he knew that we didn't expect that!

Tomorrow we can begin our next exciting adventure – in our new home, on an idyllic island – paradise!

18

Home Intrusion

Tara

After leaving the hotel, and then a stop off at the small supermarket for basic foods we might need, the taxi drops us off. A cottage by the sea along the curved shoreline, and right at the mouth of the river in fact. What could be more attractive?

Well, it isn't really a cottage: more of a clean and tidy cabin. But the locals referred to them as cottages, so cottages they are: three similarly built side by side. Cases in hand, we stand surveying the scene.

The cottage is set in a gently undulating area, almost on the edge of a sand bank, with the other cottage on either side. It is certainly incredibly beautiful, we agree, looking westward over the mouth of the river and across to the town further on. The idyllic setting is a nice distraction from any concerns we'd had about being here. We share our feelings about what it will be like, watching the sun rising over the water each morning at the eastern side of the house; and at night, sitting on the deck as the sun disappears beyond the mighty ocean to our west! We spy a couple of small church spires and only two relatively low multi-story buildings that rise above the village, set against a backdrop of steep mountains of a lush tropical rainforest. Fluffy clouds are simply hanging around the tallest peak. Truly, we voice aloud, the town's name, Kleine Paradijs, is so appropriate.

Excellent coffee growing country too, especially in the higher reaches, I'm thinking.

"No wonder the Dutch at the end of the eighteenth century saw this as a potential hideaway in which to develop new trade with secret varieties of coffee. If only I was able to paint," I say to Iain, hoping he understands I am really more than happy with my second best, getting my camera out. I so look forward to catching angles of sunrises and sunsets in this beautiful place. He releases my hand as I grab my phone to quickly capture the present moment, special for it being our first day in our new home on the island.

The building itself is of rough sawn timber planks, painted blue, with white around the casement windows, giving a sense of the Mediterranean. The veranda runs all the way round, with entrances variously placed along all sides, giving a freely accessible and open feeling. After walking around, we tried to enter from what we thought was the front door, but it clearly wasn't! It actually led into a small storeroom, and without any access to inside the rest of the building. So we try the side door which we find unlocked. This brings us into a large open room, with a large wooden table in the centre, and a small but more than adequate kitchen to the side, with all the things a couple might wish for in a holiday setting. The only areas separated off are for a bedroom to one side and a separate toilet/ bathroom/ laundry on the other. We drop our bags in the bedroom in front of the old dark wardrobe. We are just taking in the room, with typical me checking out the bed springs, when we suddenly hear a noise that brings us hurrying back to the main room.

There, just inside one of the outer doors is an intruder. Yes, another intruder! Here is a man, not running away but standing stock still, perhaps thinking if he didn't move no-one would notice him? As we emerge, he continues to stand, unblinking, glaring at us. He makes no movement as Iain walks up to him.

"What are you doing here?" Iain demands. They are now standing face to face. Seems to be a long moment in time. But I observe that the gaze of this stranger feels neither insolent nor threatening. It is just a fixed but emotionless stare down.

When he finally speaks, he has a somewhat assertive voice:

"I might ask you the same."

We both wonder if we've entered the wrong cottage, but no, looking around we see no evidence of anyone living here. Iain tells me later he vacillated between simply answering in a civil way, calling the police, or demanding the man get out. I'm glad he chose the first option, but the irritation he felt still showed through.

"We are the new tenants. What are you doing here?"

"I live here" came the immediate answer. The man remains unmoving on the spot, except for his mouth opening. His head didn't even turn to observe me, though he can hear me slowly walking to get to a chair, to give me something to use if needed. In apparent confusion and disbelief, Iain voices his concern:

"You, um, you live here?.....er... but we have, well, maybe we have the wrong house?"

After another long pause, the mouth opens again in a tone hardly audible, and as if talking to himself:

"No-one told me. But then they never do. Probably squatters, I thought. And probably noisy squatters at that. And you are not traffickers, eh? Lots of stuff gets landed here. Police half asleep. No border force checks between here and the mainland as they like to call it."

Iain didn't quite know how to continue so I now walk across, to break the tense moment.

"This is your home?" I ask him directly. The man's dark eyes now shift to focus on me.

"No."

"But you said you live here?"

"Yes, I live here" he answered, "isn't that exactly what you and your man asked me?" Then as if needing to make sure these foreigners understood, he slowly repeats one word at a time, copying Iain's Scottish accent, as if by so doing he would be better understood "And … noo, …this ….is ….nought ….my ….home."

"So you have another home somewhere else?"

"I said, this is not my home" he answers even more slowly, "I have only one home." The man is starting to sound frustrated, perhaps even agitated. So I try to settle the tension, rephrasing the question: "So, your home is somewhere else?"

"Yes, that's what I have been telling you!" he answers. My, he looks like he is thinking we are just idiots!

The man shrugs, suddenly turns, and starts toward the door when Iain stops him, putting his hand on his shoulder: "Not so fast, man: where is your home?"

"Next door, the house next door. Everyone knows that's where I live. If you are not squatters, I won't bother you. Just don't turn up your radio. I like it peaceful and quiet here."

With that, the man calmly lifts Iain's hand from his shoulder and continues swiftly and noiselessly out the door, and thankfully is gone. But we hadn't even asked the guy his name! This is such a strange experience, yet it doesn't feel suspicious, something about him, but can't put my finger on it.

Iain later tells me he was so relieved he'd not summarily dismissed the neighbour as an intruder. But now, with the adrenalin rush subsiding, and feeling relieved if not a little amused, we flop down on the sofa, only to hear an enormous squark. As quickly as we'd sat, we jump up again, adrenalin again surging. But the noisy culprit merely proves to be a child's teddy, hidden away under the cushion.

It reminds me of the teddy I had bonded with in my toddler years. I had even carried it into my teens, only for it to be gone one day when my grandmother did one of her clean-ups. I remember how I had cried for weeks and now, all of a sudden, I am hit by a sense that I had never really stopped grieving. To Iain's surprise, I hug the teddy, as passionately as I might have done if a long-lost friend returned from the dead. Iain notices the tears welling up in my eyes.

Completely uninvited, many of my childhood traumas now unexpectedly come flooding back. I feel giddy, as though I am spinning out. A few minutes ago, I was laughing with Iain. Now, with a simple fright, this incredible reaction, really quite visceral! I thought I had worked away those unhappy memories with Em, ages ago. How could such a small startle bring so much back uninvited? Iain has seen me happy and sad, but never spin out quite like this. All he does is hold me, and he does so for the next twenty minutes. He sits down beside me, with deep concern etched in his face. But he seems to know to say nothing: he is just present, arms holding me close. I feel that, deeply.

My mind gradually quietens. The past becomes a blur as vividness retreats. I'm glad there is no talk. Just being there for me - that's what I love about Iain. Being there, not saying anything, I later tell him - makes me feel he trusts and respects me. But when I share this with him, he freely admits thinking at the time "little does she know just how helpless I feel when I don't know how to fix something". How blessed I am, feeling that at such times Iain is so prepared to be selflessly, unobtrusively present with me, when as a hurting and vulnerable person, my feelings are so much more important than his own.

I am ready to move on, but I don't want to talk about what's been going on in my head, not just now. I hug him tight and then, grabbing his arm, I stand up, drag him over to the westerly windows. The setting sun is reflected over the mountains, brilliant red streaks against the clouds over the highest peak.

"That's just for us" I say quietly, pointing up and then back out to the mountains. Then I put one arm around him, the other around my teddy. "Let's have a quick bite to eat before we get some sleep. We can talk more in the morning." With the light now fading fast, we find the light switch: a single globe in the centre of the room. We notice there are no curtains, and we also discover there is no way of really locking doors, except for some very small hooks on the inside.

19

Childhood Revisited

Tara

We have settled into the cottage over the last couple of weeks. Iain tells me later that he had woken as he often did around three a.m. His worry time, he calls it. He could become fixated on a problem that needed solving. The more there were calculations such as about finances or statistics, or the more a need for clear logic, the more awake he would become. He could then lie there only to fall asleep finally around sunrise. He had learned that if he started praying for his friends one by one, he soon forgot his worries and, in the morning, realise he had fallen asleep mid prayer. He had a list and would try to remember how far he had reached so that next time that's where he would start!

Iain reported that as he'd been about to start praying for me. he'd reached over to touch me softly but immediately sat bolt upright, finding no-one in the bed next to him! And then he'd seen me, silhouetted at the open window, looking westward out to sea, a sea bathed in the brightness of a full moon. He had crept silently across the room, intending to fling his arms around me in surprise, not realising I was still holding the teddy.

But I am not caught by surprise. Always alert with good peripheral vision, I see him in the mirror in the corner of the room. I watch him rise and approach me.

For me this becomes a wonderful healing moment. I look out over the sea, the moon reflecting off the waves breaking relentlessly, running up the beach. I feel a tremendous contentment and am reminded of a joy I had never thought possible during my troubled childhood, and even less likely after the terrible experience of an abusive marriage, short though it was. In a desperate attempt to quench the pain and fill the emptiness, I had indulged my lusts, but the fleeting relationships in search of something - I knew not what - only added to my sense of enduring emptiness and a futility about any relational satisfaction. When hope is gone, and there is no meaning, nothing seems to matter.

What a contrast. Here, the once unimaginable, unattainable, impossible: I stand now with a friend with whom I have personally grown so much, even just in four short years. Yes, through the initial romance with its' normal ups and downs, there were often arguments that felt we'd never work each other out, but gradually, ever so gradually, we moved on to a relationship that has brought goodness I had not even dreamed existed. Tov – a Jewish biblical term about goodness I have recently been reading about. I now reflect on how that growth in understanding had required hard work at times. That reality had set in with our first fights, only a few months after we married. Even recently, a fleeting memory intruded: in exasperation at Iain over some stubbornness, I had thumped him, driven mad by his determination to argue a point, and then another time, when he had yelled at me, equally stubborn! But I smile now, remembering that even through those experiences, we had gained appreciation of our being two quite different but strong-minded people; that no matter what, we did respect each other. We remind ourselves often of the need not to let the sun go down on our anger, no matter what it's about!

No longer feeling so bereft or alone, I can now understand more clearly what love really is: utter and relentless commitment to making relationships work. Iain had seen that in his clinical work. I recall some of those he had shared with me which so encouraged us both, as he often observed that "the happiest most resilient couples were those who amid the inevitable turmoil and thrusts of life were there for each other, not for themselves, but for others, for family and friends". Yes, we are there for each other, but more than that, there is a purpose much, much deeper and wider than self-fulfilment. Strange paradox, really, but as one of Iain's favourite sayings puts it: "the proof of the pudding is in the eating!" How wonderful it's been that we've been able to have an open home for people to drop in. I wonder how that will eventuate here, knowing no-one really; and how will I make sure Iain as an introvert can also find enough time for the space he seems to need?

Quiet contemplation brings me back to what I am holding: the teddy and that suddenly again forcefully transports me back, but this time, no longer taken by surprise I remain calm, ready to work things through in my head. I recall being happy as a six-year-old child. My mother had taken me to the beach at Altona. We had built sandcastles together. Such undivided attention was rare. My mother was so often preoccupied, buried in a book, or always moody, just lying with her eyes closed. When she spoke, it was usually to tell me not to do something. Everything had to be super clean, neat and tidy. My grandmother did most of the looking after me, but she too was stern. But yes, that day at the beach was so different. I remember I buried teddy up to his neck in the sand in my imaginary play. She didn't seem to mind what I was doing, seeming to be uncharacteristically happy to play with me. When we got home, she gave me the biggest of hugs as she put me to bed. That too was unusual. I felt really, really happy, and I wanted it to last forever.

That happiness was shattered early the next morning. I vividly recall my grandmother screaming at my grandfather in Hindi, words I could not understand. Then there was the sound of sirens. Voices of strangers. I had crept to my bedroom door. I wanted my Mummy, but as I opened the door, my distraught grandmother told me to stay in bed and closed the door, tightly. Then another siren, more voices, this time including women. I wanted Mummy all the more, but I was afraid of my grandmother. I clutched teddy, waiting for a chance to escape. Finally, no more voices, so thinking my grandmother had gone, I had dragged a stool to the door to open it, but it was locked. I sank up against it, clutching teddy. I'd started to cry and call out for the mother I'd had yesterday, but no-one came. I had cried myself to sleep, lying on the floor.

I now vividly remember waking to that feeling of being very hungry, just when my grandfather's sister opened the door. I had not seen aunty for a long time.

"Tara, come with me. You are a lucky girl, coming on a holiday to my house." Aunty might have sounded cheery, but she certainly didn't look very happy. We got to her car: there was no mummy in sight.

"Mummy, I want mummy. Where's mummy?"

"She's not coming now. Just you."

"But I want mummy." I lay down on the footpath, clutching teddy and kicking wildly.

"Mummy has gone away. Now just be a good girl"- my aunt picked me up roughly and bundled me crying into her car. I didn't ever miss much, even then noticing my elderly aunt was clearly trying to hide her tears. Why was she crying? So I gave in, thinking I must be why she was upset.

Suddenly I am desperate to shake off the pain I am feeling. I am so relieved to find Iain is still standing next to me, his loving arms quietly holding me, knowing the unbidden tears needing to flow. I am gradually feeling less overwhelmed, and I am so glad that few memories of my pre-teen years now ever intrude.

Just one sudden flashback however returns: after going back home from staying with my aunty, and after repeatedly asking when my mother would be back from her holiday, I was finally told my mother had gone away and was not coming back. For years I blamed myself for my mother going away, wondering what I had done? What was wrong with me, that my mother didn't love me enough to stay? I learned only in my teenage years that my mother had overdosed, so then the self-blame had begun again, not just for her leaving, but for her death.

I had thought my childhood trauma had been dealt with, having talked about that with a psychologist in later teens. Though I no longer blame myself for my mother's suicide, the pain of abandonment, not being loveable, still occasionally returns. The teddy experience has triggered so many memories, and again it takes me completely by surprise. The little child is still there. Will she always be there, hiding maybe?

But now, as we move to sitting together on the bed, continuing to look towards the moonlit sea, I sense we are not alone. I had never experienced this before, so unobtrusive but comforting a presence: was this the Holy Spirit? We begin to talk about it. Then Iain intuitively suggests that a healing closure to all these feelings might be made possible if I, now the more knowing and therefore more confident adult, could talk to the little child within. I tell him how Em when I saw her professionally had worked through my attempted drowning using that very technique, I ask him if it's OK for him to help me this time? I know what I want to do, and even how to do it, but I want us to do it together. I want him to be with me, like walking hand in hand.

Gently, ever so gently, he encourages me to relax, and then as he sees me do that, leads me to imagining my little child within, teddy in hand. He reminds me that he is here beside me, my adult self. I let him know I now have a vivid picture of the little Tara, and we are both there. I am going over to her, hugging her. Silently, without words, I introduce her to Iain. Iain knows to be quiet now. I actively comfort and reassure the child within, guiding the discussion around questions of feeling responsible for my mother's behaviour. She has lots of questions. I find myself answering her, reassuring my little self that it could never be about being loveable or not. We have a internal discussion about what and who might have contributed to our mother's sad choices. She seems so rational to me, and also so trusting.

I cannot quite remember about what happens next. Iain later tells me that for the ensuing ten or so minutes of silence, I had sat entranced, followed by unexpected tears streaming from my right eye! Apparently, that indicated to Iain that I now had finished all I needed to say. Quietly he asks if I am ready. I know enough to say 'yes.' He suggests I could now hug myself, imagining the now happy child is one part of me that finally has become a relieved but importantly integrated part of who I am.

The scene fades and a gentle joy now flows, along with a sense of acceptance within me, between me and myself. I and my child part want to celebrate, to dance for joy, to run off into the sea with the teddy, and then flowing with my imagination, I really want to sit and re-play in the sand.

But the realist in me stirs - it is nearly 4 am! Iain shares his understanding of imagining as being almost as effective as actually doing. Virtual reality, so powerful! So, I had briefly indulged in my happy imaginings, unaware of how long we quietly have been here together, in absolute but comfortable silence. But right now, I suddenly feel incredibly tired. I gently tug us back to bed; time to catch some more sleep.

While all this was happening, weeks later I learn that Iain's attention had briefly been caught by a small rowboat pulling in upriver, and then he'd seen a man in a dark hooded top emerge from the shadows to meet it. The mangroves apparently could not hide him completely in the bright moonlight. But for me, at that moment I held no fears about who it was, nor why he was there...the night held far greater, more positive and lasting effects on me that excluded anything worrisome. My mourning had been turned into dancing, my sorrows into joy! Little paradise!

20

Search for Contraband

Iain

The sun and tide were both well up as Tara and I walk onto the beach with our breakfast bowls, a mug of tea for one and the other with coffee in hand. Who could ever have imagined having our own kind of private beach, right outside our front door! We sit on the sand to enjoy our breakfast, our bare feet enjoying the sand. It feels like we have gone out for a picnic. Wispy clouds and a pleasant morning breeze, all so idyllic. There's a boat with sails on the horizon, and several fishing boats that suggest this is one of the frequent activities the locals enjoy.

There's no need to talk. I sense Tara's contentment in the aftermath of last night, massively enhanced by the scene around her: she clearly does not want to disrupt it by recalling and explaining. She is visibly savouring the moment with the tranquillity surrounding us. The birds flying over join us, expressing their delight in this peaceful environment with their beautiful songs.

It strikes me that simply being with someone, present with someone you love, sitting next to someone, not talking, not touching, just being there, manifests a sense of communion, deep attachment. How un-alone I am feeling. So different from when I was living alone. And I didn't even know what I was missing then, because I had never quite experienced anything like this. The old saying, I guess: 'what you have never had, you never miss.' But I do wonder whether I'd had some sort of sense of it, if in no other area than spiritually, and this thought affirms my suspicions that burying myself in my work was my way of avoiding any awareness of the need. Experientialism contained. Not bad after all.

While I am in my own thought bubble thinking about the past, Tara, now back to her normal present awareness, nudges me.

"Iain, look!"

There, walking toward them, only meters away, is our neighbour, accompanied by the police inspector in his grey overcoat, closely followed by two uniformed police officers. They walk up to us, not the cottage.

"You know who I am, and I know who you are. We met before at the hotel" says the inspector in the gruff voice I clearly remember. I wonder how it could be at all possible that he would think we might not remember meeting.

"My men here, they need to search your house. Is that all right with you or do we need a warrant? Whatever way, you may not go back in until we are finished." He is abrupt.

"No, go right ahead. What are you looking for?"

"Contraband, drugs. And, oh, don't go away. Stay here" he demands, turning around and heading toward the cottage, following the two officers who have wasted no time to be on their way. The nameless neighbour stands there for a few seconds longer, and then shaking his head and shrugging his shoulders, he heads back to his home.

In less than fifteen minutes the inspector returns, alone. Tara is openly relieved, and says, "Well, that was quick! now we can get on with our day."

"We have found what we are looking for. We will be taking the powder back for analysis, though the marijuana speaks for itself."

"But we don't know anything about any drugs. We have only just come out here yesterday afternoon" says Tara, suddenly now somewhat distressed, but DI Visser doesn't seem to be listening.

"I need you to come back to the station, we will talk there. We will take your fingerprints. No room in the car now, and you both need more suitable clothes. When ready, come directly to the station." Again, not waiting for a reply but head down, he turns and walks back to his waiting constables. It is then that we notice our neighbour is accompanying the police.

The contentment of half an hour ago has now been replaced with a sense of foreboding, trepidation, though when we reflect more deeply later on, we also would have sensed a strange twinge of joy persevering. But there is no time for that now. As we return to the cottage, our brains feel on fire.

Even more perplexing though is what we find as we come back into the cottage. Despite there having been a supposed search, nothing looks to have been touched. Not even our yet unpacked cases had been opened. What had the police been doing here? A thousand negative scenarios fly through my head. I choose not to share these with Tara.

21

If-ing

Iain

The inspector did say we needed to go to the police station, but he didn't say straight away. So, we have taken our time to change, needing to collect ourselves together, and over our drinks.

But now, rather than settling us, we find ourselves being even more disconcerted, entertaining the most unpleasant of potentials still to come, a thorough going case of the 'what ifs.' What if the police are corrupt, or incompetent? What if they want to lock us up, falsely accuse us because, well, they are island police, and they need to solve a case? What if they have planted the material they claimed to have found? But why? How embarrassing if such false accusations were to be splashed over the local papers. I feel a strong personal anger at potential injustice. I know that Tara has experienced that before, just because of the colour of her skin, even though it is relatively light. For a fleeting moment, I ponder why I should feel so much more strongly about a potential miscarriage of justice when *I* am affected, compared with when I read about or hear of others suffering injustice. Am I just a selfish being after all?

Tara seems far less troubled than I expected. She was not so concerned about the injustice I had thought at the time. None the less, she later told me that the worst of her thoughts that had crowded in were irrationally about me: They ran something like this:

What if there is something you have never told me: a criminal history? Have you really been honest about your past? What if you are a drug dealer and the packages the police had found have been left for you? Those thoughts were just too devastating; to think of being betrayed just when for the first time in my life I had trusted someone like never before. And, yes, I'd finally experienced the wonder of secure attachment. But what if it was all a lie? It just felt like terrifying devastation might be lying ahead. But I couldn't bring myself to ask you.

No wonder my own thinking is suddenly interrupted by Tara calling out "Stop, Stop, Stop" at the top of her voice. My train of thought stops. I put my arm around her and note she is cold, and only half responds. I wonder what thoughts she might be having. It feels like she needs reassurance. I gently take hold of her hand, tightly now. She sees my loving but strained face, but is desperately trying to collect herself before speaking. Her eventual response is reassuring:

"Sorry, I was just yelling at myself, at my stream of negative thinking. A case of the 'what if's' as our friend Em would call them. But now, I just need to get a hold of myself. I thought I was on top of my 'what if-ing.' My mind is so running wild. I find myself considering the worst possible scenario. It seems to have stolen the peace I experienced only last night."

Tara was looking both sheepish and troubled. I knew that despite her childhood traumas, Tara was generally an optimist by nature. When there was a problem, she would normally and quite effectively shrug her shoulders, turn the page as it were, smile and see it as an opportunity. But clearly now she was having trouble being positive.

"'If-ing'- I like that, Tara - Em has taught you well. I should know all about that, but time to fess up: my mind has been doing exactly the same! I bet I have cooked up much worse potential scenarios than you! The gifts of a more pessimistic disposition, combined with a rich imagination!"

I want to pick up on Tara's mixed feelings, but I know she is always disinclined to recognise them as such. I note she has said 'my mind is running wild', surely indicating she is focused on her thinking, not her feelings, and wanting rational control. Not to be distracted by feelings: that works for her. In a flash I wonder if I should take her back to reflecting on her feelings. Does she need to, to be more rationally in control by letting them out? Or should I focus rationally on her thinking? Insight comes immediately: This is Tara, cool headed in crisis. Stay with the immediate, the rational, that's how she deals with stuff. If need be, I can always come back to listening and sharing feelings later. I continue:

"We shouldn't be too hard on ourselves, Tara. Nothing wrong with the 'what ifs.' Stress can make us so much more vulnerable to thinking the worst. And we have had our fair share of that over the last few days! The same police we saw at the hotel brings all that back. Quite stressful. We perceive a threat, and when we do, our mind has been designed to entertain all possibilities that make us ready for fight or flight, to ensure we are prepared, think about how to deal with whatever."

I feel as though I might sound a little patronising. Maybe it is being protective? But hang on, she is a capable intelligent person who has successfully organised and lived her own life. What makes me feel so protective? Gender stereotypes? But Tara doesn't seem to have noticed. She is clearly solution focused, here and now.

"All very well as an explanation, but, well, how do we stop being on high alert, this stuff intruding?"

"To face the 'what ifs?' Well, we need to assess the reality of the various threats."

"How do we do that?" Tara asks. I am relieved I do not at this point suggest that all we need to do is pray and trust God and everything would be OK, as I once would have done. Sure, prayer is important, but Tara often quotes me as saying, 'Yep, pray and keep your powder dry'. She has made it clear she firmly believes in personal responsibility, taking whatever action one can, as necessary. No just praying and sitting around waiting. That is such a welcome balance on me. It works, to hear a voice of reasonableness to counterbalance negative thinking. Rationality was clearing away any haze. Time to go straight on to directly answer her question. That's what she wants and needs.

"Let's think things through, point by point as they come to us. Me first. Is there any reason for us to be under any suspicion? No."

"And" Tara completing my thinking, "I suppose we need to remember that we are not required under Australian law to prove our innocence, but rather the police would need to find and provide a court with evidence that we had brought or placed the contraband there, and we haven't, so there must be another explanation."

"Yes, and in fact, there could be any number of plausible explanations" I suggest.

"If we really are under any suspicion about us, they would have arrested us, I am sure."

I go on to suggest that surely needing our fingerprints is standard procedure. There was nothing to suggest that they are other than thoroughly professional and competent.

"Our personal effects had not been touched; did you notice, Iain?" Tara asks, and I complete what I think she is saying:

"Yes, and if they thought we were involved in drugs, they should have gone through our suitcases!"

With each consideration we both feel more relaxed.

"I agree. No real sense in thinking through 'what if' negative consequences. Each just leaves you, well, unhappy. Think positively, and if it takes a bad turn, let's cross that bridge when we come to it." I notice now that Tara is recognising her feelings post hoc, now having dealt with the stuff rationally. Such a good strategy. Was that learned, or innate? What happens when people are simply emotionally overwhelmed? Later reflection needed!

To our surprise when we finally arrive at the Police station, we find it to be a relatively small stone building, cluttered with desks with small windows open to the tropical air. Inspector Dirk Visser is not to be seen. His sergeant Sabina comes out from the back and greets us in a surprisingly warm way indeed. The initial response is to think she may be trying to catch us off guard. She thanks us for coming. What is this all about? She even apologises profusely for needing to take our finger-prints. While she only cursorily explains why, she takes our prints. She goes to considerable pains to explain how our privacy and rights would be protected. The prints would be destroyed once they had served their purpose.

"You must be wondering what sort of island this is, when you have had dealings with us twice in as many days. Not a nice first impression in your planned long stay with us, eh?"

"That's right! But the drugs…?" I start to ask, when sergeant Sabina jumps in, seemingly to play down any of our concerns:

"No need to worry. They are clearly not yours. The dust on them suggests they have been there untouched for weeks, if not months. Nor were they left for you. We checked and you only arranged the rental a couple of days ago. We had a tip off from dear old Jove, that neighbour of yours. He had seen them under a bed in the room off the outside of your house. He's quite a character, quite nosey. He is well known. Most people call him Grumpy because he is so blunt that, well, he makes people think of Snow White's dwarf by that name."

She pauses a moment, but then goes on when she can see both of us were still fully engaged. It strikes me that she is probably an extravert who likes talking, thinking out loud.

"But actually, he has a heart of gold. A few years ago, when fires raged in the mountains and many were up there fighting them, the most delicious casseroles started appearing overnight at the fire shed. They were so appreciated and so good, everyone thought they must have come from a Chef at a local restaurant. But then someone checked the surveillance cameras, and it was old Jove. And, man, was he cranky when he realised he had been found out! You'd think we'd accused him of a crime! He was obviously influenced by what he remembers from Sunday school. He simply says right and left hands are not supposed to know what the other does."

I wonder why she was telling us so much, almost as if talking to friends. Is this what we can expect on the island? And then, as if suddenly aware she's been rambling and needs to get back on task, Sabina continues:

"Sorry to hold you up. Before I forget, here are your bits and pieces we collected to check for forensic evidence after the hotel incident. Just sign for them here. So, they are yours again."

As I sign for the returned evidence, Tara fossicks through the evidence bag. I see her looking at the sergeant as her hand feels around.

"Everything should be there" the sergeant reassures us as she reads an enquiring expression on Tara's face.

"No, not everything: I am missing my USB Flash Drive" says Tara.

"It's not on the list - and I don't remember seeing or picking any up."

As we were talking, the inspector has come back through the front door. Without a greeting he bluntly intrudes on the conversation:

"USB Flash Drive: how big and what is on it?"

"Scan Disk, 64 Gig. A whole lot of documents from university and public libraries I had scanned, mostly about coffee and the island, not otherwise electronically available. It was encrypted."

I watch the two officers give one another something between a knowing and an enquiring look. Then the inspector turns to me:

"Do you, or have you ever worked for, or are you or your wife in any way, directly or indirectly connected to, or friends with anyone in the West Australian or Australian Federal Police."

"I don't think so…." I start to answer.

"Simply yes or no" interrupts the inspector impatiently.

"I may at some stage have seen a policeman as a client, but other than that, no. Why do you ask?" Without answering my question, the inspector turns his questioning imperative gaze on Tara.

"No" She simply answers.

As the inspector starts to walk off after another knowing look at the sergeant, I return to my question as to relevance. Again, he doesn't answer me but instead a thought seems to have come to mind as he turns to address Tara.

"Please supply me with a backup of the drive. And if you haven't got any, I need a list of all the documents you had on the drive."

Before Tara can answer, defensively and in protest, I want to insist on him answering my question:

"That's all! and only private research information as Tara has already told you! Its 'commercial-in-confidence.' What reason might there be for anything specific to be of interest to a police enquiry? And what's it got to do with any relationship either of us might have with any police?"

"Never you mind. I can always get a warrant" the inspector mutters, appearing annoyed as he starts to walk away towards the back room, leaving Sabina looking somewhat uncomfortable.

I had wanted to mention the figures I had seen in the night among the mangroves, even though I didn't want to unsettle Tara further. But with the lack of transparency in this questioning, I feel no obligation to share it now. In fact, I decide to think positively myself, suggesting it might have been nothing to be worried about, just some night-time fishermen, nothing to do with any drugs.

My thoughts are interrupted by Sabina trying to break the awkwardness that had been created.

"I hope you don't mind, Tara, but can I ask if you have family on the island, or maybe have come from here originally?"

I wonder whether this is just personal interest or further investigative probing. I am annoyed that there might be some sort of suspicion lingering. But Tara, always quick, perceptive, and direct, takes no time to ask:

"So, is that question because you think I look like I'm a burgher?"

"Ah, well, yes. I hope you don't mind…"

"Not at all, Sabina. But my maternal grandfather was English and my grandmother from northern India. I don't know who my father was."

"Ah, so not a burgher but as I thought, like me, Anglo-Indian. Maybe we can get together over a coffee sometime?"

As we walk home, Tara says she sees Sabina as straightforward and open, and felt quite welcoming of her invitation, accepted simply as her enjoying making personal connections. But personally, I wonder whether Sabina may still be wanting to go fishing for something, but for what?

PART 3

WORK IN PARADISE...

22

Tara's Research

Tara

Sitting on the deck overlooking the sea, I can't help wondering what I have let myself into. But I know I must get going on my research – that's why I am here! So yesterday Iain joined me in a quick walking tour of the main shopping strip, before doing what I knew was first up: to find a nice little furniture Op Shop, for some bits of furniture the cottage was not endowed with. My household goods were discovered quite quickly, so we arranged for a 'man with a van' to deliver a desk with a good chair, and an extra deck chair for Iain, to be set up as my study on the west facing deck. I hoped the veranda there would generally be adequate, especially when the notorious tropical summer storms hit – none experienced here yet. Been told that won't be for a few months, according to the waitress of the cute little alfresco cafe we grabbed a bite to eat. "The worst are often even after Christmas" she had commented. The removals man had agreed to making the delivery after I got home, no earlier than 2pm. After finishing our tasty and delightful light lunch, I left Iain to enjoy further meanderings, while I quickly walked the kilometre or so home.

What a place to work! I so love being outside! Coming here has offered such a fantastic opportunity, especially with the global awareness that coffee is becoming less available, more expensive, so my research certainly offers another positive prospect. But really, am I kidding myself, thinking I can really produce enough evidence of development opportunities that my employers will be satisfied with? At the same time, produce a PhD for the Uni? Hopefully, to be of some value too!

The man with the van arrives soon after I do. He calls himself Adrian, and I introduce myself as Tara, Iain's wife. He's clearly not a great talker, so I am surprised when he offers a spontaneous remark: "I wondered who was living here – I've seen the lights on. No one has lived here for quite a while".

"Oh, so you live around here too?" I ask, wondering if he knows the mysterious Jove.

"No, but I often meet a good friend just nearby who does a lot of fishing out from here – night fishing!"

"So do you fish too, Adrian?"

"Well, yes, sometimes, especially when I need some extra cash, if there's not enough furniture removal work around. But I also help a mate out some nights, pulling his boat out and offloading his catch of the night".

Conversation ceases as he helps me carry the furniture on to the deck. He seems eager to get going, so I thank him, saying I hope we catch up again sometime. I realise afresh how I am looking forward to making friends on the island.

But Iain is still not back, so thankfully I turn to my new desk. Try out my new desk chair, which gives me some reassuring pleasure. My first real uninterrupted time to start thinking, planning, and trying to create a realistic timeline for myself, to achieve what I have undertaken to do: to rediscover the land thought to have grown a reputedly high-class coffee, some 200 years ago but somehow now lost! Maybe to find that elusive 'superior' plant! I'm hoping I might be even able to identify a number of different coffee bushes that have gone wild in the hills. How exciting, but honestly, quite daunting!

Before leaving Perth, I had found a few brief references at a local library to some Dutch coffees grown wild in the highlands here, but all quite vague. I'd visited a couple of university libraries, but found only a few academic articles, and none with practical pointers for a potentially onerous task.

There is a brief intrusion into my thought stream: the missing flash drive. It has information I need. What is the seeming interest of the police about? And why the questions as to whether we knew any Western Australian police? Puzzling. It is just a drive with some research documents. Innocuous, I would have thought. I decide there is no sense going into that right now. We have been here settling in with interruptions for long enough. I am starting to feel some urgency to get on with my work. The flash drive can wait.

I am pleased that I have already managed to spend some hours in the local KP library, scouting out possible resources. This has turned up several local books, written by some now quite elderly people who know the island well. I plan to find out where to locate these authors, and to engage them in some valuable help about local coffee growing. I have heard there are several coffee farms here but have yet to find where and how these persist.

I'm also thinking I need to regularly start exploring the hills, systematically looking for those coffee plants already known to be scattered amongst the native trees and vegetation. I seriously need to find a decent detailed map! Maybe one of the older writers has a map I could borrow. For me, details always bring an exciting illumination – never what for some is reputedly an attitude that the detail includes a disturbing thought of the devil!

Right now, I must first locate that map – and preferably an up to date one! I start generating my list: finding the local lovers of plants is number two, including authors. Number three is visiting the small local coffee growers. No 4 starts me thinking on and on… Wow, even the list is confirming the size of the job I have taken on; but I'm never daunted too long, once I start. Oh, and yes, my mind yet again returns to my flash drive and all the information on it has gone. Still, that shouldn't stop me. I try to remember whether I have backed the flash drive up to the backup drive I left with my dear friend in Perth. Will I share it with the inspector? My mind returns to the puzzle. Why on earth was he so interested? What were the knowing looks about at the police station. They seemed honest enough. They are police anyhow. Just fleetingly, I wonder whether the inspector has some connection with someone else interested in the old coffee on the island. If so, then he certainly is out of order. How perplexing, those questions about associations Iain or I might have with other police! Strange.

My thoughts are interrupted. Iain is back. I change track. Now must come my necessary interchange with him about how he is going to occupy himself, so that I have greater freedom to concentrate on my work here! Afterall, that's why we are here. I know he is fighting something that is difficult for him to accept, the fact that he is a 'kept man'! I really love this man, but goodness, conversations can be so long and complex, and take so much time! I need to negotiate how I can actually work from home, with him around all day. I hope he has some ideas that we can creatively turn into practical realities! Can't have him thinking we can live on love – nor that we are retirees! Nor that we are just here on a long holiday – all of which he may think for a while are wonderful options!

23

Quandary

Iain

It's several weeks since we retrieved our stuff from the police, so have had some time now for reflection. Perhaps in my case it is better called 'wrestling with my thoughts.' Reflection has been a habit. From early childhood I had found that I was always reflective. As an only child, I remember my long walks on the Scottish Highlands, usually alone, but never lonely. So particularly when I am stressed, I have always had a habit of withdrawing, reflecting and thinking, away from confusing emotions, slowly gaining balance. I had found the reflective practice taught in my training incredibly helpful too. Not only can I now structure my reflections to be systematic, but through a process of critical reflection on my reflection, thought of as reflexive thinking, I had been able to modify, adapt and tailor my reflections.

Now how about starting my *year* of reflection? Now that I have arrived at the expectant moment, ready to actually start, it all seems perhaps rather much, self-indulgent even. A whole year of reading and reflection. Is that balanced? Time to reflect on reflection. But do I need to? That means I am now reflecting on reflecting on reflection! I can just imagine the Leunig cartoon.

How about applying some developmental psychology to thinking about this *year* of reflection? To what end? In developmental terms I think of it as being at the doorstep of another transition in my life, given to me by an opportunity to take a break from clinical practice. I had an inkling that this might be a more permanent break, an early mid-life change, moving away from being a psychologist. After all, I became a psychologist supposedly because I wanted to understand relationships and hoped it would help me form something I was looking for but didn't quite know what. Instead, becoming a psychologist offered me a shell, a fortress from which to stand outside the world, watching analytically. But then Tara, and love broke through. Has psychology served its purpose? Why continue? And really, will that take me a year to think through? Surely I already know the answer?

This leads me to remind myself that I like to think about my work as a calling, a vocation, to achieving something worthwhile through what I do, rather than about where it gets me. I can never quite understand those who see work as a career, driven by ambition to achieve by getting places, climbing ladders. There is wisdom in the saying 'climbing the proverbial greasy pole'. Yes, I like that description. It puts it into perspective by acting as a mild pejorative. I muse on the thought that 'the subconscious is always listening' and I know how such pejorative phrases can get past any critical function of one's mind, and be taken on board, though quite subconsciously.

A major transition, eh? I know, though, only all too well how I can fool myself. Somehow there is still a quiet voice challenging me deep down. I need some external accountability. But why? What else is there for me to do here on this island? What is this about doing something useful? Is it just my protestant work ethic? Surely a year thinking is useful? Waiting on God, I tell myself.

So, maybe just ask the Creator? Sometimes it is hard to shake off the old understandings and habits of prayer from childhood. Prayer then was simply a shopping list. I remember having a long list as a seven-year-old. I wanted my relatives all to live to a thousand. I would go through them one by one. Finally, when the list got too long and I wanted to get back to reading, in a brief prayer I would simply point God to my long list, and say 'and I pray that NOW, Amen.' Needless to say, many of my older relatives have now died well before reaching their centenary! I figure that even as an adult, my understanding of anything divine is probably now no less naïve or childlike. Prayer is a mystery. Maybe Tara is right: "You don't have to understand everything. Just do it!"

But how do I not just get back to making my decision-making part of it a mechanical intercessory list, just asking what to do? How can prayer help me connect with the Creator to weave the intended meaning and purpose into my life He has created me for, yet leave me free with choice? For me, if He is not there, my life makes no sense: I am just an animal. I remember now, a commentary by Eugene Peterson on Psalm 3, about David fleeing from Absalom his son. Peterson commented that everyone's life is full of good and troubling incidents that weave into a story and that this psalm reflects a prayer at a crucial point in a story. Yes, I remind myself, that's it, prayerful living, mindful of God in every action. I recall how Peterson goes on to suggest that there are no storyless prayers, for story is to prayer what body is to soul. Life without prayer is lifeless, akin to a corpse. Intercessory prayer that is not part of story is also lifeless, like a laundry list. Makes sense. I am writing my story.

There is a season for everything: Ecclesiastics comes to mind, and I know this is a season for me to reflect. But how long that will last starts a ferment in my mind again. A whole year?

This is the season, for one short year, for a retreat. Stick to the plan. Just do it.

Still, there is an unsettled feeling. What is that all about?

24

Interruption

Tara

I've had some new insights into where my next adventure would take me, so have spent most of the morning on my laptop, Iain also sitting out on the deck. He enjoyed reflecting on our differences, and occasionally had tentatively interrupted my work, sharing his latest thoughts - they are always stimulating, but often time consuming. He clearly has relayed his understanding that differences are not just a matter of gender, nor self-discipline, but most obviously relates to differently wired brains. Despite his understanding, it still perplexes him as he asks aloud: "how can one know so much, and yet have the mind going in potentially quite different directions, and all at the same time?" I stop to check the time: no wonder I need a break - already past midday! I also now notice the sun has become less obvious – clouds are gathering, so I wonder how long it will be before the pleasant working outside will cause us to go inside, to escape the drenching rain predicted. Well, that should be a nice change at least.

Suddenly we hear a noise behind us and turn around to see a man. Ah, our neighbour, Jove! Surprised to see he has a tray in his hand, with three plates of lasagne, and three beers.

"Cooked a batch of lasagne. Forgot the freezer was full. Then I saw you. Nothing worse than waste. Hate waste. Don't tell me you are some of them vegans. You don't look pale enough. Mainland ideas, ruining the island. Used to be quiet, plain and simple here."

Without waiting for an answer or invitation, he puts down the tray and seats himself down between us, and with no further words exchanged, distributes the plates, beer, splades, and very neatly folded dark blue cloth serviettes. I smile at the details, how thoughtful this interesting man, can I say this quirky guy is? I'm sort of impressed too!

While Iain is standing still, wondering what on earth to say, weighing up any supposed potential consequences if he should encourage or even dismiss such an intrusion, I speak up, responding in the same cryptic way Jove has spoken to us.

"Perfect timing. Looks good. 'Thank God for Jove and for this big-hearted gift of food.'"

"And the beer?" asked Jove.

"The beer is included in the food" answers Iain grinning, a little pleased he has found himself answering so quickly. Jove gives him a sideways glance as he picks up his splade and starts eating.

We both look at this wonderful and generous offering. Next to the neatly placed lasagne is an artistically arranged salad, topped with a couple of nasturtium flowers, cashews, raisons, and an elegantly placed dab of mayonnaise. Just as Iain looks over to my plate and notes salad on Jove's plate too, Jove turns to him.

"No need to eat the salad. I can always compost that part of the meal."

Then, turning to me, he states:

"All home grown, the salad, even in this sandy soil. Lots of composting. Wife taught me. I collect coffee grounds from the local cafes. Magic stuff. Makes me plants grow. The wife, she loved plants. She died. She loved salads, and I didn't, not 'til after she died. Wish I could tell her now. Plants remind me of her, keep me going. There, you know all about me now. Nothing else to know."

He looks away from me and out to sea, and there is an awkward kind of silence. I noted the distress that registered on Jove's face when he mentioned his wife, but "need to be cautious" floats through my mind: this man is complex so we should respect his privacy, until he indicates he feels safe enough to speak openly with us. One day, hey! I'm grateful when Iain breaks the poignant silence with his softly voiced but broad Scottish accent:

"Well man, this is awfully neighbourly of you, kind and thoughtful, and just with perfect timing." Jove seems not to have heard the intrusion, and then looks back to me as I ask:

"So you like plants?" Without looking down, Jove picks up his beer, slowly taking a couple of sips before answering.

"You could say that."

"Great! A gardener then! Hope I can get some clues for our non-existent garden!"

The meal is enjoyed by us all, in a quiet companionable way sort of way. As we finish, suddenly the heavens open and we experience a tropical storm. Jove quickly grabs his dishes, as we thank him again, watching as he without fuss disappears next door. Time to readjust our thinking to working inside. Great meal though! Iain says he wants to read, while also watching the storm. Maybe I should take a break too - write to Em?

25

Letter to Em

Tara

Dear Em,

I promised to write and let you know how we have transitioned to the Island. I look back at all the times you have been there for me at tipping points in the past, and I am now so appreciative of our friendship since Iain and I got together. A careful and fully informed transition from the original professional relationship. And we did it, responsibly!

I am always so grateful that you fill a role I often missed, having lost my mother so young. So I do miss being able to catch up in person with you, Em, but I find writing stuff is also good for sorting some things out in my head too. So I hope that my long emails won't be too onerous for you!

What are you up to in your garden? I guess all the wonderful native plants are serially blooming, and your brilliant roses still flowering. I just love the view from your patio, over the pond, the native LillyPilly hedges, and even looking up through to Kings Park and the Botanic Gardens. Always loved cycling through that whole area – the trees are spectacular! And so close to everything in beautiful Perth – and Fremantle too. So glad the fires have not been too worrisome for you this past year – terrible for a lot of Australia! Hope WA continues to remain fairly safe, not feeling too isolated in terms of COVID, and hopefully without too many restrictions in Perth. Wonderful to remember how you and Jack are always so welcoming of visitors – be a while before that will happen here I guess! But shouldn't speak too soon - an interesting neighbour spontaneously brought us a cooked lunch, which was a really nice welcoming gesture!

We do hope you can visit sometime, Em: this is such a beautiful bit of paradise! Been here now for over a month, and we are already slipping into a healthy routine. We feel like we are on a beautiful retreat, though I personally know I must get more earnestly into my project here. Quite enjoying our little cottage by the sea, at the mouth of a local river – haven't spotted its name yet!

You know how Iain can turn into a couch potato, thinking, talking, reading and writing, and how I am always prompting him to get active each day. Well, I am glad to say he is enjoying being in a new place, so it's a great opportunity for rousing him with a potential new routine - inspiration is what he needs, hey! Most mornings now we both love walking, or me swimming/running along the beach before breakfast - there's nothing so magnificent as watching the sun rise, is there! The wide stretch of the skies beyond the waters is just amazing, Em – and the clouds like today will create an even more wonderful sunset! Very different in the tropics – never really cold, regardless. Sometimes though, I worry to think that much of this beauty is under threat from sea rising due to climate change. Why can't people see the truth right in front of them? I think I know your answer, Em!

It's certainly been an interesting few weeks. I must share a few things that have created conflicting emotions about this place. It *is* a remarkably beautiful tropical paradise, and we have settled into the loveliest though basic of seaside cottages. So, though everyone tells us it is such a peaceful and safe island, surprised that we had dealings with the police right from the start! First there was an intruder in our hotel room, and then second, it seems I've lost my encrypted flash drive, the one that had a lot of research documents I had been given "in commercial confidence." Bizarre, really! Glad I left a copy with you - could you send it to me soon, please? Thanks...The police here seem to be really interested in it. No idea why! You know the statement, never rains but it pours! So, just as we were coming along the beach one morning last week, after a great run, we saw a police car pull up, and my first thought was that they were probably coming to ask about the flash drive again.

Anyhow, out steps the friendly sergeant Sabina we had met at the hotel break-in. She looked very serious, and, with her, an important looking uniformed female officer. We were introduced to her just as the Superintendent of Police on the island! They asked if they could come in and talk, privately. It made me recall scenes of police knocking at someone's door, to tell them a family member had been killed in an accident or something equally grim. Momentarily fear gripped my heart. I had finally allowed myself to grow close to Iain: what if tragedy like that happened here? So, I wanted to get a quick answer from them as to whether they were the bearers of bad news. But to cut a long story short, it wasn't bad news! - in fact, a funny twist: tell you soon!

You know, Em, how Iain was so looking forward to being away from any temptation to work professionally, taking a year off for much needed time out, in reflection, away from stressors that tempt Iain to self-medicate with a little more wine than Paul recommends for one's stomach's sake! Well, he tells me he had been feeling some unease about the year being a little self-indulgent that he put down to his protestant work ethic, and thinking he had dealt with it a few days ago, the police visit has thrown him back to a real quandary. This is where I will value your thoughts, so I can help him sort out a way to make an important decision.

It seems that the police had done their homework on us. The observant sergeant had noted my bible next to the computer when they attended because of the break-in at the hotel. Then they'd done a complete check on us, including using our fingerprints, on the pretext of a package of the drugs our neighbour Jove had found at the cottage here some days later! They gave us a clean bill, but they had looked Iain up and found out he was a psychologist, with special interests around organisational structures on the one hand, and personality on the other. They took the latter to mean he would be interested in profiling! They had done such a thorough going search - also noted that he'd had some notes from teaching counselling at the Perth College of Divinity. No anonymity even here, Em!

Initially some general chatting had focused on how we were finding the island, during which I had opportunity to inform them about our reason for our time at KP, principally for my own coffee research. The police people then moved on to Iain, asking what he thought about various religions. He told them of my Hindu and bi-cultural backgrounds, which he mentioned naturally made him very appreciative of both cultural and religious differences. Conversation became quite informal and relaxed then, but typically, I was getting impatient and asked the real reason for their visit. That's when finally, the chief superintendent said she hoped I didn't mind, but they were really sounding Iain out before wanting to encourage him to respond positively to an upcoming job offer! They had really come to ask Iain to think about filling a vacant position of Police Chaplain! Can you believe that?

It seems the island has been unable to fill that position for some time; needed for one to two days a week, and also at times, they've wanted a consulting police psychologist on a need's basis, to work with them collegially on crime. They pointed out that the chaplain role is an initiative to be funded by the local churches. You can imagine: we both sat in stunned silence.

To be honest, it has felt somewhat as an intrusion. Iain came here not wanting to be known as a psychologist! He expected to spoil himself, with the ultimate sort-out through a year off. He'd promised himself this would enable him to become more resilient, less overwhelmed by client issues! Of course I understood and had encouraged him, knowing that as an introvert, he saw this retreat year as a necessity, not an indulgence after years of being totally available to others.

You know how conscientious he is, Em, so he feels quite conflicted. He worries about what will happen with his retreat year. He agonises over everything and often says "I just wish God would tell me! Then I wouldn't have to struggle with all the conflicting issues". He also feels there is just a deafening silence, and that's something I can't fix for him either!

Em, he really should let them know his decision by the end of the next week or so, and well, I would so appreciate your thoughts and prayers. In fact, I know he'd love you just to tell us what you think he should do, but I know from experience that you are so wise and sensible, and would simply throw the decision back to him ;-)

We both really look forward to hearing from you soon. Keep well and safe!

Love you, and say hi to Jack from us both,

Tara

26

Guidance and Silence

Iain

I thought I had dealt with my protestant work ethic challenging my planned year of reading and reflection. I was just getting to be happy with my planned structure, making sure it didn't just become an undisciplined meander. I had set some goals and targets. I had carefully arranged a sequence of books to read around core issues. Sure, there was still a little nagging thought that a year is a long time. But hey, in convincing myself I decided this was like doing a course, and who knows, maybe it could morph into something like writing?

But three days ago, just as I was finally settled, the unsolicited police intrusion. I remind myself yet again that I had put your hand to the plough, and now was not a time to go through another reconsideration yet again! There is an internal argument that one should never be so rigid as to not be open to grasp an opportunity. Be adaptable and responsive? But this is to be my sabbatical! Yes, that's it. A sabbatical. Like a Sunday, its justified. There will always be a need here or there. I need to stay firm, stick with my plan, and make the decision. I need to be resolute.

OK, I will be saying 'no' to the request. It is settled. Now an enjoyable morning reading awaits.

I start to read. But when I get to the end of a page I find I have taken nothing in. The intrusion has left me conflicted, and I have got to say, disturbed. A part of me is bringing up worthwhile possibilities. I cannot stop the churning. A thought comes in: is this some sort of divine nudge, and if so, how would it be confirmed? Or is it simply an intrusion and a distraction by the enemy to effectively derail the efficacy of my retreat? Would it be selfish or wise to refuse? Why hadn't my Creator let me know before I started all the planning? How do I get this conflict out of my head? I put the book down in frustration.

Ugh, and then Tara has frustratingly not offered any nudge one way or another. She just confirms that she saw it as absolutely the right time for me to retreat, read and reflect, and if I thought it should take one hundred percent of my time for twelve months, then fine. But she has gone on to suggest in a not too subtle way, that maybe here was an opportunity to explore things in some complementary way through doing. Easy for her to suggest, I'd thought: she is so much into doing. 'Do first and think after' she would joke, and I would answer 'Think first, contemplate it having been done, and move on to the next thinking!'

I give in and to get rid of this distraction once and for all, I am back to pondering about accepting the current work offer. Maybe I need to consider it as strictly only part time. Ah, maybe that's it? But I know how time and emotionally consuming my work has been in the past. Would part-time mean that my time for reflection would be hijacked by work-think demands?

OK, time to do a decision sheet. I pick up my iPad and turn to the notes app. Pros and cons I write under headings of the three alternatives: one, the other or a combination. Nothing very much comes to convince me. Well, I think, how about SWOT headings under each alternative?

Just lots of points appear, but nothing sufficient to convince me of the option I want to see come out on top.

Tara said she has written about it to Em. Maybe I should just wait on her reply and treat her advice as drawing a straw! I ponder: how can I know if the two who had come with the invitation were indeed some sorts of messenger sent to challenge me, or on the other hand to distract me?

Yes, I decide, it seems there is nothing for it but to wait on what Em answers to Tara's email. I am tired of thinking, and over thinking this. Accountability, I tell myself. A part of me is quite happy with this, remembering how enthusiastic she was on hearing what I was planning. I kind of expect she will be 'on my side' telling me what I want to hear! I quickly convince myself that Em is always dependable, wise, and very encouraging, especially when thinking about anything challenging or contentious. Yes, what she advises will be the go.

27

Em's Reply

Em

Hi TARA!!!!,

Great to hear from you, and really, quite soon after you arrived! Thanks for filling me in.

I can't wait to plan a trip out to your beautiful island. I neglect the computer as much as possible these days – too many alternatives that keep me happily occupied, with spring in the air, tending the garden. The natural world our Creator has given us has so much beauty in it, doesn't it - I love joining in with this creative potential – sometimes alone, as well as with others when restrictions allow.

Am really happy with long emails – so much more satisfying than scrappy bits that require frequent clarification because too brief! So any time, Tara – though sometimes it may take a few days before I answer. ☹

But your email comes as a complete surprise! Not only about the unexpected police matters, but more particularly, about the job request!

That being so urgent, needing to find an answer for Iain, and you both, really, well, it prompts me to ask several questions:

Should he think about the old question of whether this is another demand that highlights the tyranny of the urgent, and for whom?

OR rather, as I would suggest, is this an important request, but one he shouldn't feel bullied into making, for a quick decision for others?

Might be useful to think about how long the need has been on the island for someone to fill the job...i.e. this gives him some necessary breathing space while considering the implications:

- this could also create a practice precedent the employer should allow for Iain, to be maintained should he take on such a job. Afterall,
- he will always be someone who needs time and space to reflect, so why would he let them think a hurried decision should be expected now, right from the get-go?!!

One of the things I'm sure he would be advising others is to make a "for and against list" when trying to come to a decision. Prayerful consideration also enables us to more confidently trust our discernment of which list will determine our decision: More of the "yes do" list needs to far outweigh the "don't do" list if he believes the job is his. Of course, some of these will include quite rational matters, but don't forget, as a compassionate person, Iain as a strongly feeling guy needs to acknowledge and consider the more emotional aspects of his life. Encourage him to be honest, Tara, and unapologetic. Knowing himself so well, such individual ways of seeing and perceiving are quite clearly God-given gifts that deserve proper attention. He also has had experiences that will undoubtedly have impacted his capacity to engage in demanding tasks, so he shouldn't ever feel he should just forget these – they have become part of the unique man he is. Interesting, isn't it, Tara, that such experiences are the very things which for both of you have contributed to making you the people who were attracted to each other!

By the way, his list should also include how his decision may personally impact on *you*, Tara, and of course, what you together may be planning, like for the future – family? ☺ Not heard anything, and don't need to, but life's demands can very quickly take control, unless we take responsibility for making choices too.

I also wonder, if *after* an agreed time to reflect and *before* answering re the job, whether it may be important to consider a part-time option? At least as he eases into the job. Or maybe, if taken on full-time, Iain should feel up to designating what an allotted paid time should be given for job reflection, and should include timeout for further training etc if needed.

It seems the offer has not included much about the job description, has it, so maybe *he* has a great opportunity here for spelling this out. Realistically he needs to assess what areas he would be really interested in taking on, thus potentially be ruling out others.

Quite exciting possibilities for Iain, Tara, that I'm sure he would do a great job, of anything asked of him. Just remember however that a loving God doesn't have a blueprint for what we should do. He wonderfully gives His children the joy of making our desires known, so clarification of what these really *are,* before asking for His confirmation of the way ahead. He will shut the door if what Iain simply thinks is *an* option but one that He knows will not be the best. Sometimes the silence we feel is simply there for us to take time to grasp the what ifs, the hows, and to fully assess if this is what we really want to do. Look up Psalm 37:3 – 5, verses that may encourage you both, as they often have me!

I look forward to hearing what together you have decided is the right choice!!

❤ to you both.

Em

28

Contentment

Tara

I remind myself: unbelievable as I seems, it is almost twenty years since my disastrous arranged marriage at seventeen. Though I never again sought comfort from the sea's embrace, and though some scars remain, it is now its memories of fun in play, fantasies, and affection for the sea that I love to recall, and I do so, so often. Even in the most severe storm, the sea feels somewhat like a friend, wild and free. In surfing, I feel as though we form a team, dancing in time, or wrestling to surprise each other. I love the spontaneity, the exhilaration of the power with which I hurtle forward, and how the arms of a wave can come crashing in on top of me, only for me then to ride it out. I laugh back at the roar of the water. I am free!

It's high tide, so I had wondered down to the beach with Iain, then drew back to watch small but strong rivulets of water rushing across rocks that then run out on the sand, creating a lacey edge that disappears into the sand, watching just as I had done as a child. The sea is relentless: whether it be a small eddying trickle here or a big surfing wave there. It mesmerizes me into what Iain has called a form of mindfulness. It's like looking into the flames of a fire. It spawns reflection, and somehow not just in the evening, even more so for me in the morning. The sun's early rays are lighting the clouds and shooting through the gaps. I sense the cool of a tropical morning, the breeze ever so softly caressing my face, so gently tossing my hair aside, and playfully rippling through the loose cool cotton of my sarong. Even the breeze feels like a friend.

In the silence together, Iain too looks content in this opportunity to reflect together. We stand there, quietly and gently embracing, looking out to sea, neither of us wanting to break the moment.

After a while Iain finally breaks the silence, beautifully using a few descriptive words with the soft Scottish accent I so love. While I know that I am just happy to stand there, soaking it all in while feeling close to him, I am aware that for Iain, it's the words themselves that are important, and these so sensitively are again an important facilitator.

"Relating. Relationships. Tara, how could I have ever put that aside, never to have known that I really needed it? I guess you never know what you have been missing until you experience something. Like God." He falls silent again. I wonder about his "Like God."

Finally, it's time to go. The day calls us forward – things we have separately planned to do. As we walk, he reiterates what he has said before. He had never expected to be happy for long, always expecting any such moments to be dashed. Everywhere he looked, there seemed to be an unquestioning and relentless pursuit of happiness. And yet that happiness seemed so fragile and transient for the most part. Was it happiness he is feeling this morning, or is the contentment something else? It seems so difficult for him to differentiate feelings sufficiently to understand how they are different, if at all, and then to understand how they work. And he's the psychologist! He often asks himself, how is it possible that, even when stressed or seemingly unhappy, there is now an underlying contentment, maybe even what could be called peace?

29

Who are They?

Iain

It felt only like yesterday that, after a late walk into the dying light of day, Tara and I had come home to a moonlit veranda, fearful of what the lights in the distance we'd caught sight of in our cottage could mean, only to find two large candles and a tureen of delicious steaming food. Real love from someone who hides. When love swallows up fear, the impact is unforgettable. And, this time, some blood-red serviettes with pure white dinner rolls sitting on top. Will Jove ever reveal who he really is?

The evening had passed as has the relaxation that came with dinner in the moon and candlelight. Right now, today however, I am again feeling a little resentful that my planned reading and reflections are potentially going to be hijacked. Of course, Em's reply to Tara didn't tell me what to decide. She only confirmed the process I already knew, far too wise to fall into a trap of telling someone else what to do.

So, I am still not sure of what I should be doing. Its back to me. Well, better check out the appointment given me to meet with the ministers. They might make it clear that this is not the job for me!

So, I am on my way. I don't know what to expect. The ministers' association is meeting in a room off a church hall. I knock. The door flies open, and a stocky man puts out his hand to shake mine. I guess he is in his late sixties, maybe even early seventies.

"You must be Iain then, unless you are someone coming to get something from our food store…. No, you don't look hungry, and you look too well dressed! You must be Iain, and if you are, then do come in, come in." The man is still shaking my hand as he now starts energetically pulling me into the room. Without waiting for an answer, he goes on: "Right on time, right on time, that's good, that's good. Here is a seat, take a seat, any seat is just fine."

I take in the scene. The room presents as a storeroom with boxes, chairs and folded trestle tables piled up around all walls and in front of the window. Two fawn plastic topped trestle tables have been pushed together to form a square in the only clear space. Around them, seven chairs. Five serious looking faces have now all turned towards me. I have been distracted taking it all in and need to collect myself: what was it that he just said again?

Ah yes, 'any seat is just fine.' Before I can work out which of the two might be his, the stocky man takes his seat leaving me the only chair remaining.

"Ah, Iain, thank you for coming."

It then crosses my mind that it might be amusing to say I was looking for the food store. As I look around, the clutter was matched by the differences in the people around the table. I am surprised to see the police sergeant, Sabina, sitting in the middle. Before I can say 'thank you' or even 'hello,' a slender lady with short grey hair and wearing a clerical collar under a black short-sleeved cotton shirt at the far side of the table starts speaking.

"Welcome, Iain - we know who you are. Thank you for considering taking on the police chaplaincy. We are quite encouraged to hope we may finally have someone to fill the gap. Pastor Sabina has been quite effusive about you and says she has done due diligence on you."

I think to myself: I hope they know I am only considering.

"We will start off each introducing ourselves - and as we do, we will let you know what each of is about, so you can think as to if and how you will fit in well with us. Are you comfortable with that?"

I nod that I understand and pause to think, but before I can say anything, the slim lady continues.

"Good, well, since you have no questions, let me start. I am Judy, and for me and my lot the central task of the church is to help people realise the presence of God in every part of everyday life."

Without pause, the person next to Judy speaks, a quiet soft voice.

"I am Carmelite Sister Mary-Martha, standing in for Father Pat. My passion is for prayer. Prayer that encompasses community and service, to change the world for God."

I recognise the next speaker:

"Yacob van der Leer … we know each other - ah, yes, well, the Bible, it is de rule book for life, if we haf correct exegesis. Preach de Word, and I don't know why we need anything more. Just de gospel. Call people to repent and believe."

I nod, then turn to look across from Judy. There I see the big man who seems to look straight up the table, as if past me:

"Bob, Reverend Bob Wesley." Turning to the others he continues: "The sermon on the mount is it all in a nutshell for me, the battle of our lives as Christians is to live by it. We are called to holiness."

The next person speaks:

"And as you know, I am Sabina; and in the fellowship where I am one of the leaders, we are convinced that we are called to use all our spiritual gifts, and in the power of the Holy Spirit."

I smile in acknowledgement, as without allowing a pause, the stocky man who'd welcomed me at the door, now sitting on my left starts to speak.

"And I'm Jim, unfortunately not Jim Beam, but Jim Booth!" I smile on understanding his implied meaning...

"and for me and my lot, well, you know, we, well, we see our job as being compassionate, acting as the hands and feet of Christ. Not too keen, not at all, on telling people they are all horrible broken sinners."

He glances ever so briefly over to Jacob van der Leer and then across to Bob Wesley, with a grin that says he is enjoying an opportunity to take a poke.

"I think people all know they are no angels, you know, of the good kind. Don't need to keep telling them. Just makes them, you know, people, normal people that is, just feel, well, feel worse than even they should. They, well, just want to hide. Its doing, not preaching they need. Doing means, how can I say it, showing acceptance, you know, of, of people themselves first. They need that. Otherwise, they can't accept others. When we accept them, well, they start accepting themselves, magical, and then, maybe, just maybe mind, they can start to accept God loves them, even a little bit".

With a big sigh, shaking his head, he goes on now murmuring to himself:

"Jimmy me-boy, stop preaching. It's about doing!"

30

Expectations

Iain

I now sense all eyes on me, with an unspoken invitation that it is my turn. I have been pondering an appropriate way to match their by-lines. I'm still not quite sure who is checking out who: am I here to interview them, after all they have invited me, or is it for them to interview me? No-one has asked for a CV and certainly I have not put in any application. I'm not sure I even want the job. This leaves me feeling completely free and unconcerned about any outcome. I need to convince no-one of anything. So, my sense is to simply reciprocate in the same way, assuming a peer-to-peer relationship.

"Yes, well, let me confirm I am Iain, simply accompanying my wife Tara, who is a sensory scientist, currently researching coffee. Having been intent on taking a year off from professional practice as a psychologist, I was not intending to let anyone on the island know what my training has been, but circumstances, well, beyond my control seem to have thwarted that! So here I am, through no design of my own, questioning if God is pushing me. I now am also wondering about your expectations of a psychologist as a chaplain."

There is quite a long silence.

"I guess we all have different expectations" the offer first up is from Sabina.

"And some of us aren't sure as to whether you have enough Bible knowledge to qualify" comes from van der Leer.

"But he is a psychologist - and surely that's enough" suggests Jim.

"If you all have different *goals* for a chaplain, maybe I need to talk to each of you individually. But for now, just for now, what do you see a chaplain typically doing day-to-day?"

"Counselling, talking with people on the job. Being there alongside them" suggests Sabina.

"Talking through issues as people face stresses, being there. Talking about family life" is Jim's response.

"Sharing the Gospel," van der Leer's comment is loud and clear.

"Praying for them, and maybe with them," suggests Mary-Martha.

"Helping them to be honest, truthful, living better lives, staying out of trouble," quietly spoken comment from Bob.

"I would see you providing therapy for individuals." It is Judy.

I make a short attempt to sum up their mixed expectations:

"You all seem to see one-on-one counselling type sessions. Would you envisage any educative role? Maybe even think of that in terms of a teacher teaching, or a coach coaching. And, where there is need, do you see that as possible and within groups?"

"So, does that mean you teach from the Bible as the way to live, then?" asks Jacob.

"You think this position should be an evangelistic one, Jacob?" I asked.

"Yes, most certainly" comes Jacob's immediate reply, to which Bob breaks in:

"Don't put that on the poor fellow, Jacob: the walk of faith isn't just about evangelising – it's about living, and serving everyday people's needs…" and then Judy interrupts:

"OK, you two, not a time to argue. We need to know more about how Iain sees himself working as a psychologist employed in some form of Christian ministry if he is to take up the position."

"Thanks, Judy. Yes, as yet I have not thought through everything about doing this job. I am not even sure what it means to be a chaplain as a psychologist. Perhaps it is more about my style. In a non-clinical role, I would be listening and sharing; both talking and walking *with* people. Like a fellow journey person, but one who can share my understanding as a psychologist, to enable them to learn, a bit like relating to people as I did back at my last church in Perth. I see my role as about empowering, so people can have confidence in having some sort of better control."

There is a brief pause as I collect my thoughts, and I surprise myself by what I say next:

"What attracts me to possibly taking on this position is that I, and hopefully you also see this as offering support to the whole person. It is you, the church, offering a glass of water in His Name through making someone like me available."

I pause to let people take in what I have been saying, but almost immediately Jacob comes in again.

"Would you share the gospel?"

Jim jumps in grinning:

"That can be in word and in action; it's not all about what you say you know, Jacob."

"So would you pray with people?" asks Mary-Martha.

"Of course he would, if they asked for it!" That from Judy, but Mary-Martha continues:

"Well, I think it is always good to tell people you are praying for them, even if they don't ask. Even the most determined atheists always seem to appreciate that when they are in a pickle."

As I listen, I am reminded of the many times when my parents would talk about me as a young child, seemingly oblivious to my presence. As their discussion goes on, I allow my thinking to take off in its own direction. I find myself considering the various influences on the person formation of such differing people I'm observing here, all with differing understandings, divergent theological emphasise, yet all desiring to know God. Such a disparate lot, I am thinking, and probably thrown together here for lack of more similar-minded colleagues that would be available in a bigger city on the mainland. And yet it strikes me, there is a wonderful unspoken commonality among them, not just necessity surely, that brings a sense of togetherness. It brings to mind the phrase 'all one in Christ.'

My attention returns fully to the group. They continue fully engaged in a lively discussion, still seemingly oblivious to my presence. The thought crosses my mind that if I simply slipped out of the room, no-one would even notice.

I cough, and it works: I get their attention. I briefly thank them, saying it's been good to meet them all.

"So, where do we go from here?" asks Jim.

"I am not entirely clear that this is my vocation at this point in time."

Phew! Good reminder to make, for myself as much as them. A way forward?

"I think I need to write a brief job description that may clarify things for me, but also for you all. And because I do need to feel confident about making the right decision, please give me at least a week or two, so that prayerful consideration can also be made by us all. How about we meet again in a fortnight? In the meantime, I will send you my understanding of the job I think you may want me to be taking on, and one that I would be happy to take on."

31

Shopping in Paradise

Tara

Well, this morning I'm giving myself a chance to explore the world of people and shops here. Just to know a bit more about what is available, and what I might need to expect may only be procured online. I should check out the postal services here too – time delays may be big, with only two or three flights per week to this side of the island.

We had a brief rain shower overnight, which has freshened up the already lush green all around. The sun is warm, and it's reasonably humid, so I hope to find a couple of new cotton shifts or tops at least, to fit in with our permanently tropical new environment! So good to shop without Iain – he's always hopeless in knowing what looks best on me, so his opinions often make me doubt my own conclusions. He's going off to the Minister's Association meeting – hope it helps him decide about taking the job or not. To me, it could be a great thing, but I'm happy either way – so long as he finds other activities that will keep him out of my way when I'm working!

I wander down the main street, taking in the general atmosphere of bright, clean, and almost holiday air, with an unhurried number of people quietly doing their shopping. There are numbers of public open areas, with bush tables and seats inviting anyone to stay awhile and enjoy! They are planted out with typical tropical palms, including plants such as the stately eye-catching heliconias, and the tall white-flowering tree strelitzias being a few that I recognise, yes and even some frangipanis – they must flower all year round here! What colour, what beauty! And the aromas are wonderful, each having their own distinctive attractions! It all slows me down; time to appreciate this gorgeous world that, for who knows how long, will be home for us, not simply an all too quickly passing vacation!

Between the frequent parks, there are quite a number of small shops, all very inviting, and most with happy music flowing out on to the street. I'm told there is only one large shopping centre here, which along with various restaurants also houses both a Woolies supermarket and several retail clothing shops, a chemist, hardware, and some of the medical suites. I choose to leave that option for another day, just to enjoy the intimacy and fun of exploring the more interesting local shops. Many of these suggest they were built after the war, with a strong influence of Dutch single-fronted, two story connected shop fronts. One shop in particular draws me in – "Feminine outfits for everyone!" I'm hopeful there'll be something here I like and not too pricey. The lady running the shop bounces up to me. She is obviously a colourful character, wearing a bright loose-fitting sleeveless top over incredibly short shorts.

"Hello, I'm Bella – you must be new here! How long is your holiday? Are you on your own, or have you left him home, snoring off last night's big night, hey?!!" Well, such a full-on but genuinely friendly, open-faced person who clearly loves chatting. Reminds me of what we might experience at some hairdressers back in Perth, or even as I remember of

Melbourne! No boundaries, yet here I can't really say it feels inappropriate. I warm to her approach, but cautiously respond:

"Hi Bella, nice to meet you! I'm Tara – been here a few weeks now, but not really on holiday. I have a research job which will keep us here for some time, maybe even a year or so". I think that might be sufficient, expecting she will now ask me what I am looking for. But no, on she goes: " Oh, right, so what is your work? And you say us – is that with your partner? What does he or she do?"

I decide to give a brief reply that is not rude but gives a message that I'm here to find out what shopping is like on the island. Tricky! How much gossip goes on in this lovely environment? I know it's sometimes difficult to do, but I think creating our own boundary is so important, even when we can accept others often don't!

"Well, my husband and I have been asked to look into a number of work options. But today, while he's otherwise occupied, I'm hoping you might show me some tops suitable for coping with the increasing humidity. It seems to be getting a little more intense since we arrived." I smile at her, showing no hard feelings.

"Oh sorry! I get carried away when anyone I don't know comes in! I just love meeting new people! This side of Rustenberg has very few holiday makers. The tourists mostly head to the other side! So, what can I entice you to buy? Shorts? Tops? Or maybe even something for eveningwear?" I am relieved – she is quick on the uptake, so I invite her to show me something of all of her suggestions for day wear, in my size, and only as long as there aren't other customers to serve. I am pleased that she is off on a mission, which leaves me some time to just float around, checking out what is available. A quiet morning for her, and Bella happily focuses on tempting me to try before I buy. After selecting three items, which she agrees really suit me, and while folding them and taking my money, I feel that asking her some questions is now appropriate. She answers these without hesitation. This includes volunteering her own background, her own love of the island, and her having wanted to go away to study fashion designing, but her family couldn't afford that. She then spontaneously adds that she loves reading, and tells me about the library resources, and how she belongs to a book club.

"We mostly read light books, but you'd be welcome to come, Tara – good way to meet a few locals!" Ready now to push on, I say "I'll think about that, and thanks again, Bella." I turn towards the door through which I notice a girl starting to enter, but then she suddenly stops as she spies me! Immediately she is out the door and off down the street. Her hair reminds me of someone….yes, that straight hair which had stuck out from a hoodie, with a notable purple streak – all clearly visible now without the hood. And that scent again. Do I ask who she is? How much should I give away? I send a quick SMS above, seeking wisdom, as I pause before turning back to Bella.

"I think I've seen that girl before somewhere, Bella – do you know her?"

"Oh yes, that's Kendra. She often pops in, just to chat. A bit lost, I think, but has a good heart" Bella opines. I feel it ok to ask further about the mystery girl – would the theft and mystery of my flash drive perhaps find an answer here?

"So this Kendra - is she naturally afraid of strangers, seeing me here? Or do you think she might also have recognised me, perhaps from where I'd seen her?... Just curious about people too, Bella!" I smile, gently offering her a connection between us that relates to our mutual love of interacting with people.

"Well, she's not normally afraid of people, no. So, yes, now I think about it, it was funny how she took off just now! Where do you think you saw her, Tara?" Again, I need to be careful, so I answer vaguely.

"Oh, I think it was at the hotel we stayed in when we first arrived. Does she work at the Ibis?"

"No, I'm pretty sure not – in fact I don't think she even has a job at the moment! She is good friends with Kyle, a nice young guy who also seems a bit lost, the last couple of years. I've heard they both may be playing with drugs…a few young ones doing them more recently, more's the pity. Especially a problem round the other side of Rustenberg – we hear about bigger drug issues there! But I wonder why she reacted to seeing you?"

"Who knows, Bella – perhaps drugs are effecting her confidence with strangers!" I offer a simple explanation that might add to a conversation continuance.

The dialogue does continue, as Bella shares something else that again piques my interest:

"It is funny, and I don't know whether this is relevant to anything, but Kendra often raps on about wishing she could find the place on the mountain where the mythical supreme coffee grew. She seems to dream about finding it, as if this would be the magical solution to her current need for money! I myself know what it's like to dream, but not about this sort of drug-inspired nonsense." We both laugh, sharing an apparent common attitude that increases my feeling comfortable with this, mm, maybe thirty-year-old? She doesn't know how much she has contributed to my increased sense that we are going to feel accepted here. I turn to go.

"Anyway, thanks again, Bella – loved meeting you and thanks for helping me choose. We've similar skin colour, which probably helps, hey!"

"Yes, you must perhaps be Anglo-Indian too?" "Yes" I interject before she continues: "No problems with that here; we're all pretty much of mixed or diverse origins, so you'll fit in well! See you soon, I hope!"

I continue my wander along the longish street scape, my shopping carried in a brightly coloured locally branded bag, "Bought in Paradise." Stopping for a bite of lunch and a locally grown and freshly ground coffee, I have time to reflect on 'Kendra' – clearly identified to me by the purple streak Iain had spotted as 'he now she' rushed past. Oh, and

I now remember he'd mentioned the opium scent – maybe that's what I'd smelt as she came into the shop. But probably the real stuff, I suspect, not the perfume! I wonder whether this latest info will ever be useful. Probably not – but not to worry: que sera, sera!

I turn my thoughts to my research planning, as I head home for an afternoon back on the deck. The thoughts about Kendra are quickly filed into a different compartment of my mind – "later with Iain". How good that we are so close to the township, and no high traffic!

32

Divine Puppeteer

Tara

I look up from my laptop, drawing my windblown hair away from my face, just to see Iain coming out on to the deck, moving quietly so as not to invade my workplace. He knows I like to keep to my planned schedule, but he also knows I will feel conflicted: dying to hear how the meeting with the ministers had gone. I wonder if it had helped him make a decision re the job offered him. So, he pre-empts my having to ask by saying he needs a coffee: would I also like one? I understood exactly what he is doing, and with a quick peck in response to his kiss, and a "yes please", I return to finish typing up the insights of the day, knowing I can accept and handle interruptions better than he can: my think bubbles are never so deep as his.

Several minutes later Iain returns with our coffees. He sits quietly in one of the deck chairs, slowly sipping his coffee, and clearly enjoying gazing out to sea. Just a few remaining puffy clouds today. Must be half an hour or so before I finally finish for the day. I close my laptop and turn to give him my full attention, and slowly savour the last drops of my cold coffee.

"Productive morning?" he asks.

"Wonderfully productive. Show you what I bought later. And a good afternoon too. How about you?"

"Interesting" he responded, clearly quite reflective.

"Not productive?"

"Not sure. A lot to think through!"

"So, are you going to take the job they offered?"

"I think I might, but only after we can agree on what it is about, what they see it achieving."

"Ah, so you couldn't agree on purpose?" I ask, ever the realist, wanting to get to the specific action planned. However, I have come to realise that understanding and fully exploring the context before acting is really important for Iain. So I should have expected his circumlocutious answer:

"Well, they are a bunch of very different people, nice people, all with quite different ideas and understandings as to what the Kingdom of God is all about, and …. even differently as to anyway to progress it…and you should've seen the room, Tara! a bit like them really, a bit piled up all over the place" grins Iain.

Then, still not directly answering my question, he starts describing the different people and aspects of the meeting that are important in his considerations. Not long into recounting, I break in, my surfing instincts always driving me to quickly ascertain the essentials before riding into action. Otherwise, I have learned we could be going off in all sorts of tangents, interesting yes, but not right now. I have been working and I need a break from thinking: surfing awaits.

"So, an interesting group. You seem to be describing a lack of common purpose rather than real disagreements. Bit problematic for you, hey? What do you think you need to clarify, if you are to be really interested in taking this job? Such a mixed group - could take you months to decide!"

"Well, yes, that's exactly it, exactly it. Potentially months to decide, so I found myself asking what you might do!"

We both laugh, with me hopefully finding that a good aspiration: focus, to the point.

"So, I left saying I would get back to them with a job description. If they like how I would see the job, and accept that, well then yes for the job, but if not, then it is not meant to be. They seemed happy to go along with that – so I have not yet made my decision."

"So how are you going to decide?" I ask trying not to be too impatient. Surfing can wait a few moments, but not too much longer.

"Dunno. I have to work on it. But I agreed to come up with something before next fortnight's meeting. I know everything I have said and thought about having to take responsibility, but at the moment I just wish God would tell me straight out"

"The divine puppeteer - Seems like the way we've been made though means we'd resent being treated like puppets. Created in His image: choice, responsibility, and self-control core to our being!"

"I know what you are saying, Tara, but surely our Creator could on this one occasion simply tell me if it's His purpose for me to take the job" - Iain sounds a little frustrated.

"If you took on the job simply because He told you to, every time there was a frustration, you would feel justified in venting a little resentment at Him, wouldn't you? And maybe even feel a bit deserving, or earning of His grace: might that start to creep in?"

"I guess so…just don't want to give up a year of recuperation," Iain's voice trails off into reflection.

I pause, as I see Iain going internal. After a sigh I try to keep this brief.

"I don't like thinking of Jesus as simply a 'boss' Iain. Maybe 'Lord' Yes, who has a right to ask us to do whatever. He asks, not tells us. It's not a relationship that involves any owing, like reciprocal paybacks are required. We can't buy or earn real relationships. It's about walking together, grace and love."

Suddenly I'm worried that I'm bashing him over the head, so I go silent again for several minutes, letting him think through where he is at, before feeling its Ok to continue.

"I am sure the best way will be where you find yourself. You will work it out. He hasn't given us reason for nothing."

"Yeah, I know! Knowing what is that best way is often hard. But a vision now and then wouldn't go astray. Take Paul and Peter, in the book of Acts, they had visions! 'Young men will see visions, old men dream dreams' - you don't think I am still young enough to qualify for a vision?" Iain jests now, easing the tension.

I do remember reading this prophecy from the old prophet Joel.

"If you are asking for visions, maybe remember what Lewis wrote: he warns us in his book on prayer to be careful what we ask for!"

I continue after another pause:

"I wonder Iain, I really wonder how convinced you might be by an experience of a vision anyway: would you really just follow it, believing it was indisputably from God? You've said in the past that as a psychologist, if you had a vision, you might well explain it away as an impending psychosis!"

"Gosh, desires, eh? That re-opens a whole bag of conflicting thoughts: innate dispositions, needs, wants, desires, indulgence, self-discipline, self-control, dying-to-self, servanthood, talents, gifts, abilities….mm. Desires, such a knotted question."

"Absolutely knotted bag of worms" I quickly break in, "but not all need to be visited right now to find an answer!" I feel a little impatient. Mercifully Iain nods his head. Time to wind up.

We enjoy some silence, as we watch the returning fishing boats, and see a beautiful yacht out on the horizon. The waves rolling in now beckon me to action. Within minutes I'm off, enjoying riding my surfboard. Iain is still standing, watching, gazing out and perhaps reminiscing about how we got together? And who would have thought that we would come to a place like this?

Out there on my board, all the energy locked up while sitting at the computer, talking, researching and writing is suddenly released! Must do this strenuous activity more often; running too - not the slow walking that Iain prefers and often drags me into!

33

Paradise Eludes

Iain

I woke early, wanting to sneak out from the tousle-haired shiny dark mop that lay next to me. I quietly slip out, noting the refreshing cool morning sea breeze. Time to untangle the knot, once and for all! This has become all consumingly ridiculous. Fair enough, though, not to do it with Tara. It's my decision and I realise I was almost bullying her into making it for me. Coffee, prayer, mind mapping, and then a decision sheet as Em had reminded us. I am sure I will get the clarity I need. Simple process. From the deck overlooking the sea, I am looking forward to the first signs of the sun rising behind me.

Desire pops up. What is the place of a heart's desire? There is a dream behind my desire. Peace. The moon and candle lit night on the veranda: deep down I yearn for that to be what life is all about, 24/7! It feels like a foretaste of paradise. Clinical practice presents a psychologist with a constant stream of the pain and problems of a broken, fallen world. No one comes to a psych to share how good life is. I have earned a break. Just for a year, surely, a bit of respite is OK. I feel smug, yet somehow, disquieted. Life is not just about making this world a paradise: there has to be a bigger purpose in this space of time than making oneself comfortable.

Paradise will be, but perhaps for now we can only experience glimpses when there is love. That's what Jove blessed us with on the veranda. It is knowing the Creator that gives me a sense of being more than a blip on a speck in space. No doubt, the Creator has a purpose for me to enjoy Him but also with that to bring a little bit of paradise to other people's lives as well. But does that mean always helping them deal with their problems and pain? The vicariousness inherent in hearing story after story of pain is draining, and even the slightest notion of paradise can seem an impossible dream as some sort of burn-out seems to take hold. Must I go back to that again? Is it time? Am I right to sense I am being called back? Granted, though, with a slightly different role….

God's presence is known by faith, though, not by sight I remind myself. Inevitably it is rarely in the moment, but it is later, in hindsight, that I recognize how I have been prompted or led. That's it! In asking for guidance and wisdom, my stream of consciousness needs to be open. So, brainstorming needs to be free thinking, not directed, a sort of mindfulness after asking the questions. Sure, it is hard, trying to understand what my sub-conscious mind might be bringing up: discerning what is from Him and what is from me? I need to I disentangle my predilections and foibles from what His Spirit might be impressing on me. Surely His Spirit really communes with my subconscious spirit, to lead me into the truth, as Jesus had promised his followers, saying that is why he sent His Spirit.

I purposefully stare mindfully and semi-focussed into the distance, first turning to the horizon way out over the sea, then looking along the beach. Just as I relax and the brainstorm starts rolling, another intrusive thought enters: why on earth couldn't I just be sent a messenger?

Just then I am distracted by two joggers in the distance in the emerging daylight. I muse to myself: maybe God *is* sending a couple of ministering angels after all! Hey, I have to stop my mind coming up with idiotic distractions! I purposefully look back down to my iPad, then close my eyes to lock out the external and to focus inwardly.

All has gone quiet in my head so after a few minutes I open my eyes, only to see that the joggers have reached the cottage and are standing looking in my direction. Oh no, it's Jacob van der Leer and Inspector Visser jogging together. What an unlikely pair!

Too late to go inside. They've seen me raise my head and are now coming up to the deck. I smile as I joke to myself that they might be the ministering angels I had desired.

PART 4

MURDER SHATTERS PARADISE...

34

Decision Time

Iain

"Good morning, Jan," van der Leer speaks with the strong Dutch accent I am getting accustomed to, an accent in which it is difficult to pronounce Iain. "Glad to see you are a man of prayer first thing to start de day. And your dark wife, she has I assume gone out already to buy a field?" he asks, attempting humour by referring to a verse in Proverbs about a good wife. Without invitation, the two sweating men insensitively climb onto the deck and sit themselves down in the two chairs. Boundaries? But then this is an island community and I remind myself that this is a familiar place for van der Leer. I look to the inspector, ever the quizzical look on his face, now dripping with sweat.

"G'day fellers," I find myself saying, while trying to think of a clever retort for van der Leer, but only a stumbling one comes to me:

"And Jacob, you think your fitness is more important than starting with prayer?"

It was the inspector who answered, the friendliness of his jocular mood a complete contrast to when I had seen him previously.

"Prayer without works is dead - I learned that much in Sunday School - This is work for Jacob. He thinks he has to convert this stubborn atheist!" First time I've recognised the clear difference between these two: Jacob migrated here well into adult years, but Dirk, well, perhaps he was even born here.

"Ya, exactly, you are hard verk, Dirk! After all dese years as your friend, I still do not understand what your fight mit God is all about." Van der Leer, joking, so incongruent with my first impressions about him, now clearly in a banter with his accomplice.

"You don't listen, Jacob. Only tell me: how can you fight with someone who does not exist?" is Dirk's gruffly spoken rebuttal.

"Evidence, evidence" retorts van der Leer. "I hear you." He turns to me: "Jan, Dirk is always telling me about evidence; dat when you are tackling a crime, you cannot dismiss de plausible possibilities just because dere is a lack of evidence! I tell him we can only prove dat something is, not isn't. Agnosticism yes, but atheism: nay, it is not logical."

I shake my head, not at what was being said, but because of the way the conversation had started. Such a non-predicated launch into a serious discussion. Their banter went on for a few minutes, almost oblivious of me until the inspector suddenly stops answering Jacob, and turns to me.

"You see, Iain, we have this argument often, but I tell Jacob each time that I think there is not just a lack of evidence for a god, but rather there is irrefutable evidence that there cannot be a god, at least not a good god worth following. But Jacob doesn't hear me."

There was a sudden and unexpected serious tone now in the inspector's voice. He sounded more personally invested, far from the gruff-voiced policeman dispassionately on duty and in charge.

"Jacob knows - so much of what I have seen in what every day ordinary people do is disturbing. Have you not seen it in your work too, Iain? Nice ordinary, good people yet committing heinous crimes."

He seemed unusually loquacious as he then again turns to me.

"You have no answer to that, do you?" His wry smile suggests to me he thinks he has check mated me.

I am searching for something to say that Dirk wouldn't see as me joining van der Leer when we hear movement inside the cottage. I turn, relieved to see Tara through the window, then walking towards us carrying a tray. She starts to speak to announce her intrusion as she walks through the open doorway.

"And this dark wife thought these Caucasian imperialists might need a drink, after all the sweating in our nice tropical climate! Not made for it maybe?" she says, with a mischievous giggle in her voice.

As a realist, she enjoys being direct, and she enjoys challenging potential insults, her racist rejoinders all included with a sense of fun, thriving on repartee and word plays. True, when she was younger, she had told me her insecurities had seen her taking such comments very personally. Working through her identity issues with Em, embracing being made in the image of God, had brought her to a place of not only comfortable self-acceptance but celebration in who she'd been created to be.

Jacob, oblivious to his earlier potential insult, could not resist a retort, and picked up on her challenge with typical dry Dutch humour.

"Ah, ya, it is a burden you know, hafing to live here and suffer all the humidity for de sake of de Kingdom. We white skins were created for colder northern climates, and I often wonder why He has then sent us here - It is good dat you appreciate the heavy cross we haf to carry, Tara. And, ya, all because I haf my friend here who I haf to convert!"

It was the inspector who breaks in.

"I thought you were a Calvinist, Jacob: predivination, no, pre something, ...predestination, isn't it that what you believe - we don't have any choice, do we? So, why does that mean anything might be up to you?"

Dirk had picked up on the jostling and jesting. It struck me that with the tail end of Jacob's comment and Dirk's response, we were witnessing a relaxation away from work, a rapport and friendship between two apparently quite different men, but were they so different? What has made for such a friendship between a determined atheist and a serious Christian? This thought brought me to ask:

"So, you two look like you're good friends, but you have such different beliefs!"

There is a loud silence after both had nodded yes; then after looking at one another and a poignant pause, the inspector speaks first, but not to answer my question:

"So you really are a psychologist, I see, not prone to wasting any time before you dig down! The island's police need you. Not just as chaplain, but consultant. Observant. Curious. Analytical. Forensic. I know more about you than you realise. Sabina was right. Have you decided yet?"

I turn to Jacob, with Tara watching closely.

"I came here to take the year off from work, to reflect and think. From our meeting the other day, I am not at all sure that all the ministers are convinced about the need, nor agreed on what the position should achieve - especially you, Jacob."

"Ya, dat is right, I don't see any need, but to be honest mid you, I don't tink dat matters in regard to your decision. If you decide God wants you to do dis - yes or no. If yes, our church will support you."

"I don't understand" I am perplexed. "What's the rationale for supporting something for which you see no need?"

"I denk de way to explain is to use de word 'hinges'- it hinges on dis: just because *I* don't see a need does not mean dat dere *is* no need, and dat God is not showing someone else de need. Or maybe calling dem to make de need known or would have dat need fulfilled! It is not for me to convince you, but you to show me, convince me even. Has he given you a vision for dis?"

This indeed leaves me pondering. Finally I answer calmly, though this does not reflect how I'm feeling.

"To tell you the truth, Jacob, I am not sure what to think. Haven't had any vision. As I said, I had really planned on a year of thinking and praying, to recuperate, work through some issues, and review where I am to head in the future - a once in a lifetime opportunity! I wanted to be with my wife as she embarked on her research and I thought that, with work unlikely here, this was a golden prospect. Then turmoil. I came out here this morning to sort it all out and, wanting easy answers, I had been wishing for a messenger from God!" I pause, then continue with a smiling face and a wink: "and then, well, you two came along and, well, you sort of intruded!"

The inspector now comes into the conversation, and I notice his usually gruff voice is back, though sounding almost reflective. And no longer just with short abrupt sentences:

"All common sense to me. No need for any spiritual hocus-pocus. What's the evidence? What's a reasonable decision, based on the evidence? The island's police need a forensic psychologist. Murderers have escaped justice. Stressed police traumatised by helplessness in seeing horrendous sights, bloodied corpses; deserve the best pastoral care and counselling. There is a gaping big hole. Everyone these days seems to be focused on their careers. So, we have trouble getting anyone qualified wanting to come to the island: not good for careers. You are qualified. You are here. The churches are willing to support you; the police to employ you. How can you stand idly by, or walk the other side of the road, dreaming of a paradise?" His definite voice then goes very quiet:

"There is no paradise, Iain. Only in dreams. And dreams get shattered."

The inspector has never used my name before. He looks away, almost as though embarrassed, his moment of unusually eloquent passion subsiding. Now he is just staring out to sea, as an awkward silence descends.

The picture of the parable of the Good Samaritan, generated from the words of an atheist; this wasn't what I expected or wanted to hear! Something inside is fighting, mustering every possible argument to justify what I convinced myself I needed, deserved. Ah, did not even Jesus, with crowds needing his ministry, still push off in a boat to…. get well needed respite? Hadn't Jesus once said: 'The poor you always have with you' - and wasn't this a year for getting close to Him - surely there is a time to be quiet, a season for everything.

I have not answered Dirk, and the silence is starting to feel even more awkward. What can I say? These are times Tara usually helps me out, but she too is silent. Distracting myself from dealing with the moment, I defensively move myself to the observer position. I wonder what tragedy has befallen the inspector. Finally, Jacob breaks in changing the subject.

"So, Iain, you see why Dirk is my best friend, no?"

I am relieved.

"Yes, but I am still curious about what looks like close friendship between two people with such different beliefs." Ah, I have changed the subject. But the inspector is not about to let me escape. He knows what I am up to!

"What does that have to do with taking the job?" he asks.

"I asked my question first" I replied trying to use humour to avoid having to answer. I can't handle this.

"I was married to Jacob's sister." His voice is quite subdued and catches me by surprise.

"So, it is family, not friendship that brings you together?" Tara softly asks. What a relief, finally Tara has come into the conversation. But there is another brief silence, broken by van der Leer.

"No, friendship, then family followed." Jacob van der Leer is looking towards Dirk, and I am surprised to see the inspector's eyes slightly watering up. What to say next? 'Was married' I had noted, yet still friends. What was the pain experienced here by a man who otherwise looked so much in control? And then I notice that the blunt van der Leer is also quite emotional. I don't have to decide where to move the conversation, for it is Dirk who finally speaks, just detectably struggling to regain control.

"Psychologists: they get to you!"

I am feeling more than a little mystified by this. I didn't think I had invited any of this discussion. How is it that I sense a battle? What sort of power struggle is this?

"You were the one who wanted to walk this way this morning!" comes van der Leer's unexpected remark directed at Dirk.

"Dutchmen love arguing. Pig headed. Trying to convert each other. That's friendship."

The bluntness of each of their comments is clear; but with it the awkwardness has now gone; discussion now back on safe, jocular, self-deprecating ground; we all relax, even showing it with a little bit of quiet, reassuring laughter.

Jacob stands up, seizing the moment.

"Time to go and leave these two in peace to have their breakfast."

But the inspector isn't about to let his bone go. He never does. That I will learn in days to come is his trademark. He wants to push me for an answer.

"Well, Iain, I have answered your question. Now, how long is the procrastination with that praying stuff?"

"Leave the man alone to work out his own decisions, Dirk" edges in Jacob, still standing and ready to leave. I am starting to appreciate Jacob for letting me off the inspector's hook. But it's Tara who now gives the inspector permission to drop his bone.

"Don't worry, I have already challenged Iain to decide before we have lunch today!"

But it doesn't have to wait until lunch. As Jacob and Dirk disappear back down the beach and I reflect on our discussion, I realise I have my answer. Unexpectedly, inexplicably, I experience an intense sense of confirming joy. He *has* sent His ministering angel, a pugnacious atheist. What more do I need but enjoy God's humour? The battle is over.

35

Engagement

Iain

It had been good to write the job description, based around what I believe I have to offer, and on what I consider to be my capabilities and background that I could bring to the job. I was really surprised by how clarifying these had been, convincing me of the rightness to accept this challenging but hugely exciting new job possibility. My reasons *for* accepting far outweigh the againsts!

I am now even more astonished by how at the minister's association meeting, *all* had simply accepted my proposal, and without a single murmur for an amendment! I simply say that I take their consensus as the final indicator that I believe I've been called to the job. I assure them that it's been a battle: I had other things I had planned to do, set my heart on, and thought were His plan. But then, along had come some challenges to my plans. I didn't know what my wife had been praying for me, but now I do, and here I am, out of her hair. They laugh.

We break for morning tea. After that the change in focus is immediate. Judy leads the charge.

"We need to decide on a commissioning service."

I am surprised by the ease and sense of unity around the planned action, considering the diversity of the group that had looked so irreconcilable in my previous meeting with them. I guess it is because they have a history of collaborating on organising events together like a commissioning. Such a service just required some amendments to a pre-existing template, and so indeed it is the organising Judy again who leads by pulling out a commissioning liturgy. Sister Mary-Martha really likes it, Jim says it worked so well last time, van der Leer acknowledges it represents 'all things decent and in order,' and Sabina asks if she could be in charge of the music. It is Jim they decide who should give the address. There is a little bit of discussion after Bob Wesley asks if there was to be any laying on of hands. Jim jumps in to say yes and reminds people that all have that rite in common, and so it indicates unity in action, while also allowing everyone to hold quite different denominational interpretations as to what it represents.

The remaining discussion is about a review of the Christmas Carols regularly held in the town, and also the upcoming Easter and ANZAC events. Purpose is unspoken.

At the end of the meeting, I am surprised to find that a sense of belonging amongst colleagues has somehow begun to emerge. It reminds me that I had never liked being a tourist, anywhere. I realise that I had been feeling a bit like a tourist on the island. No roots. No connections, no sense of purposeful engagement. In the past, if I went anywhere, it was to conferences. Conferences are good for me because they are about sharing things in common, in the pursuit of a purpose that is interesting and worthwhile. Yes, that's the feeling growing here already.

We all stand up, picking up our bags to head off. I am so looking forward to getting home and sharing with Tara. However, just as I head for the door, Jim Booth comes across and invites me to what is apparently their regular lunch after each association meeting. I make a brief call to

Tara to let her know I will not be home for lunch and that all has been finalised. She sounds happy, and typically, jokingly confirms that with me out of her hair, she'll be able to get some more work done! Neither of us are on holiday anymore she points out! Darn it, I am dispensable.

Now sitting on the front deck of the hotel bistro, we look out across the road, straight down the main jetty. Not bad if this is to mark the new beginning of 'working.' It is as people relax that I like listening and observing, to come to know and understand them better. But as I listen to various current concerns, about this parishioner and that building's maintenance, I start to understand that being in ministry here might look inviting, but the stresses and strains can be heavy. There are probably few cosy relaxed meals: always a need for serious sharing and mutual support. So that is what brings such a somewhat disparate group together, I surmise: they are on an island with few immediate interactions with colleagues from their own denominations. No information yet as to what lies on the other side of Rustenberg.

Listening and learning brings me to reality, to realise that my job as a chaplain will not be easy either. Their unspoken invitation to be a member is welcome. I am starting to realise the association will be an important group if I am not to be too self-reliant, nor alternatively risk an unhealthy co-dependence on Tara. I just hope I can give back as much as I will no doubt receive. In my practice, I had seen various clergy. But here the relationship will need to be as a colleague, not as a clinician. I need to think that through. It is so easy to default back to previous modus operandi. I am becoming conscious of the need to work differently. This is an opportunity for adaptation, creativity. I am seriously so glad I'd written the job description!

Just then my thinking is interrupted by Bob Wesley:

"Iain, you look in deep thought. Observing us no doubt. What are you thinking about us? Do you have us all worked out? Reading our minds, eh?"

I know he is joking with the last phrase, but it is one that makes me cringe. Before I can answer, Jim chips in:

"I guess you are a behaviourist – nothing to work out, eh? Just need a handy way to how to modify us or challenge our irrational beliefs? The counsellor we had in the drop-in centre used to say that. Good value, she was - did a lot of good. Wasn't the philosophical type. All the better for it." He winks at Judy to let her know he was teasing her.

"Or the theological type" put in Bob seriously.

By this Judy is now drawn into the discussion. She displays a capacity for getting people to focus.

"Iain, here we are, we are supporting you. You obviously can sit and listen. But I would like to hear more from you. So, what's your orientation, your philosophy? How do you put your psychology together with your theology?"

How on earth can I answer that in five seconds, so I try to put it succinctly, to state my position without referring to my journey.

"I suspect that there is something intrinsically interesting for me in the understanding aspect. My initial training was heavily behaviourally focused, but I've moved on: further up and deeper in as C S Lewis says, and not just about our faith journeys but also our professional ones. So I am old enough to know now there are no simple answers. People are not just their behaviours. They have personalities.

"I'd love to hear a little of your journey" comes Mary-Martha's straightforward request.

"Well not now if you are going to be very long" intrudes Jacob. "I haff an udder appointment. Keep it short if you must." It occurs to me that it was kind of flattering that he would not want to miss anything I might be saying. Interesting. All are now looking at me expectantly, so I sense a need to go on without further debate. Judy confirms it, her organising capacity again on display:

"Given the short time, I would like to hear specifically about your orientation, and how you got there."

"A big ask, but I'll try. I don't have Tara here to keep me brief. You will have to do that, Jacob. Anyone, feel free to go anytime. It's not everyone's interest to know."

I take a few seconds to collect my thoughts. Ah, yes, at the beginning! How to make it relevant? Goodness knows. I will try to end up with time for questions.

"In my study and training there was a strong emphasis on environmental explanations for human behaviour. Cognitive behaviour therapy fitted well with my Christian world view, where one takes full responsibility because there is choice. It offered irrational beliefs and behavioural conditioning as one, if not as adequate explanations for all behaviour, at least as a realistic and practical means for effecting change. I could teach people how to gain and exercise control, for isn't that why people seek counselling from a psychologist? In some way they feel stuck.

"My practice also involved me in assessing learning difficulties and disabilities. That involved understanding intelligence. Sure, fluid intelligence is about what we have learned, and acquired. Its environmental. That fitted my blank slate assumptions, you know that 'give me a child until she/he is six' idea. I'd been comfortable with that.

"But then that's not all to intelligence either. There is a component called crystalized intelligence, considered an innate inherited individual difference, an intellectual disposition. This opened me up to thinking more broadly about individual differences, dispositional psychology, genomes, phenotypes, and to personality differences and preferences."

Enough of that, I need to bring things back to relevance here and now: not as to their personalities in relation to their discussions and interactions, but rather to their food. I continue:

"Since Tara has come into my life, there has been a further exciting development. It is about the food each of us likes. Why did you order what you did for lunch? Maybe the choice you say was guided by needing to watch diet or budget, by choosing to be a carnivore, vegetarian or vegan. But what would you have *liked* to eat? And if it is different from what you actually ate, why did you not, and does *anything* explain your capacity for self-control?"

Time is at a premium. I don't want them to start talking, just thinking.

"I am aware from working on stuff with Tara that there is good research evidence to suggest that a sweet tooth is linked to the Big-Five agreeableness factor. People who are by nature friendlier are more likely to like sweet food!"

I let it sink in as I look around, seeing each of them grinning. But I press on, not allowing for an interruption.

"And as for the drinks, Tara has made me aware of differing preferred flavour profiles, of individual palates, and I have become a little interested in if and how these might be associated with personality traits."

I pause, long enough for it to sink in, but still signalling it was not time for questions.

"As for character, the sort of ethics and morality one is inclined to, there is nothing substantive related to preferred foods. And as for what and how people like coffee, there is a lot written based on surmise, but really, no substantive evidence.

"So, to sum it all up, I have been challenged to find that so much of who we are, what we can do, what we want to do, what we like, who we get on with, how we think and understand even, and dare I suggest, even our spirituality and theological inclinations, they are all in part at least expressions of our genes, manifesting through our personalities, our natural predispositions.

"This raises some serious questions for me. Like, if so much of who we are is the result or our dispositions, for what are we really responsible? What if we are dispositionally inclined to addictions, like gambling, sex, or getting wealthy? Why the good I would I do not, and the evil I would not, that is what I do?"

I look around the group. During the ensuing brief Q&A, a lively but brief interactive discussion. I am heartened by the range of stimulating questions asked I am not used to being asked. I feel it has been a satisfying time together, even though from many different viewpoints.

36

Work Begins

Tara

At last! Iain is off to work: his chaplaincy to the Police. I am delighted with the prospect of getting some space without having to ask him what will occupy his thinking for the day. I am excited about my work, with plans clearly written up on my computer, and a way of recording daily activities that helps me see some real progress. My first task is done: I now have a current map, so will head off tomorrow to walk the main dirt track identified as 'Bean There' – sounds like there was some coffee humour amongst the golden oldies!

I'm looking forward to meeting up this afternoon with the first of two elderly historical writers, whose names and addresses I received in an email from Sabina. She had offered to find these for me, since she has a good knowledge of islanders, having been here for many years. I am starting to feel a little less isolated too – I don't need lots of people around me, but I admit, life without close friends can be quite depressing. Oh no, shouldn't use that word – let's just say, life without friends can make us feel quite disconnected!

The first lady on my list lives almost within a stone's throw, so I walk there after lunch, and open her cute little front gate, only to find she is out waiting for me in her garden: what a nice connection already!

"Hello, you must be Tara: I thought I'd welcome you out here so I can show you my garden." I quickly give her my hand, saying "And it is so nice to meet you out here, Mrs Johnstone – what a lovely spot near the river and such a lovely lush tropical garden!"

I feel even more relaxed as she asks me to call her Mabes:

"Makes me feel young again, you know, hearing a young thing using the nickname my family called me when I was young" she says with a warm smile.

A wonderful half hour passes quickly, as this little white-haired lady proudly points out the various tropical plants and trees she and her late husband Paul had planted many years ago. Most of them I have never seen, I tell her. She is quick on the uptake.

"Oh yes, I guess you know many of the Australian natives, coming from Perth, is that right, dear?" she asks, checking her memory is correct.

I affirm her assumption before moving on, letting her know I'd grown up in Melbourne, so am also aware of some of the more exotic trees, but mostly ones that grow best in a cold climate. Surprisingly, I find it so easy to share of myself with this bright and likeable lady. Already I do feel safe sharing with her: so much to like, but I also gather she will be able to teach me so much about local flora. I feel quite excited! After her invitation, we move inside into her open windowed and cool back sitting room.

"Cooler in here, Tara - Comfy chairs, and a view out on the river that is most relaxing."

She hands me some fruit juice, already poured and waiting for us, as we slowly begin a wonderful near two-hour discussion of her knowledge of the island. This included her take on the locals –

"mostly very friendly, dear, and they're always so willing to help if I need a hand" she assures me, along with saying "and you will quickly be accepted too, my dear, so long as you take time to listen to their stories first!"

What a gem! I think Iain will really get on well with her too. Finally, I also feel comfortable enough to ask her if she has any family members living on Rustenberg. After a conspicuous pause, she shares a few sentences of an only child; she had left home as a late teenager, moving in with apparent drug friends on the alternate major town over the mountain. It seems it is only reached by plane or boat from KP.

"Gabbie was always a bit untamed, determined to do what she wanted to" she said quietly, "and eventually, only came home for a while, when she was pregnant with her son." She paused again, looking out the window with sadness etched on her face. I felt no verbal response was needed as she quietly continued:

"When Ronnie was three, she left him here for my husband and I to look after. We kept up a contact through friends who knew where she had gone, until we learnt she had died of an overdose."

I feel her incredible grief, and murmured my own limited understanding of her sorrow, recognising I have little real appreciation of what all that had meant to her. But I know I need to ask further about the child.

"I'm so sorry, Mabes – and I can't imagine how you coped, raising Ronnie after losing your only daughter!"

"Yes it was tough, Tara, and we tried everything possible to prevent Robbie from falling in with the same crowd. He was a happy enough child, and we loved him. Used to go to the combined youth group run at the community centre. Unfortunately, he had a lot of his mother in him, and was determined to leave school as soon as he turned 15. He wasn't cruel or unkind to us, but it was not long before he wanted to explore the mainland, so he headed off for Darwin. My husband tried to trace his whereabouts, but without success."

"Oh dear, Mabes, that must have been crushing for you both... Have you heard anything since?"

"No, my dear, but I live in faith that he might turn up one day, recalling how we had truly loved him, and wanted only the best for him. I keep my hopes positive – keeps me looking on the bright side, Tara! That's why gardening is so important to me – feeds me no end of positive energy" she says now with a smile. "And he must be about your age now, Tara...that makes your coming here wonderful to me...some young life around...and even more wonderful because you love plants and growing things."

I find her optimism inspiring, and gently take her hand in mine, thanking her for sharing.

As if to finish off this sad element in our conversation, Mabes then brightly asks if I'd like to read her last small but detailed book, written some ten years before. She said it had helped her fill in her day in the years after Robbie had left such a hole. As I gratefully flip through its pages, I can see it shows her keen interest in and love of the island and its flora. The book also includes numbers of quite beautiful photos of private gardens that are regularly open to the public. She has also included interesting facts and reflections about the various landmarks; lots here that will clearly be worth investigating. Her book 'Come See our Beautiful Eilandt' had been sponsored by the local council, as a tourist guide. It has a clear map, though as Mabes points out has had a revision of which she is pretty sure, but which is available at the Visitor Centre, right next to the library.

Eventually I see Mabes is tiring after all our talk: from what she has said, I decide she must be eighty at least! I suggest I will come back another day, after I've devoured her book, which I assure her I will return!

I'm so eager to find out all she can tell me through its illustrated and well-written pages.

"And I hope you will be happy to give me some more clues about the best places for me to explore, and maybe where people now grow, and also *used* to grow coffee in the past?" I tentatively ask, alerting her to one of the reasons I had chosen her as my first interviewee on the island!

"Of course, I will, Tara! I will look forward to digging out some of my old memories, and I think you won't be too bored!" She laughs, and I laugh too: she is such an inspiration! As she waves me off, she calls out:

"and just come when it suits you, my dear – I'm always home, apart from a bit of shopping and my time at the library on Wednesday mornings – oh, and Sundays, when I usually go to Mass."

I return home very stimulated, enthused, and eager to share with Iain my delightful introduction to the people and plants in this my new workplace. As I walk home, I reflect over many things shared during our two way and quite personal interchange, recognising there was something special about it: a conversation you'd expect between two friends!

Suddenly I am aware of feeling deeply moved: I have just made my first new friend on this island – definitely not a paradise lost for me! But unexpectedly, I now also feel terribly disturbed: the gentle quiet picture of Mabes becomes the almost forgotten picture of the grandmother I had left more than 15 years ago! My goodness, my thoughts become almost scrambled, with an avalanche of questions long buried. What may have happened to Nani, to Dada too? Surely, they must have died! What would have happened to their house, their estate? I wonder what they did with all my childhood toys, and the clothes I'd left behind? How could I have just totally shelved them, as if I had no relationship with them?

Deliberately, I had refused to think about my ex, but my grandparents: Had they really missed me, worried about me? How had they managed their own feelings about their only grandchild, suddenly gone without trace? How had I simply become so preoccupied with me, so self-centred? Had the ordeals of my childhood meant I had found it simply easier to dismiss any who had been involved in those traumas? Shut off that period of my life as if it never happened, rather than face and deal with the heavy issues? And why now should these issues erupt?

I find unwelcome and massively unexpected tears pouring down my face, so I quickly find a hidden track back to our cottage. I feel devastated: self-deprecation and loathing uppermost in my thoughts. How can I think Iain doesn't feel some of the same negative feelings about me, an uncaring dislocated grandchild, with no sense of attachment to those who cared for me in those formative years? What does this predict about my own future relationships?

I stumble home and throw myself on the bed. I had been so exhilarated after sharing time with Mabes, but now, I'm exhausted. Such emotional turmoil, completely foreign to me as an adult. Gradually though, the tears seem to dry up, as I close my eyes, praying that this latest self-revelation might somehow enable an important growth in me that will mean Iain will not abandon me!

37

The Inspector's Wife

Iain

The local Kleine Paradijs police station is an old building constructed for the tropical climate well before the advent of any electricity, let alone air conditioning. The Dutch colonial imprint is evident. Built by people from a cold climate, it shows the influences of the Dutch East India Company architecture that can also still be seen in Indonesia. Solid stone walls are surrounded by a veranda. Set on the lower rise of the hills behind the town, the outlook over the sea is expansive and appealing.

Inside though, there is little charm. There are louvre windows with frosted glass, the sort with chicken wire embedded. All the windows are barred, giving a sense it is more of a prison. A motley lot of desks are crowded against one another, with just sufficient space to walk in between. Some spaces need to be negotiated sideways, and only by lifting over one's head anything being carried. The only relief from the tropical warmth is via ceiling fans, almost always on. I am told there was once an air conditioner, but it was useless, removed as it was blocking a much-needed window. Other than the open space with all the desks that are behind the counter, there are two interview rooms and a narrow passage leading to toilets and holding cells. Signage is old and fading, and interestingly still in both Dutch and English, bringing a sense of history. It leaves me imagining the many things that must have taken place here over the centuries. That sense alone gives me a feeling that this building is part of the fabric of the local culture. There is however one sign of up-to-date modernity: sparkling new computer screens.

Clearly, there is a strong incentive for police to be out on the beat or to meet elsewhere at one of the many charming street-side stalls and beach side bars. It is not unusual to see a police officer or two working out there in their uniforms, daytime with their mobile devices, and then in casual clothes immediately after work. So, this is where I now find myself spending much of my chaplaincy time.

For now, it is after work, and there are eight of us, chatting around a table, mainly about the upcoming football match this week which will see the Freemantle Dockers play Geelong. As a West Australian dependency, even though almost six hours flight away, the Dockers are seen as the local club, but two at the table grew up in Victoria and are clearly barracking for Geelong. As yet the Covid pandemic has not prevented the all-important competition from continuing. Any discussion like this is fun if not relaxing: no problems, nothing hangs on it ultimately, everyone knows something about it and can pretend to be an expert; there is competition and excitement, and individuals can identify a sense of belonging to a tribe. As Tara has observed, with nothing ultimately hanging on it, it's a perfect distraction from real life, keeping people at a safe distance, unlike talking about politics or religion. Little wonder sport enjoys such a central position in the Australian culture.

I find it even more relaxing as I am enjoying a cold India Pale Ale from a West Australian Craft brewery. This offers an opportunity for some to tease about drinking fancy beer: the implication in their eyes typecasts me. One even rags me by suggesting rhetorically that I probably prefer beach volleyball or even perhaps synchronised swimming to Aussie Rules! All of us laugh. But I am not about to disclose my personal problem with addictions that I nicely keep under control.

Despite this all being in fun, there is a serious underscore: it offers a framework of a sort of typecasting for understanding people. I am sure as they go home it will be part of how they are coming to view me. At the same time though, when we meet at work, it will offer a good commonality for me to start listening before talking, as I grow into my chaplaincy role. Right now though, while by nature an observer, I am quite intentional in sharing my knowledge of the various Dockers' players. I think I perceive, inch by slow inch, acceptance from my new colleagues, and hopefully some sort of identity with them is arising.

I ring Tara to let her know where I am. She is enjoying time with the new elderly contact re plants on the island. I relax. One by one the group grows smaller until finally it is just Dirk and I, and I am about to leave. Dirk has been quietly observing. Two observers now together doesn't exactly make for much of a discussion. Before I can get up to go, however, Dirk asks me how I think I am being accepted. To gain some thinking time, I turn the question around: how does he perceive I am going? His answer is as always, direct if not a little cryptic:

"You are on the way. Good tactics. Nothing too personal."

So, he notes deliberate tactics on my part. Do the others also think I am being tactical, I wonder, and if so, does it come over as non-genuine? In tune with him, I stay simple:

"Yes, just about rapport and trust building. Acceptance, trust, a thin line between them. Some necessary boundaries too, I'm afraid."

"Take your time. Looks like you are patient."

I agree. It takes time, even as an appointed chaplain, to have them come to a point where they may be willing to share personally. I am sensing just how different, *quite* different this on-the-job work is, compared with people who come into a private consultation with me as a psychologist. There had been debate as to whether they should know I am also a registered psychologist, but in the end, it was agreed the only ethical way meant people would need to know. Otherwise, how would it look when I am consulted regarding the psychology, the forensics of some offenders. So to Dirk I continue:

"I am feeling my way between roles. Boundaries will need to be different. I remember learning about the difference in expert and referent relationships. A prophet in his own land – as I become known and accepted, there will always be the question of becoming."

Dirk looks at me quizzically. He states simply:

"It's not what we become, its who we are." I enjoy his raspy voice.

"I guess you are implying I should just be myself. Tara is always challenging me about overthinking, not trying to work out what people might want or need me to be, but simply straight forwardly be me, as I am, there for people, take it or leave it."

"Got it. Exactly what my wife used to say."

I can't work out why he is suddenly turning away from me, though the further crack in his voice does not escape me. I recalled him saying that he was married to Jacob's sister, and now here he is again speaking in the past tense. Yet now I note it was his wife, but not *past* wife. Is this an invitation to ask more? Is this the time, with evening closing in, or is it time to go home to dinner? It feels intuitively important, opportune to enquire by reflection. The answer might just take a few more minutes.

"Your wife, um, she, she um, used to say?" That should leave room for plenty of choice, no unwanted nosiness. He picks up on my request incisively, as if he had purposefully steered me toward asking. The answer is as brief as always and catches me off balance. Turning to face me again, his normally focused and somewhat intense blue eyes are now a little sorrowful, and at the same time there is a hint of anger:

"Yes. She's dead. Murdered."

How am I to respond to that? He had spoken in a tone that could be taken to imply I should know. Maybe not. It's one of these moments where I instinctively know the best thing to do is simply reflect, not ask any question with any specificity as to what when why etc. How do I convey I am feeling his pain? One word is all I can reflect with.

"Murdered?"

There is a silence as Dirk continues to look straight at me, almost in a stare. Should I speak, or wait? It needs to be in his time, allowing for his collecting of thoughts as to what he will say. I have probed enough. I wait. I have de-focused my eyes as well, but if I continue to directly engage with his eyes much longer, it will become uncomfortable - as if I am pressing him to hurry. It is at such moments of seeming discomfort that we typically start talking again, if nothing more than to break a sense of awkwardness. I need to signal I am still present with him, but also give him room to take whatever time he needs. He is not Tara. I cannot put my arms around him. The silence, it needs to be comfortable. Ever so gently I move my eyes to now stare unfocused, in thought, at the drink in his hand. He knows what I am doing. He follows my lead and lowers his eyes to my drink. We sit there for a full seven minutes. I am present with this man. I feel it. In the clinical setting, I would probably reach out and touch him on the shoulder, but not here. Somehow, here intuitively I know not to. Finally, Dirk looks back up, and so do I.

"Your Tara, somehow…. When I saw her. … And how she tells you: 'be yourself'. That's Hedi. Hedi…. Always herself. Her own person. Straight. Forthright. Uncluttered. Social worker. Others before self. Could be ridiculously funny. Not dark humour though. Tall, blond, slim like Jacob, unmistakably Dutch. Thighs of a bike rider."

It isn't the answer I expect. In the pause that follows, Dirk again looks down at my drink, unfocused. It is a further moment to collect his thoughts and this time it is I who follows suit to give it to him. The sense of pain, his pain, is slowly ebbing, as I consciously focus to be more cognitive. I resist any temptation to say anything. In less than a minute he looks up again.

"You read papers? It was in the West Australian. You would have seen it if you were there three years ago."

All I can do is shake my head slowly for 'no.' It is not time for me to elaborate. Lines of distress along with anger now appear on Dirk's face as tears well up.

"I've seen many bodies, many ugly murders... But nothing prepared me."

His knuckles become white around the beer he is holding, and the other hand forms a fist which he brings down slowly onto the table. We have caught the attention of the barman across the way. A quiet seems to descend, even though no one else is looking. Dirk's voice drops to a near whisper.

"Blood everywhere. She had put up a fight. That was my Hedi, a fighter, always but for others; then, it had to be for herself, alone. I was not there, Iain, I was not there. I should have been home."

Dirk looks to continue, but he pauses again, and then:

"They wouldn't let me in on the case. Never solved. I am not allowed access to any files. Not even today."

There was a further silence. No need for words. Dirk quietly and yet more determinedly speaks directly at me. His passion is back:

"You see why we need a chaplain? Coppers carry so much. You listened. You didn't interrupt. We need that. Not religious stuff. No platitudes. Don't try to tell me any God was there, or here now. Evidence: can't be. Doesn't make sense!"

How can I ever, even think for one moment, let alone suggest, that I understand? No, I don't, but I do experience his pain, and sense the frustrated sense of helplessness that just magnifies it all. I have no answers, nor do I need any. I need to be myself, honest, no fluffing around.

I am glad for the tears in *my* eyes. They speak a thousand words. But nonetheless, it is time to speak.

"No, it doesn't make sense. I agree with you, Dirk, evidence is paramount in making sense, otherwise we simply get nonsense."

Suffering and wellbeing is stuff that had been the focus of much thinking in my journey as an evidence-based practitioner. But now is not the time for debating God, suffering and evidence. Now is a time simply for affirming and being present. Ah, and not 'becoming,' but simply 'being there.' In the silence that follows, I am suddenly aware of a presence far greater than myself, of the One Who has personally suffered and is more grieved by suffering and pain than we can ever understand. It's a knowing that is evidence based, not dependent on feeling. In time to come, just maybe, I will be privileged to bring some healing to the pain evident in Dirk's post-traumatic stress.

We have sat fully ten minutes just in one another's company, with me just taking it all in, before finally Dirk speaks.

"Iain, from Tara - the flash drive, the information, it is so important."

It is as if he has changed the subject, but then I would have expected him to change his tone to an authoritarian demanding one. No, his voice is quiet still, in tune with what we have just been sharing and I need clarification.

"Important for solving a murder?" I ask quietly.

"Yes" responds Dirk simply and quietly. With a nod he gets up and walks away, noiseless but deliberate.

38

Grief Beckons

Iain

Last night any sharing of the experiences of our separate days had been pushed aside until we'd had refreshing and rejuvenating sleep. We both were seemingly too tired, or maybe unwilling to confront our respective reactions. But over our breakfasts on the veranda, with the calm sea settling our different emotions, we agreed to share. Tara had insisted I share what my day had meant to me. Probably the heaviest reporting I could have made would have been to reveal Dirk's wife's tragic murder. Somehow, I felt Tara was not ready for this, an indescribable pain he must still carry. I told her of the time getting to know various police members, and simply mentioned that Dirk had told me something intensely personal. Sometime later, I thought, but not now. And Tara, thinking no doubt 'professional in confidence' did not ask further about my day. That left me silently wondering if and how my call to the police chaplaincy might be involved with this unsolved tragedy. I often take comfort from the common phrase: 'God only knows.'

So our discussion finally had turned, to Tara sharing her own grief, her intensely personal reaction in response to Mabe's life story. Naturally needing to support each other, we had spent quite a time sharing the pain she had experienced, not only to allow her to debrief, but also to reassure Tara of my absolute love – I wasn't going anywhere! In fact, hearing Mabes' story and Tara's personal response, suddenly I too was confronted by my own past, and my own inadequate response to my early life in Scotland. How come *I* had never perceived my own psychological repression of the things that had traumatised me? How had I simply run away from the past, without concern for my own behaviours, let alone much thought about how my choices may have seriously affected others? How infrequently had I thought about my ex, or the family I'd left behind, and even less frequently did I even care about how they might have coped without me! Was my own lack of attachment to important others any less deficient than what Tara's had been? And how could I have so easily missed these maladaptive patterns of behaving, given my intense psychological training that identified such mechanisms so clearly? … Impacts that must have been felt on *both* our attachment styles, that would have made connecting for us so much more difficult!

We both wept together, as we each shared our individual griefs on how we had dealt with our pasts. Eventually we could positively express our wonder at how love covers a multitude of sins – yet we also could acknowledge how at times love can also make us so blind to the truth! We affirmed our need to review any past pains that continue to impact our attachment style to each other. A work in progress.

A new chapter now seems possible, with an honesty that has been self-protectively kept at bay, repressed for many years. But I was then extra glad I had decided to park my conversation with the inspector. This was not the time for looking at more pain; our own equilibrium must be gained first. Not that facing our own issues should be allowed to become an all-consuming preoccupation. Balance. Balance in self-care, and stewardship of our giftings in being there for others. It *seems* so clear to me now.... Time will tell!

39

The Other Side

Iain

Some time elapses before we take to the beach, to quietly walk off our emotionally charged awareness of each other and our personal grief. The vast open ocean, so refreshing! My phone rings, but there's no caller ID. We really don't want to be interrupted - but finally, we agree I should pick up.

"Iain?"

"Yes" I reply sharply.

"There is a young officer who needs your help, around the northern side of the Island."

It takes me a few seconds to place the voice, but the context of 'young officer' confirms recognition enough for me: this is the Superintendent. And we'd only met so briefly! Hardly know her! What are the protocols around how I should address her? Her title or first name? It might be an Australian territory, but it is an island with its own sub-culture, and we are noticing a few conservative elements. As for the police culture, that's altogether new ground.

"OK."

"When can you go?" The superintendent doesn't sound like someone who goes on with unnecessary small talk. I realise that for the moment I do not need to use her title or name.

"My thinking had been to go cross there next week sometime to familiarise myself with the people there. Could be then?"

"No, needs to be tomorrow."

As blunt as the inspector! What sort of culture awaits me with this woman of few words? She reiterates urgency:

"We need you to be there. Tomorrow. Probationary Constable Lexie is a new recruit. She's fresh from Perth, and has been desperately missing family. She has just had news from a friend that her boyfriend back in Perth has started going out with someone else. I have given her the day off, but it's not for me to advise her whether I think she should or shouldn't go back to Perth."

A caring culture it seems, or is it that they just want people back to work? Time will tell.

"I, I um, I don't have a car. We had been thinking we might not need one, just our bikes, and just hire one when needed. My wife is planning to rent one for the day to visit some coffee plantations next week re her research."

The Superintendent's response again was immediate.

"She can do her initial visiting tomorrow. It's a golden opportunity for you to meet the officers in the small station we have over there. Good excuse. Talk with the officer in charge. Essential to see the lie of the land."

I am a little taken aback by how commanding she is. I have not even started yet she is already organising Tara as well! She could be the inspector's twin! Instinctively I want to push back; I need to set boundaries, and all I can think is to say:

"Well, this is a bit sudden. We had some other arrangements. I am not sure what Tara has planned. I will need to check." But the superintendent didn't seem to be listening to me.

"There's the police Land Rover, with a constable all set to drive you across. After dropping you off in town, he can take your wife to whatever plantation she decides she wants to drop in to. He can check the gun lockers and licences. Needs to be done about now; all responsible and efficient use of police time."

I wanted to continue my protest, but carefully. I knew Tara would be much more adaptable than I, but I still needed to set a precedent round boundaries and control. The superintendent's language was full of imperatives: musts, should, and needs. There was little if any of the language of choice: like could, maybe, can you, like to, does it suit? At least she acknowledged that Tara had a choice! And yet I couldn't help feeling that she demonstrated some sort of respect for others, nonetheless. Perhaps it was the implied concern for the officer, and the implied thoughtfulness in working Tara into a plan.

"Tara, that's my wife…"

"Yes, I know."

Ah, she is listening, and quick to signal I need not provide unnecessary detail.

"Tara has yet to organise where she will drop in. And it may be a bit late to give notice."

Again, the immediate response indicates someone who is very quick thinking.

"Iain, this is an Island. We do things when we need to do them. We don't spend a lot of time planning. All the plantation owners know me. I know them. On an island like this, everyone likes to think they know the superintendent, personally. Ring me back in an hour to tell me which plantation Tara wants to visit, and I will ring them tonight to tell them she is coming."

I note it wasn't 'if you ring me back…' I don't want to capitulate completely.

Slowly I say "OK, that's all good. I will check with Tara if it suits, and which plantation. And get back to you."

"I expect your call in an hour then."

There was a click before I could say goodbye: a conversation interrupted, not finished. Meanwhile I check with Tara – as predicted, she is quite excited to make her initial visit to her next research participator tomorrow. In fact, she looks incredulous, and she shakes her head.

"Wow Iain, exploring the northern side of the island, a driver, free transport and with a local as a tour guide providing a personal introduction, and all part of my work! Who has to think about that? Ring her back. Tell her I am delighted! Paradise happens after all!"

40

Real Coffee Costs

Tara

I'm blown away with how quickly things are now progressing! One full-on day spent getting to know myself more through getting to know my first friend on the island. Then the next day, another full-on one visiting the other side of the island, followed by a deep dreamless sleep. So today I'm needing space – too many people suddenly in my brain. I've told Iain I need to go for a long early morning run on the beach. Alone! Wonder what exercise he will choose to clear his mind: the deck chair I suppose! How different we are! Yet so great we can share honestly.

As I run, I start to recall yesterday. The police landrover had come to pick us up, and there was not only the constable, but to our surprise, sitting in the back, the police superintendent. It all began with the Super telling Iain to sit next to the driver as she invited me into the back seat. As I sat down, she had told me to call her Joan, though she said nothing to Iain. Immediately I was struck by some similarities with the blunt and direct DI Dirk. But then also differences, as she clearly likes to socialize and engage in personal chatter. She also explained that the island values people's adaptability, with an expectation of all being able to makes changes more frequently but less predictably than the tides that surround it!

From the outset of this trip, I had listened to various conversations: first at the central Police station, then in the police four-wheel drive vehicle, and later on as we dropped in on a number of coffee plantations. Regardless of context or with whom we interacted; Joan communicated an incisive understanding that living on this island can be both tricky but also very rewarding. I'll try to capture some of those details, but really, it was a very full day, and I don't want to needlessly bore you!

I had accepted this opportunity in the belief that going with a real local would make this a more enjoyable experience – and with one who had only ever spent a short time away on the mainland for police training; otherwise, Joan has lived her entire life in KP.

I always find it fascinating to recall what is discovered by just listening to answers that emerge from asking a few but significant questions. But it is also clear to me that along with asking and listening, it's so crucial that the questioner shows a genuine interest in the person, along with indicating a real desire to understand and simply accept the other's insights and opinions. No pretending, just being genuine! Living with Iain has greatly enhanced that understanding for me: seeing him interacting with people, regardless of their abilities, backgrounds, and even when not particularly interested in the direction of the conversation, this has modelled a respectful caring attitude that allows people to feel connected. That quality of listening had not been part of my upbringing, so growing this new habit has involved a lot of practice, obviously needed to make such a new skill gradually but surely become a more natural, almost automatic response to people.

So, while listening to Joan, I learned much about her as a person: a forthrightness mixed with a genuine concern that the right thing be encouraged. There was also no indication that she would act any differently with people outside the workplace. The constable driving us was himself a native of the island, whose wider family had lived for generations throughout the mountain range, and there were oblique references to some non-conforming relatives! Yet Joan treated him with utmost respect, to which he responded in similar but quiet and deferential politeness. I remember wondering if the choice of this constable had been deliberate, making any police matter less threatening to the locals. Some of her conversation with him quite naturally related to what his task of the day entailed: checking the gun lockers of the plantation owners and any other farmlets with gun licenses. Clearly Joan modelled an attitude that would give no grounds for interacting with people other than with due diligence, surrounded by always being courteous.

We'd driven directly to the small village on the north-western, more windward side of Rustenberg, over a well-made but narrow winding road around the side of the mountain range. It took almost two hours, allowing for several brief stops to photograph some very special views: some up the mountain, caught in morning sunlight and shade, and other locally known land features - like the cave that had obviously given way after years of tropical rains. Apparently at times, this drop creates an amazing waterfall, directly cascading on to a meandering rocky river many metres below. Can't wait till that happens!

The hanging plants and the tall flowering palm-like leaves were also just wonderful to capture on camera, to later hopefully be identified – maybe by Mabes? The village itself was perched on a cliff top, with magnificent views out to the Indian Ocean. In a way I wished Iain and I had gone alone, with time to explore, walk, scramble down the rocks and check out the flora and the birdlife – but that I knew would have to wait.

I briefly met one of the local constables, but then left Iain to this his first challenge as a chaplain. I sensed he was needing to focus and establish his role, not the least being that it involves the expectations of an unfamiliar Super woman boss! As he kissed me before I left with her and our driver, he whispered:

"I'm glad you're taking Joan with you!" I whispered back jestingly: "Is that about me, or you?" He squeezed my arm.

Heading up this more southerly side of the mountain via a different route from the one we'd taken to the village, Shoal Haven, it was great to see there were large areas of land that were still massively covered by native forests, though these trees were not so large as some Australian mainland forests. Much of the conversation shared between us made me want to read up about the indigenous wildlife that until now, I had assumed would mimic Cape York Australia. I also reflected on Perth and wondered how much the Indian ocean winds here are in some way like those experienced from the Fremantle Doctor, and how they may have impacted on these somewhat smaller trees seen here. The further up we travelled, the cooler it became, and we were not even near the top of the rugged mountain! In fact, though Joan had told me to bring a jacket, I didn't believe it would be needed. How wrong I was!

I had also been somewhat apprehensive about how Joan might interact with the two particular plantation people she had committed to introducing to me. I had wondered if because of her position, she might have been quite an encumbrance to my research opportunity, making it difficult to get past first base, but surprisingly, the opposite was the case. For example, Joan introduced me to my first local grower - Matius, someone she knew who had grown coffee within a small cooperative run by a large international company. Matius had recently retired early, due to a knee injury. But if Joan's relationship with Matius was typical of how she treated other plantation holders, it was apparent that even the local manual workers held her in great respect but were also not afraid of her. Joan sensibly had freely given me the opportunity to converse alone with Matius about various aspects of coffee growing on the island, choosing to go and find his wife. Mita had remained inside their tiny but beautifully maintained house, surrounded by flowers and tropical trees. Joan seemed to know her way around here quite comfortably, even with the family.

I had valued the time with Matius, as he'd showed me around his small but productive garden – I was particularly excited to see his few prized coffee trees. He also happily shared some aspects about his work as a labourer, which seemed to be really quite intensive. Sometimes, I reflect as I write, I am glad I'd been brought up a city girl! We drink our coffee with little regard for the incredible and tedious work of manually picking each beautiful and aromatic cherry! But Matius had been born into a poor family. It had survived by subsistence farming, living on a small plot of land they had cleared. Even as a child he had wanted to do something for his family, so as a young teenager had gladly accepted a physically demanding job working for a big company, planting trees over a rugged and steep tract of land. He finally had "graduated" to picking cherries, normally called coffee beans, then sorting them: many hours of tedious work. But Matius had appreciated the income he received that eventually enabled him to build a simple but comfortable home in somewhat of a Dutch farmhouse style for his then young, part-Indonesian wife. They loved living in a safe though isolated place, which meant they held no fears for the future wellbeing of their own children. I decided to ask about the myth of there being a special coffee plant, and where to look for it, but Matius quickly put such a possibility to nought, declaring that was simply a myth, with no truth in it. The strength of his response was somewhat surprising, but I assumed another planned visit with him in a few weeks' time might explain his reaction. I wondered silently but decided to be more careful in future when checking out what locals believed about coffee.

I discovered Joan happily chatting on the back veranda with Mita, enjoying a relaxed home-squeezed tropical fruit drink. Hearing their conversation about family members, and how they were managing since Matius was no longer employed, I reflected again on Joan's capabilities:

not only as an efficient and organizing woman, yet quite able to adapt to whatever the situation demanded of her. Also surprising but importantly to me, there was clear evidence of her genuine interest in whoever that involved. Joan was able to inform me of so many factors surrounding such people as Matius. Her comments about Matius and Mita again demonstrated her acceptance of people who have backgrounds, abilities, and even certain values very different from her own. So, when we drove on to the next person I'd shown an interest in meeting, I felt more than a little relieved that Joan was not going to make my life more difficult, in regard to my research project at least. I could retain a bit of a question mark about how she might impact Iain in his chaplaincy work, but time would tell!

On our way further up the mountain, I had phoned Tony Mancini about visiting him. He appeared to be understandably reserved, so I knew I had to be careful. Poor cellular phone reception didn't help. En route, conversation with Joan was helpful, respectfully sharing insights on Tony's background were invaluable. Like knowing he'd migrated from Europe as a young man with his wife and a growing family, after completing studies in business management. The second world war had not been kind to his family of origin, so he'd escaped to a peaceful island setting, hoping to regain a more positive perspective on life for the future. Joan knew enough about Tony that meant I should expect he would be cautious in sharing much about his work, but not to take this as personal rejection, but rather, his protecting the company's work practices that needed to be safeguarded.

Joan went on to explain how this man had now become a success-ful businessman, having established a worthwhile coffee distributing company. This had raised the coffee industry on the island from merely a group of small semi-impoverished farmers surviving locally to one that had gained good export markets. A keen organising mind, col-laborative despite shyness, he had been intent on supporting the local farmers in adopting more efficient and improved farming practices. Eventually he had succeeded in a getting groups of farmers into forming two co-operatives, each cooperative working on improved processing and their own unique marketing. With the marketing had come better prices. With better incomes, greater focus on education. However, with that, many of the growers' children were forced to go off Rustenberg for their tertiary education and better jobs. This brought an increasing depletion of farm workers, resulting in a serious labour shortage. The Australian visa system for indentured labour has its difficulties on the island. Policing it requires tact and collaboration, Joan explains. Hence, she takes every opportunity to visit and talk.

My short visit to Tony was wonderfully invigorating. However, this man was quite reserved, and would need patient and measured questioning before letting anything out of the bag! But he did offer to perhaps lend me a book he was now writing about his island experiences – if or when I returned. He suggested this be after his wife returned from visiting their daughter and her family in Adelaide – another three weeks to wait! I warmly accepted his implied invitation, with some excitement.

There were numerous opportunities during the day to discover a vastly wide-ranging set of questions that I now must find answers to, before making any definitive conclusions about where my research would take me. For example, on a practical level, would I be able to photograph the existing coffee trees across the hills, without upsetting the propriety demanded by the owners, and how many varieties would be found to be economically worthwhile? Would the myth about an unknown coffee be still remembered, well enough to point me in the right direction? And were current landholders open to discussions or were they bound to silence?

The visit has made me conscious of deeper ethical and moral questions. Coffee, the world's third most traded commodity, is valued as the drug that more than any other fires affluent productivity. Yet is so dependent on impoverished farm producers, and keeping them, well, at least somewhat impoverished. Each Arabica cherry is selectively picked by hand, allowing the green fruit to fully red ripen on the bush, making the harvesting an expensive, long and arduous task over several months. In other parts of the world, Robusta coffees are more easily and even more readily disposed to being mechanically strip picked, with the whole trees shaken to release the coffee cherries, all at the same time.

So in Rustenberg not only is the cost challenging, and hugely impacted by an evaporating younger labour force, but there appears to be looming problems from climate change, threatening to devastate production under its current methods. How can the remaining somewhat impoverished smallholding farmers adapt? Where is the money for developing varieties that can adapt to the changes ahead? Where are the other younger Tony Mancinis, to make this a more equitable industry, where laborers get a reasonable return for their hard labours? Do we consumers need to reconsider how we value our coffee?

And here I am, looking for a remarkable bean. Who will stand to profit? The company and university I'm contracted to? And who will own my intellectual property, each in part paying for my work? Or will the locals really benefit? This has me asking myself: Who am I working for? One moment I feel in paradise, the next I'm caught up in a conflicting conundrum. No wonder I need this early morning run! And alone? Do I not want to talk to Iain about this? If so, why?

Sensitivity must be maintained, I recognise now more clearly, even after this one day of exploring, potential directions for the way ahead that no longer looks so clear and simple. But in all of this, I know I have found one more friend who is I believe trustworthy: Joan the Superintendent – I hope she will feel as comfortable with me as I feel about her. It remains to be seen. I'm also mightily encouraged by the general feel of people within the community, at least so far. And finding the now elderly coffee guru to be a writer was another exciting element.

Surely, I reflect, returning to my deck desk to summarize the day: there is much to work through. Iain's ways must be rubbing off a little, all this sitting down! But its not about me, I tell myself as I sit. I always find that liberating. Is that counter-intuitive, or counter-cultural? I know about givers and takers. Pretty obvious. Grant's book comes to mind. I can create my own utopia paradise by just ignoring, or not seeing the inconvenient things, telling myself they are all too big for little me to handle. Alternatively, I could become a self-sacrificing activist. Maybe that would make me feel good? Both though would be about me, and that's not OK! I recall talking through how real love is not about feeling good, nor about brownie points for self-sacrifice. It's about considered wise effective action. I reflect on how giving means I will receive what I need, but not if the giving is so I receive. That would make me a taker. Counter-cultural indeed, but it works! The Micah challenge comes to mind: seek justice, love mercy, and always walk in humility with God.

How amazing is this: an opportunity for thinking, for personal development, but also running in harness with practical caring for others. Plenty around me on this bit of paradise who need encouragement and assistance, even growing coffee! And doubly wonderful when in real friendship with others of like mind! Thank God for the selfless workers!

41

Bush Walk

Tara

Having been inspired by my discussions on plants with Mabes, and now saddled with a revised map of the whole island, I set off quite early on my first mountain exploration alone. Enough of heavy talk. It is a time I need to be alone. Plants are restorative. Drink bottle and light lunch in my backpack, I decide on a route that will take me a good part of the day. What a glorious day – temperatures during the day are almost predictably between 25 and 30, and with slightly cooler overnight temperatures, we've rarely experienced any lower than 20 degrees. No winters here, and definitely all quite dry: locals reported some of these seasons have had as little as 50 mms. No wonder Rustenberg is thought to be an idyllic place to live, especially if you don't have to work outside in the tropical wet summers! But we are so glad it is really a largely undiscovered secret hideaway. No great influx of tourists to disturb our peaceful retreat, this side of the mountain at least.

I wonder again about coffee growing here, with natural water in winters often not available unless piped. I had discovered from Matius that in some years, they had even had to hand water some of the young newly established trees, making their busy manual harvesting time between April and August extremely labour intensive. This was also confirmed by Tony Mancini, who had himself funded an installation of a simple irrigation system for some of the larger farms, for those unusually dry years. As I walk the tracks further up the mountain, it seems to become quite lush, so I reflect that this can't have been such a dry year - great for coffee growers, picking their beautiful and freshly ripened cherries!

My mind remains ever aware of changes to the flora, and to my surprise, once outside the actual town, I find the native growth also has changed with the rising altitude. My camera is also ever on the ready: I am so glad digital photos can easily be uploaded, with never a fear of memory loss. Up into the forest, with the air decidedly cooler, the trees now are taller, and less tropical in their leafage. I suddenly spy some small coffee shrubs. I wonder how old these are, and whether they are at full height. Based on my knowledge so far, they would certainly not rate being called trees, so I need to take some leaf samples as well. Glad I thought to include some small containers, recording by numbers on my map where these are found.

The deeper into the "jungle" I go, I find more evidence of coffee trees that had apparently naturalised, gone wild as it were. There are several different varieties. I am increasingly excited: what if I find one with red berries still attached that I may be able to identify, and maybe even as unique? And what if such a plant might be the one thought to be the superior coffee others have only dreamed about? I sit down to reflect on how exciting this would be, as well as to recover some vigour. A delightful spot, with a great outlook: I can just spot some water. How exciting: it's the sun shining off the ocean in the distance! Can't smell the sea, but seeing it always has an incredible capacity to make me feel relaxed. I quietly pull out my lunch, musing on the solitude that I so love. Hooray for a thermos of coffee!

Just as I sit down, I notice smoke rising a short distance away. Someone must have lit a fire for their lunch. My impulse is to go see, to say a friendly hi to some other hiker; but something warns me to be careful in checking it out. I decide to finish eating, before wrapping up my remains, safely storing them in my backpack. I quietly begin to walk towards the smoke, spying a small tent, and two people sitting nearby. They are talking quite loudly, covering any noise my approach might create. Stepping a little closer, I then pause as I realize who one of them is: Jove! I faintly hear him saying "But you *have* to find that drive, Kendra, we really need it! We must have it, Kendra! Don't you understand?"

Its Kendra then – and she says loudly, imperiously: "But I don't have it, Jove! Don't you understand?! I needed the money!"

"So what have you done with it, Kendra?" I can see Jove has stood up, as if making his point more strongly, though his voice softens so that it is even harder for me to hear.

"I sold it to Matius – he promised if I got it, he would give me $200, and that was too good to pass up!" She also now stands up, and it looks frighteningly like a huge disagreement will erupt. Their voices become more indistinct, as my heart pounds in my head.

By now I am rapidly becoming quite nervous, worrying what might happen if they discover me there. So ever so quietly I start backing away, the same way I'd come! My internal praying changes, needing to stay calm, quiet, and careful – no longer asking for wisdom about what I should say, but rather how I can maintain clear-headed cautious movements, so I can safely arrive home without being discovered! I feel my legs shaking, as I also sense my heart pumping so hard, I fear they may hear it! Oh, how I long to be home, yet there is such a long walk ahead of me. Please God, give me quiet confidence!

42

Betrayal

How Tara reached home in such a short time was something she could never quite believe possible. But some things were never to be forgotten, so she so urgently and accurately reflected on her experience with Iain. Naturally, as soon as she had allowed her shaking body to be held and comforted, Iain had to restrain himself from reiterating his question:

"Tara, what's happened? What has upset you so?" He knew from past times that when Tara's emotions were disturbed, he needed to be patient, just to hold and wait. Only then to ask for the facts.

Finally Tara could speak, initially in short sentences that stated clearly what she had seen in the bush, who she had seen, and what she had heard. Then she more honestly admitted how she had reacted in her determination to get away without being discovered. Only after these basic facts were shared could the questioning begin.

"Tara, did you see quite clearly that it was our neighbour Jove? Might you be mistaken?"

"Oh no, I am certain – he always wears the same sort of shorts, and I would know his voice anywhere. Besides I heard him call her Kendra, and she called him Jove – no doubts there! I was not dreaming, Iain! But I am still totally rattled!"

"Understandably, Tara – and I'm really sorry I wasn't there with you!"

Iain himself is feeling bewildered, with a mixed number of memories floating through his mind about times they had shared with Jove, and though knowing he was a bit 'different', their absolute trust in this gentle neighbour was never really in doubt.

Tara verbalises some of her own thoughts: "I can't believe we have treated him so innocently, as if he can be trusted, Iain! We've not locked our house, we have shared meals with him, and yet we find out he is involved with stealing our flash drive. If I didn't see it with my own eyes, I wouldn't believe it! I feel so stupid, so utterly unwise! What can we do with all this, Iain? Golly, has he just befriended us to snoop and raid my research? And why? What's that got to do with anyone else?"

Iain is also battling with his feelings of betrayal: questioning his own sensibilities, his previous trust in his own perceptions of humans and their credibility! How could he have been so wrong regarding Jove? Tara too is confronted by her own inexperience, her gullibility, believing that people are naturally good – except for the few who are found guilty of awful crimes! Why did this have to happen here, when things were beginning to look really positive for them on this island?

It was some time before they had gone over every possible glitch in their thinking that might explain any wrong conclusions about Jove and his involvement with Kendra and their flash drive. Tara was adamant about all she had heard, and for her there was no mistaking the truth: Jove was not to be trusted. And afterall, she had always known Kendra was guilty: now she had even more evidence – from her own mouth!

"I need to go see Dirk, Tara – I really think he has more info about all this that may help us understand what's going on."

"Why do you think he would be any clearer than we are, Iain?"

"Well, I haven't shared with you all that he told me earlier, Tara... about his wife".

"What is that?" Tara asks, now seeming a little less shaken. Iain believes she is now more able to cope with what he needs to divulge, and realises there really is no alternative now.

"Dirk told me his wife, Hedi, was murdered, three years ago, but no person was found responsible". Iain hardly paused before adding "and because he was excluded from the inquiry, Dirk has felt really angry towards everyone, including the God he can't believe exists. Apparently, the case closed way before every possibility was followed through. I think he thinks there has been a cover-up. Someone has been paid off."

Tara explodes quickly: "That's absolutely terrible, Iain! How come such injustice, and for such an honest, personally committed man like Dirk! Never to have that crime against him and his wife resolved is unbelievable! Has he tried to have the case reopened? Does he suspect someone? Is the corruption within the police force on the island? And he, an inspector in that very force?"

"I'm not sure, Tara, but at least now with some new evidence, re-opening the case should be more possible. That's why I need to talk with him ASAP – will you come with me, Tara? I'd rather not leave you here alone".

"Of course, Iain. Maybe he would come here? But I can't even begin to imagine there is anything connected with what is *on* my drive that relates to a murder – it sounds ridiculous!"

"I know, Babe, but one thing that Dirk has reiterated, right from when he learned there was a missing flash drive, is that he must have that drive! He strongly seems to think there *is* some connection – perhaps he will tell us, now that we're more implicated!"

"So, is it actually possible that Jove and Kendra together may have been involved in Hedi's murder, Iain? How could we have got this so wrong?"

Tara clearly finds this all so unbelievable, even now in the face of the facts. She questions what in her own research might unravel now, and that becomes a real worry. Suddenly she remembers she'd asked Em to find and send her the encrypted backup drive, stored with her, and which should arrive any day. But then she also recalls she now does know who has the stolen one. Kendra had admitted selling it to Matius.

"And my goodness, Iain, to think that I have spoken openly with Matius, thinking he may be helpful in my researching coffee plantations – just a few days ago! Why on earth does *he* want my flash drive? What's on it? Could he be a murderer? But, come to think about it, I now recall his very adamant rejoinder about the coffee myth, saying that of course there was no truth in that – VERY adamant in fact! And I didn't think at the time to question him further...oh gosh, I can't believe this is happening!"

Iain too is thoughtful about this whole fearful saga, and particularly concerned for Tara's safety. He can't ignore the fact that so much of her work is done alone, and often means she explores quite isolated places on the island. He sits at their table, clearly engulfed in his own thoughts, until Tara again excitedly suddenly grabs his arm.

"And Iain, if there's something on my drive, encrypted so that even *I* don't yet know what I'm involved in, what if it means we also are in some danger?" Tara begins to shake again, as the reality hits her, exposing their potential vulnerability.

Iain is now alert, committed to clarifying this as quickly as possible, as he turns to grab his mobile, saying:

"The sooner we get Dirk alerted to this new information, the sooner we can feel less stressed, at least by getting answers to some of our questions. I know Dirk - he will make sure now that both Jove and Kendra are brought in for questioning! But I still can't believe, Tara, that our friend Jove is potentially guilty of some crime. It just doesn't make sense! Everything we know about him, even like his taking food out to this pathetically isolated girl spells care, not crime; speaks about things we can't yet know but that clearly need to be known. Let's get Dirk over, hey Tara? Then we'll also feel a little safer too, and less in the dark!"

Just as Iain goes to call Dirk, he suddenly notices a figure near the open window that quickly move out of sight. Has someone been listening in on their conversation? Was it Jove? Startling Tara, Iain rushes past her to the door, but by the time he gets outside, the figure has disappeared.

43

Suspicion Moves

Dirk

A phone call from Iain. He sounds distressed - unusual for him to so quickly cut to the chase.

"We are being stalked after Tara overheard stuff about the flash drive you are so interested in, and I think they know she overheard them."

I waste no time in getting to their cottage. As I approach, I see them sitting on the back deck. A third chair, I notice.

"Hello Tara, Iain. What's up?" I can see both are very tense. They direct me to sit.

"Thanks for coming, Dirk: Tara has just had a shocking experience. Somehow your earlier request for the flash drive now seems related to what you shared with me about Hedi's death, which of course I have only just now shared with Tara; so, Tara, you start this ball rolling."

"Dirk, earlier today, well, I went on a trek into the mountains, following a lovely walking track, looking for wild coffee bushes. While stopped for lunch, I noticed some smoke rising near Craggy Point. Thinking I might find some fellow walkers, maybe in a picnic area, I started to walk over. As I got closer, through the thicket I saw a tiny tent. I could hear voices, and to my surprise, recognised that one was Jove, *our* Jove. I was relaxed, but before moving forward, I listened briefly just in case it might be a private conversation that I shouldn't barge in on. Then I saw who Jove was talking to: Kendra!

"That was not the biggest surprise; what I heard Jove say next stopped me dead in my tracks. He was really firmly speaking, telling Kendra 'You must give me the flash drive. Then she said 'I can't, because I sold it" and she admitted, for $200! And you know who to? To Matius, the guy I just interviewed last week about coffee growing!"

My response is just to listen - must let Tara talk. Fully attentive of course. No questions.

"Now when I got home and tell Iain about my experience, we find a stalker has been listening at the open window. What is going on?

"A stalker?" I finally interject reflectively.

"Yes, a stalker: but vanished as soon as we opened the door! It's really made me feel even more stirred up."

"Frightened, feeling very unsafe, Dirk" Iain interjects before Tara continued:

"I don't understand what is so important about my flash drive. No one but me knows what's on it, though haven't got to the encrypted stuff yet. I can tell you it's only some records I copied in libraries and some records from my previous employer. He's the one who is part funding my research. What use is all that to Matius? Or you for that matter?"

No opportunity to explain now - Tara is on a roll.

"Iain has just told me about your wife. I am really, really sorry, Dirk. Unbelievable that it is still unsolved! But how on earth can you think that a flash drive you know nothing about can have any useful clues? And then, to find Jove is mixed up in this is just so, so, well, distressing! We trusted him! We thought he was different, but never thinking he would be involved in something, something that looks, well, like it might be serious crime! This is all so confusing. You owe us an explanation, Dirk!"

As Tara draws breath, Iain then cuts in, perhaps frustrated that I am not saying much:

"We are clearly quite disturbed. Can you understand that, Dirk? As Tara says, we need some explanation at least, and from you, right now!" Iain is obviously stirred up. I completely understand.

Both fall silent, but I'm aware I am not free to give them the full explanation they are asking for. One thing though, I must at the very least reassure them about Jove.

"You two just have to trust me. As for Jove? I know for a fact he's as safe as! Utterly trustworthy. You'll just have to believe me. Both of you."

"Hang on, Dirk, you're the first one to point to needing the evidence before trusting anyone, and right now, *I* have the evidence that points to Jove as being *un*trustworthy! I knew that Kendra was probably the one who took the flash drive, having identified her that one day by her hair as the one who rushed out of our hotel room. But I couldn't have dreamt that she would have anything going with Jove!"

"Tara, tell me what you saw. The scene." It's not a time for explanations, at least not yet.

"A very small tent. She must be staying there. Looks like he is visiting her. But why would he be there with her?"

"So what sort of things is Jove known for doing? Habits die hard. Isn't that what he's most likely doing in this case, Tara?"

"Well, if you mean his habit of bringing people food.... yes. OK, there was a dish there that was clearly warmed on the fire, so he may have taken that to her, I guess. But if he is trustworthy, what ...what about his questioning Kendra about the drive? I accept I only heard a small part of a larger conversation, but the question about his wanting to get that drive back! *Why* would Jove know about it, let alone be wanting it, you tell me that, Dirk!"

There's nothing left for me but to answer Tara and Iain.

"I have to ask you both to keep this conversation completely confidential, because a lot is potentially riding on that: can you assure me we are speaking off the record, and between honest trusting friends who seek the truth?"

"Absolutely Dirk!" They both answer almost in unison, but very quietly.

I know I need to go on, to reiterate my understanding that something was indeed potentially connected with my wife's murder. I need to tread carefully.

I share some selected details of my discussions with police from Perth. About *why* I thought Hedi had been murdered. My incredible wife. A gentle and more caring social worker could not be found. Hedi's life was always spent seeking ways to alleviate someone's struggles. Always sharing their pain. Life was never easy for local people surviving on simply growing coffee. Briefly I recall my dearest wife, so suddenly taken from me. I pause to catch my emotions, before I must now force myself back to the task in hand. I lower my voice.

"Tara, just the night before she died, Hedi had told me she had some insights, some important information she'd like to share with me about her recent interchanges with some of the farmers – but she said she wanted to sleep on it. She wasn't sure if the information was privileged. I was called out to work, and during that time, she died, an unexplainable, cruel, heartless, violent death."

I stop – unwelcome grief now catches me. Embarrassed - they both see my tears well up. I'm unable to speak for some minutes. Relieved: at least they respectfully remain quiet. Yet present: Tara acknowledges that, resting her hand on my shoulder. I don't usually like anyone touching me, but now I find this gives me strength. They are good people. I sense possible valued friendship may yet lie ahead.

"Its OK - let's go on" I finally manage to whisper before saying more clearly:

"I searched Hedi's notes but found nothing except a note in her to-do list that caught my attention: 'Check with Gena where flash drive is safe.' But, before I could check with Gena what it might mean, she died in that unfortunate road accident the next day."

There is silence for a minute or two. Iain then quietly begins some sensitive questions.

"But Dirk, even if the locals couldn't believe one of them could have done this, why didn't the Perth constabulary take up the case, seeking to know the truth?"

I am still gathering myself together. I can't answer Iain quickly enough before Tara follows up.

"Yes, and Dirk, did you not feel free to do some of your own investigating, even in your own time?"

I can finally answer them: "Unfortunately, plenty of people too quickly come to conclusions. No understanding. Prejudiced views. I only have hunches about the corruption which had the case closed too soon. Could be wrong. But that was very much against my wishes!"

"So, Dirk, do your hunches include local police?"

I think: good question, Tara, but I can't answer that directly without creating more fears. Or, maybe even giving too much away. I simply say:

"I do know there are some people on the island who would appear trustworthy. Upright citizens. Not all though are what they seem. I assure you, Jove is not one of them. I would trust him with my life." I pause. How much to tell?

"I think it suffice to say one thing. It has been my instinct to encourage him if he ever had the opportunity, to ask Kendra about the flash drive. That is based on pure trust. Not only of mine for him, but also because of Kendra's trust in him."

"How come Kendra trusts Jove, Dirk?" Tara and Ian are both looking enquiringly at me. I don't take in who asked.

"When Hedi died, Kendra was terribly cut up. My wife had been a great personal support to her – Kendra being a motherless child. When she began really going off the rails after the, the um, murder, Jove stepped up. Showed some genuine care for her. From time to time - depending on what she was up to. Jove was the one person who displayed consistent counter-cultural, unselfish behaviour she could not doubt! … Nor could I, ever!"

"Sounds incredibly Christ-like living, Dirk!" Iain speaks softly, without judgement I know…and how I wish I could believe! I slowly reply.

"Indeed, sometimes even made me wonder …. When I see a person like Jove …. but still, the cruel unsolved death of my innocent, my wife …. Confirms my disbelief in any loving God."

I mustn't get side-tracked.

"Tara, you now know my dilemma. The evidence I need to open the murder case. I believe there is something that is encrypted on your flash drive. Information on it from the researcher Gena who was here before you. Crucial evidence for solving my wife's murder."

They both look at me as they take in what I have said. I focus back at them both. Iain and Tara need to be careful. Who really was the stalker? Not Jove. Two things are clear. To my mind, their trust in Jove is crucial to their feeling safe with their neighbour. But, I wonder, are they safe here right now?

"Your observation of Jove and Kendra have confirmed to me that indeed there is a flash drive that Kendra has stolen.'

I purposefully think out loud.

"We now know that she has sold it on to Matius. What we don't know is if Kendra had stolen it *for* Matius…. Or alternatively: Did she approach him and offer it to him? And why on earth, we are left to wonder, was he interested in a USB drive…."

"A drive that he could not have known anything about?" offered Iain.

There is a silence as I let our discussion sink in. After a while Iain continues with the next question:

"Dirk, has Kendra ever been known to be violent? I mean, is Tara at risk here? Do you think it may have been *her*, stalking us before?"

I reply quickly: "Never violent. Soft as butter. Needy, just needy. Makes stupid decisions!"

Enough of this discussion. I don't want to let them know I very much doubt it would have been Kendra. I think I know who it was, but I don't want to tell them who. Someone quite sinister. I now need to deal with the immediate situation.

"Tonight, you must stay at my home. Just so at daybreak, we will all go across to the other side of the island. Pay Matius a visit, hopefully get the flash drive. Tara, I need you there to identify the flash drive. Iain, as a witness. Now, time for food. Take-away on the way to my place. I will order it now. You grab some overnight clothes."

44

The Dark Side

Iain

It is barely daybreak and Dirk wakes us for breakfast. No time to make small talk, though our thoughts race – staying in this place, the home of an incredible unsolved crime! We have only just finished eating when a police SUV pulls up, and an officer we had not met before comes to the door. Dirk introduces her as the other sergeant, Maranda. I remember she was away for my first police catchup.

"Search warrant?" he asks her, ever brief.

"Got it." She replies just as briefly.

When we get to the car, we see that there is a second officer, and as we get in, we are introduced to the relatively young constable, Jim Bakker. Dirk motions for Tara to get in the front with a gruff:

"All the men in the back."

We head west out of town, the rising sun behind us, still largely hidden in the dark of the mountain. It is a clear day. Tara, ever sociable, starts chatting to the driver. It's the usual polite introductory chatter, hiding some of the tension we all understandably are feeling.

"You been on the Island for very long?" Tara asks.

"Four and a bit years" she answers.

"What brought you to the Island?"

"Ah, that's a long story. My uncle is rather senior in the police in WA and, well, I was sick of people claiming I must be getting special treatment so when I wanted to get my sergeants promotion, I decided that I wanted to do that out of the state. There was a position going here so I applied for it, and got it."

"As a sergeant?"

"Yes, I had already passed my exams, of course."

"And how do you find living on the island?"

Before she can answer, Constable Jim in the back breaks in:

"Its relaxed. Everyone knows everyone. Back home in WA a policeman is a little fish in a big bowl. Here, well, they respect you, old culture, and you're kind of a big fish in a small bowl, if you get my meaning. Though, if I must say, other than work, if you are single like we are, well it can get a bit.... kind of mundane." Obviously Jim is unafraid to speak his mind, even with the DI beside him. Dirk is deep in thought, ignoring their trivial chitchat.

"But there are plenty of clubs and singles bars," Maranda broke back into the chatter, as the constable trailed off. "Plenty of night life if you like that sort of thing. How have you two found being here?"

Before either Tara or I can answer, Dirk breaks in.

"20 minutes to Matius's house. The plan. When we pull up, I engage Matius and his wife. If he denies everything, what are you to do, sergeant?"

"Serve the warrant."

"And then?"

"Start searching in his office."

"And you, constable?"

"If there is no resistance, start searching in the office with Maranda. Then, we go to the bedroom, then the kitchen."

"Good. Make sure you search together. No room for accusations of planting evidence. And Tara and Iain, stay close to me. Tara: describe the drive."

Tara describes it as a distinctly red USB drive, with 'Coffee Research' labelling it.

"When you find the flash drive, bring it straight out to us outside, so Tara can identify it and we can charge Matius with receiving stolen goods."

"But it is such a small thing" suggests the constable. And Dirk turns to him to explain.

"It promises to provide evidence that identifies a murderer. Matius paid for an encrypted drive. Why would a coffee farmer buy stolen goods? Conclusion: cover it up. Encrypted, it's no use to him other than to destroy incriminating evidence. No hypothesis about secret coffee information. Hope he has not already destroyed the drive. Otherwise, all we have is the evidence of an unreliable witness that he bought it from. Getting the drive would seal the case. Tara here can identify and unlock it. Bingo! Meanwhile, after the search, drive or no drive, we arrest Matius."

"But we don't have room in the car" says the constable.

"All taken care of. Sabina and another constable are following behind. Delayed ten to 15 minutes. In the divvy van. Back-up just in case. Not too much fuss when we first arrive. Give Matius a chance to come clean. The extras can join in the search if need be."

"I don't think Dirk thinks we can do a good enough job, Jim!" jokes Maranda, but somehow, I sense a serious undertone that bespeaks covert defensiveness. Dirk does not engage. There is silence as we approach.

We drive up the farm driveway, rounding the bend to the farmhouse Tara had described to me. We pull up in front of the porch that extends out from the front door. There is a simple functionality with a muted influence of Dutch colonial design.

Dirk asks the two officers to accompany him as he goes to the door, after instructing us to stay in the car. The two walk behind him. He presses the doorbell and there's a wait. No response. I check my watch, 8am. Then I hear him knocking. Again, no response. They talk - I assume Dirk is suggesting they go round the back when around the corner of the house come three armed men. Two are carrying impressive looking rifles and the man in the middle has what I recognise to be a shot gun. I see the officers each move their hands onto the revolvers in their holsters. The approaching men stop.

The man in the middle steps forward, moves his right hand away from his weapon and stretches it out. I cannot hear but can lip read the predictable:

"Dirk, good to see you. What brings you here? Looking for someone, something?"

"That's Matius," Tara whispers to me as I wind my window down to listen. Dirk doesn't waste any time with pleasantries.

"It's not a social call, Matius. We require you and your friends here to put your firearms down."

"This is my own private property, and all licenced and legal...what's the worry?"

"Put the firearms down, NOW!" The demeanour of the three now changes as they tense up, but slowly comply. Without a further word, the two constables walk forward and pick up the firearms, and in each case they can be seen checking that safety catches are on before coming back to stand with Dirk. The situation looks even more tense.

"Matius Korfemann, we have information that suggests you have knowingly received a stolen good or goods, and there is a suspicion you may have conspired to have it stolen in the first place."

Matius looks puzzled, possibly to the point of seemingly overacting, and the men with him laugh.

"Got the wrong man there if you think that," one of the men says with another short laugh.

"Yea, Matius is one of the most honest and straight forward fellows I know" says the other. But Dirk looks undeterred.

"Did you or did you not pay one Kendra Thompson two hundred dollars for a computer flash drive, knowing it had been stolen?"

"And what if I did? Its only a tiny computer part."

"Hardly innocent when you pay two hundred dollars for a ten-dollar drive. There must be something of significant importance on it, worth at least paying twenty times its value." It's the sergeant cutting in. Dirk gives Maranda a look that clearly says 'leave this to me.'

"The girl was out of money and rang me, desperate, offering me the drive, with some mumbo jumbo that it had important coffee information on it. How was I to know it was stolen. I felt sorry for her. She was obviously out of money. I thought if I paid her for it, I wasn't just giving her money for nothing. I was going to check out the drive and see if I could work out who it belonged to and return it. But its encrypted."

Now the constable interrupts:

"So, you, a supposedly poor farmer, drove for an hour to give a girl two hundred dollars for a flash drive that could be simply useless, possibly stolen, only so that you could give it back to an owner? That doesn't make sense….. unless of course there was an expectation of really important information …. maybe you are aware that there *was* a drive with important information concerning an unsolved murder?"

The sergeant then immediately continues:

"A murder in which you were once a suspect."

It sounds more like an interview in a police interview room after an arrest.

"No evidence" responds Matius, hands now on his hips with an air of defiance.

"Matius. The drive. Do you have it?" Dirk asks, assertively taking charge again, with a sharp look to silence the two enthusiastic officers.

"Why, yes. Would you like me to get it?"

"No, stay here. If I get the evidence, I will arrest you on suspicion of murder. I have the owner who can decrypt it right here. Where is it?"

One of the men now speaks up. He is clearly annoyed if not aggressive, certainly not congenial. Tension has racked up a notch.

"If we are not under arrest or under suspicion, we demand our weapons back, now! You have no right to hold them."

Dirk ignores them.

"Matius, where's the drive!"

"In my office. Top drawer old oak desk. My office, its the spare bedroom, second on the right." He sounds resigned.

"And, anyone in the house?"

"Mita. She is out" comes the sullen reply.

Still holding the firearms, the officers look to Dirk for instructions.

"They can hold their guns. Magazines to me."

The front door opens easily as the officers enter to retrieve the drive. The two men start to argue with Dirk, one demanding their magazines back, the other accusing the police of stupidity, when a shot rings out from inside the house. I reach across the seat to grasp Tara's shoulder.

45

Guilty

Tara

I freeze at the sound of the shot, but then, after a pause long enough for me to jump into the back seat with Iain, we hear what sounds like another shot followed almost immediately by a third.

We see Dirk pull out his mobile phone and make a call. The three men are looking on with expressions somewhere between surprised and troubled. Still talking on the phone, we see Dirk hand the two men their magazines, and Matius his shot gun. They move into a huddle for what looks like they are listening in on the phone conversation. Within seconds one of the men gives his rifle to Dirk and breaks away to walk unarmed toward the house.

It is all so confusing. I can't figure out what is going on. Iain also looks dumbfounded.

Just then I realise a car has pulled up behind us. It's the backup police vehicle. Sabina and another officer jump out and run straight for the door, drawing their revolvers as they run.

Just as the three get to the door it opens, and out staggers Jim the constable, limping badly.

"She shot me, she shot me!" he yells. "We found the drive and she said she was going to destroy it as it would incriminate her – she is your murderer."

Sabina and the accompanying officer step forward, one each side of the constable, but not merely to support him: I see them take his gun and handcuff him, at which he starts yelling again:

"What are you doing? She shot me, she shot me, what are you doing? I tried to stop her destroying the drive – I was arresting her, I was going to come out for help when she pulled her gun and shot me, I, I fired in self-defence. Self-defence! Can't you see I have been shot? Inspector, help me!"

I manage to speak through my very dry lips: "Why are they hand-cuffing him, Iain? - it's absurd. He needs medical attention. Surely!"

Iain is shaking his head as he softly answers with "Beats me, Babe - but there must be a reason." We are both flabbergasted.

I then notice Dirk has ignored the injured man, and is now at the front door with Matius's offsider, and they all then go inside!

"Iain, they are going in, unarmed. It could be a trap"!

"Dirk is no fool, Tara. But it beats me why he is going in with a suspect's friend."

We watch closely and silently wait. We have no words. It all seems so surreal, as if we are not conscious of ourselves. We feel detached. Onlookers. Things look and feel like they are in slow motion. Iain later explains that in any potentially traumatic crisis, this reaction is a survival mechanism, which leaves one ready for full concentration on fight or flight. Time seems to slow down.

Sabina and her colleague lay Jim down not far from their police van. His hands are cuffed in front of him as they lay him back on the soft lawn. We hear him continue to complain loudly that he is being mistreated and needs an ambulance, that he is bleeding to death. Neither Sabina nor the other officer engage and it not very long before Matius's friend comes out of the house, and jogs towards us. He is carrying what looks like one of those fancy kitchen knives and scissors, and some bandages in his other hand.

He kneels next to the distressed constable who asks what he is going to do. To our surprise we hear him say:

"I am a doctor." Then after a brief pause:

"Your colleague is alive, just. Helicopter is coming. Meanwhile let's look at this leg." We watch as he cuts away the bloodied trouser leg, and as he runs the bandage around it, he loudly announces:

"Minor flesh wound. Bullet gone right through. You can safely take him to hospital in your van." And the now apparent Doctor flashes a brief grin at the guy on the ground.

With that he walks briskly back to the house as Dirk emerges. Dirk immediately goes over to Matius and his other accomplice sitting on the lawn. We can hear their strange and unexplainable conversation.

"Sorry Matius. Your spare room is a mess. Last thing I expected. Shooting and blood. Guess though should have predicted violence from Bakker. Just didn't think they'd go that far. Not between friends. We *will* get it all cleaned up."

"Glad to help." we hear Matius reply. "The hidden surveillance camera and mic worked I assume?"

Some light is gradually dawning, at least about his being not considered guilty by Dirk, who then also turned to Matius's friend.

"Thank you for setting it up. Yes, all recorded, and Sabina was able to watch. On her iPad. Back around the bend where she had parked."

Dirk rises from his haunches and comes over, sitting down heavily into the passenger seat. He doesn't turn around to us but simply puts his head into his hands and sobs, ever so softly. We sit there for a full ten minutes. He's really overwhelmed, and I so feel for him – such a mix of emotions he has no way of dealing with right now. I am so glad Iain and I can emotionally *and* physically support each other. Just being together, feeling safe!

A helicopter arrives; paramedics hurry out and over to the house with their bags and a stretcher. Another police car arrives, and I recognise the officers from Shoal Haven. An ambulance arrives. We see the injured constable taken on board, all the while complaining about being mistreated. A police officer accompanies him as the ambulance also leaves.

Sabina now comes over and sits down in the driver's seat. She too knows not to say anything until finally, Dirk raises his head. She speaks quietly but confidently:

"We've got them, Dirk, at last, full unsolicited confession, all on tape."

She then turns to us to explain. As we obviously look puzzled.

"It seems Jim Bakker murdered Hedi when she wouldn't hand over a drive with drug trafficking information she had been given, and which they believed incriminated them. But Hedi didn't have the drive. We now know she had already passed it on to her friend Gena, your predecessor, Tara, for safekeeping."

We are stunned, but eager to let Sabina complete the puzzle that had so bewildered us.

"It also potentially explains Gena's fatal accident the next day. There is a record of her calling in at the station saying she had crucial evidence on a disk for Dirk, but wouldn't leave it. We have a police report, but no dash-cam, of Jim and Maranda pursuing Gena an hour later, on a narrow coastal road where she ran off and over a cliff, instantly to her death. We now suspect their pursuit was not a traffic offence but rather to retrieve the drive, but we surmise they can't have found it on the body.

"We knew that Jim Bakker had been on your very plane coming back from Perth, seated across the aisle from you. He may have overheard you talking about your predecessor and having a drive from her. Putting things together, he most likely suspected it could be the lost incriminating drive! So that too may explain why Bakker sent Kendra to retrieve it. But she wouldn't part with it, instead contacted Matius. The rest is history. All needs to come out in court. So, it goes without saying – until then, everything must now remain in strict confidence."

Dirk has been listening, patiently in silence. He now turns around to us. Having collected himself, he speaks very quietly.

"Thank you for coming. Sorry to put you through this. Glad I didn't need your drive just now, Tara. Iain and Sabina, I guess you've been praying. Thank that God of yours and Hedi's. Get Him to tell her we have her murderers now. Oh, and just maybe tell her…. This atheist might just have a glimmer of hope... Can't leave her there without me one day."

Tears were streaming down his face as he turned back to Sabina:

"Enough for now. Home, Sergeant, home. Get these people safely home. We have fortunately lost our untrustworthy driver."

46

Missing Pieces

You may be the reader who likes to guess how the conclusions made in Tara and Iain's story were possible. But others of you may really need to know more of what really happened to enable the mystery to be resolved. If the latter, read on, so you are no longer left in the dark.

When Sabina and Dirk had heard that Tara had a flash drive with encrypted material included from her predecessor, they had spoken about it among the officers as potentially having clues, only to notice that two of their colleagues had asked a lot of questions.

On retrieval of the contraband drugs, though clearly handled with gloves, they had found a hair which on DNA testing was identified as belonging to Sergeant Maranda. Dirk had then gained information from Perth for why she was on the police data base at all. She had been charged back in WA for possession of drugs, but the charges had been mysteriously dropped for undocumented reasons, but fortunately her DNA details had not been removed from the record. She had then moved to KP on Rustenberg.

Kendra had told Jove that Constable Jim Bakker had approached her and offered her drugs in return for stealing a flash drive from some new arrivals in the local Ibis Hotel. But, attractive as some free drugs had been in motivating her, Jim gave her the creeps, so she had maintained to him she had lost the drive when running away from the hotel. Later Sergeant Maranda, not believing her, had also come by, questioning her, and threatening to arrest her after a thorough search or, alternatively, a promise of six months free drugs and enough to become a dealer if she found the drive and handed it over. Frightened, and thinking no one would believe her, she continued to deny having the drive.

Feeling like she was in some sort of danger, out of fear Kendra had sought advice from Jove one day when again he had brought her food. He said he would check it out and get back to her. Jove had previously gone to Dirk who confidentially requested Jove get the drive from Kendra when he next saw her.

Meanwhile Dirk spoke with Matius. He'd then offered to get the flash drive, offering to buy it from Kendra on the pretext that it contained important coffee research. Kendra seemed only too glad to get rid of it. Kendra had then contacted Jove when she was again out of food and camped in the bush. That was when he took the opportunity, that Tara had serendipitously overheard, to ask her for the drive.

No one as yet had a clue as to whether there was indeed any incriminating evidence on the drive that identified a drug ring or Hedi's murderer. (Tara's copy will finally reveal all.) By this time, however, Dirk had come to suspect either or both Sergeant Maranda and Constable Bakker, hence his setting up the mock situation at Matius's house, expecting the two suspect officers would jump at an opportunity to dispose of the drive on being sent in to recover it.

What was recorded in the Matius office, you may wonder? Clearly within minutes, Maranda found the drive, exactly where Matius has said it was. She had then gone on to tell Jim, all on record, that she was putting it in her shoe and would keep it as insurance, should he ever turn on her or try to pin Hedi's murder on her. Another few minutes revealed their plan to say they could find no suspect drive, only those in the box carried out.

The recording then showed Bakker becoming angry. He clearly has a short fuse and is heard saying that she *knew* he'd had no alternative but to do away with Hedi and had then searched her place when she refused to give up the evidence that could put them both away. The video recording indicated that with drawn gun, Bakker menacingly demanded Maranda hand over the drive or he would become violent. She laughed at him before he shot her in the chest. She fell. He quickly took her gun and placing the recovered drive on the floor, put a bullet through it. He then put her gun in her limp hand, pointed it at his thigh and pushed her finger to pull the trigger. After taking a moment to arrange her body and checking for a pulse, presumably finding none, he put his own pistol in its holster and was then seen hobbling out of the room.

Have you wondered why the flash drive became so important? Remember the man sitting opposite on the plane, seeming to be curious about Tara's computing? What information had Bakker then obtained, perhaps identifying himself as a police officer, in his brief interchange with the flight steward? A look at the flight passenger manifest no doubt revealed the names of the two sitting across the aisle. Was it perhaps divine Providence that had alerted him to his potential solution for averting any incriminating evidence that such a flash drive might have? His follow-up actions in trying to retrieve the flash drive via Kendra in the end brought about his own demise – the murderer who for three years thought he'd got away with it!

AUTHORS POSTSCRIPT

Digging in Paradise takes place in an attractive island, promising much but ultimately just an imperfect setting. In a sense, while we may not be living in an idyllic island paradise, we are all digging for utopia: trying to find or to create peace, happiness, contentment, joy, even while the rest of the world may seem to be falling apart.

In 1943 Psychologist Abraham Maslow proposed an organisation of human needs for wellbeing into a hierarchical pyramid subsequently named after him. Fulfilling higher order needs depend on lower-level needs having been met first. The basic two primary levels are physiological (food, water, warmth, rest) and safety (personal security etc) needs. The secondary level is about psychological needs: love and belonging, then self-esteem, encompassing needs for mutual respect, self-confidence, and identity.

Iain and Tara could be seen as comfortably secure in terms of their primary needs. However, their respective individual histories have not fostered any confidence in love and belonging. Surprisingly though, and perhaps because of their professional and academic achievements, they nonetheless experience a reasonable confidence and sense of self-acceptance.

We note that Iain's pursuit of psychology has, in part at least, been in an attempt to understand himself. But still we note that his balm for his lack of love and a sense of belonging has been his resorting to various addictions, and finally that of workaholism. As a confirmed bachelor prior to marriage to Tara, he has used his psychology as an escape, not a solution. Work so frequently becomes an escape route from unresolved issues.

Tara, approaching mid-thirties, also finds herself still determined to avoid the vulnerabilities of intimacy. Yet as commonly experienced in life, it is not *reason* but her *emotions* that raise to the surface her subconsciously deeply repressed and denied personal needs. From repeatedly troubled and largely subconscious memories, when these are confronted and appropriately handled, the broad light of consciousness can help remove what can hold us all captive to a dark past, histories that frequently prevent a sense of wholeness and wellbeing that all humans pursue.

The light from the Truth makes it more possible that we can be set free, to enjoy the opportunities and relationships we desire to experience, even in an imperfect world!

FURTHER REFLECTIONS

- A quick first question: if you usually let first impressions guide your lasting ones, what did you expect from the book cover? We hope you were not disappointed!
- We believe serious thinking always involves reflection: not just to acquire some information, but in order to make sense of that knowledge. Regular and personal reflection, even reflexively on our *previous* reflections, enables greater understanding. Often this will involve reflections about others, considering why the world is the way it is, why people do the things they do. But inevitably we gain most benefit from self-reflections. Then we start to grasp why we do the things we don't want to do, and to leave undone the things we believe we should complete!
- Some of us start this process as young people, trying to make sense of life; others begin this journey at middle age or more, and sadly often too late, or only after life has thrown some enormous challenges that almost beggar belief. How about you?
- We do wonder if this book has caused you the reader to seriously reflect on things in your own life that may still pop up from time to time, creating negative thinking that you'd rather not hang

on to? What insights have Iain and Tara's experiences left you to wonder if you might apply some elements of their responses to your behaviours?

- Or maybe reflections have floated in your mind about what other people you relate to voraciously hold on to, with some behaviours that are less than healthy. Perhaps you've gained some insights that allow you to reflect on *why* these issues remain – and questions may arise that perhaps you may need to reflect on further, particularly as you encourage those you care for with greater patience, and more understanding. Consider the role that fear may play, for example, preventing movement forward or making good choices that would bring about imperative change.

- Are there certain psychological understandings just waiting for you to read about, so that you too can feel some relief? With greater knowledge can come restorative understanding. Terms like repression; sublimation; attachment theory; formative years; authoritarian and permissive control versus authoritative leadership; parenting styles; trauma; unconscious versus conscious beliefs; mindfulness.

- When it comes to making important decisions, what procedures do you normally adopt? Some struggle, as Iain did…others clearly know that instantaneous magical answers will always be questionable at best, and likely to lead one down an irrational pathway, where God inevitably must get blamed! Discerning the way ahead includes hearing others out, before wisely evaluating the rationale, the feelings, and always needs an honest appraisal of our personal agenda, by which we can get deluded, unless shared with another trusted and wise confidante.

- Has Iain and Tara's journey of only a few short years helped you reflect on your own individual strengths, as well as any weaknesses that may get in the way of better relationships? In this story we hope you have gained a greater appreciation of how we differ as individuals: in personality, backgrounds, and cultures.

- As in real life, when the psychological aspects become immersed in our spiritual, philosophical as well as personal responses to ethical issues, we may even see those we love with greater clarity and acknowledgement. Like the issues surrounding the growing of coffee, wider personal considerations may have caused you to reflect on the goods you buy, with best deals perhaps uppermost, or alternatively thoughts of how the producers of such goods may not be receiving due rewards for their labours.

- Our lives can become increasingly complex, demanding a growing need to reflect and seek wisdom. Learning to listen more sensitively, knowing when to speak or when to keep silence. Check out what passive aggressive communication includes, and how this is often misunderstood.

- As individuals, we not only have different personalities, seen in our different ways of perceiving, seeing, different ways of thinking; we can also have very different behavioural habits, and even values – sometimes learned, modelled by important others, while others have formed strong reactive patterns to what has been experienced. Perhaps you have also glimpsed potential choices individuals make without consciously realising that those opportunities only come with deeper reflections. Many such personal reflections are often kept private, and consequently are not activated.

- Many life-changing reflections however often result most effectively from reflections deliberated between people: with an honesty of sharing that can only be possible with trust. Have you thought about the changes that took place within and between the main characters? Like when they were able to have confidence in the trustworthiness of those with whom they shared life's experiences, or like when feelings were listened to: no comments, criticism or evaluation, just simply accepted. Understand how important it is to be a mirror, simply reflecting back another's feelings and beliefs.

- Read up about "problem ownership" that often care givers remain ignorant of, expecting to solve other people's problems rather than being facilitators so that the other becomes more able to face and deal with his or her own problem. Support does not mean you need to carry or take responsibility for what is not yours to own. Psychological terms such as transference, countertransference may also need to be understood in learning to listen effectively, without becoming over-burdened.

- In relation to observing the journeys frequently made by individuals who experience constant life battles, consider Viktor Frankl's 3 questions that remain so pertinent today, where identity and choice is often considered only after mistakes are made. The order is important: 1. Who am I? 2. Where am I going? Then 3. Who goes with me? When this practice is better understood, a simplified journey can mean some unnecessary failures and hurts may be avoided. Consider further the meaning shared in the phrase: when God says I'm ok, then I am!

- Is there a Jove character in your life? What does she/he mean to you? We wonder if such a character can provide a growing appreciation and acceptance that contributes to your understanding of what life is about? Or maybe Jove is someone who is simply annoyingly vague or perhaps complexly confronting!

- When you reflect on the happenings on the island, have you considered your own standpoint on coincidences in life? Perhaps gaining a fresh perception of how the most appalling things in life can finally become meaningful, and useful to bring about good. Where sunshine after rain reflects joy that follows sorrow, and a peace that follows pain. How do we challenge our very human desire for perfection in this life, but where brokenness virtually makes this an impossible pursuit?

If this book has raised some psychological issues about which you would like to gain greater insight, keep a watch for our new book soon to be released, in 2022: **A Psychologist's Casebook, Published by Ark House.** This book has many deidentified real-life examples encountered within the therapeutic context, with details of approaches used to alleviate long-held patterns of unacceptable behaviours or problematic stressors. It also will highlight how real-life people have recovered from traumas, both recent and long-term, with treatment outcomes explored that include some like those experienced by Iain and Tara. Each chapter of that book will focus on different psychological issues and the treatment options affectively applied, with honest reporting of the sense of personal well-being and possible relief gained, and with a clear rationale for why these results were or were not achieved.

You may also like to access our blog:
PsychologicalDigs.blogspot.com

JOHN ROODENBURG PHD FAPS FCEDP FCOUNSP

John's primary school teaching experience was followed by many years as a practicing developmental psychologist in country Victoria, Australia. A mid-career quantitative PhD from The University of Melbourne saw him return to his passion of teaching but this time in tertiary education. John was awarded the 2020 Australian Psychological Society's National Award of Distinction in recognition of his work at Monash University leading the Graduate E&D course and directorship of the Krongold Clinic, as well as four years as National Chair of the College of E&D. With his wife and colleague Esther, his research passion has been modelling individual differences in thinking.

ESTHER ROODENBURG PHD BMUS BA DIPED PGDIPCOUNS

 After initial secondary teaching experience, followed by raising 5 children with her husband John, Esther's many years as a community-based psychologist was then further explored within her own more qualitative PhD, into individual differences in ways of thinking. She joined John in the University setting, teaching counselling and clinical psychology to Educational and Developmental graduate students. Her teaching included sharing her experiences of a broad case-based range of therapeutic approaches, with a practical application of well-developed theory-based psychological understandings. These are evident in this book and also in a forthcoming book: *A Psychologists Casebook*, Ark House, 2022.